# DEADLY
# CRY

BOOKS BY ANGELA MARSONS

Detective Kim Stone series
*First Blood*
*Silent Scream*
*Evil Games*
*Lost Girls*
*Play Dead*
*Blood Lines*
*Dead Souls*
*Broken Bones*
*Dying Truth*
*Fatal Promise*
*Dead Memories*
*Child's Play*
*Killing Mind*

Other Books
*Dear Mother* (previously published as *The Middle Child*)
*The Forgotten Woman* (previously published as *My Name Is*)

# Angela MARSONS
# DEADLY CRY

bookouture

Published by Bookouture in 2020

An imprint of Storyfire Ltd.
Carmelite House
50 Victoria Embankment
London EC4Y 0DZ

www.bookouture.com

ISBN: 978-1-83888-733-9
eBook ISBN: 978-1-83888-732-2

*This book is dedicated to Lynda Allen*
*My sister and my friend.*

# PROLOGUE

*'Mummy, Mummy, look at this,' I cry, holding out my arm. I am trying to hold back the tears, but one droplet escapes and rolls over my cheek. I am relieved I have caught her at the front door.*

*'Not now, sweetie, I'm late for work,' she replies, not even looking my way.*

*'Please, Mummy, look, it hurts,' I say, thrusting it at her. 'There's even a red mark, here, on my arm.'*

*She puts down her handbag and grabs my arm roughly. Her face has hardened. She is annoyed with me. That hurts me too, but in a different way.*

*'Where?' she snaps, causing me to shrink back from her.*

*'Th… there.' I point.*

*She looks more closely. 'There's nothing there. Stop being such a silly baby.'*

*Now the tears break free and the sobbing starts. I want to wrap my arms around her legs and stop her from leaving. There is something there. The skin is still smarting from the fingers twisting my flesh.*

*She gives me back my arm and with it a gentle shove away.*

*'And don't disturb Daddy with your silliness. He has an important conference call this morning.'*

*She regards me for just a minute, as though weighing up whether to lean down and kiss me before she leaves. My heart hammers with hope.*

*I wait.*

*The urge passes and I see a dozen thoughts about the day ahead enter her mind. She smiles weakly, as though she knows that there is more she should do.*

*She turns and leaves, closing the door with finality.*

*I go back to my room with an empty feeling; it's as if someone has scooped out my insides.*

*It won't be long until fresh marks appear. How many more times will I try to explain?*

*Because she doesn't listen.*

*No one ever does.*

# CHAPTER ONE

'Oh, Bryant, make them turn it off,' Kim moaned, covering her eyes with her hands. Just ten minutes she'd wanted. She'd told Bryant to pull up in front of the café so that he could buy her a much-needed latte after their Diversity Awareness refresher at Brierley Hill.

Treating people differently because of colour, age, race or gender was not something she needed a morning of death by PowerPoint presentation to understand. She had no bias towards or against anyone and was generally rude to everyone.

'Bryant, I'm begging,' she said to the detective sergeant, glancing back at the television. It seemed that wherever she went, there was no escaping the impending visit of the celebrity Z-lister, Tyra Brooks, famous for sleeping with a prominent, married footballer and then writing a kiss-and-tell book about it.

Every local news programme or bulletin mentioned her book tour and signing at the imaginatively named The Book Store, in the shopping centre in Halesowen, at the end of the week.

Even here, at a half-filled, back-street café in Brierley Hill, the small television was repeating the girl's history, interspersed with clips of Superintendent Lena Wiley from West Mercia urging peace and order across the nine scheduled events in the Midlands.

'New Age celeb, guv,' Bryant said, trying to get the attention of the café owner, who had his back turned and was watching the news himself. 'It's all wags, shags and reality TV these days. I remember when you had to be skilled at something to be—'

'Okay, let's get out of here,' she said, finishing her drink. She didn't disagree with her colleague, but she wasn't wearing the right shoes for a trip down memory lane.

Bryant looked dolefully at the rest of his sandwich before following her out the door.

'What the?…' Kim said as she collided with a uniformed security guard from one of the stores. Another was running across the road, radio in hand.

She knew many of the stores were members of a Retail Watch Scheme where they shared information and intelligence on local criminals. Sightings of known shoplifters and troublemakers were communicated between the small network so that each could be on the lookout for trouble in their individual stores.

She turned to follow.

'Guv…'

'Police business, Bryant,' she said, quickening her step.

In her experience, store security would only leave their own premises if someone on the network had called for urgent assistance, normally for a shoplifter getting violent, some other kind of public order offence or something involving children.

Kim followed the security officers into the Shop N Save store nestled between a bank and a Blue Cross charity shop. She navigated the long, narrow aisles filled with bargains and low-priced items, ranging from home furnishings to toys to food products.

A row of tills was located right at the back of the store. She could hear no shouting or any other indication of a scuffle as she approached a small huddle of people.

'Move aside,' Kim said to the security guys as Bryant showed his identification.

The bodies moved to reveal a little girl, aged four or five, clutching a small, grey bear that had been taken from a toy rack beside the tills.

'What's going on?' Kim asked, moving to the centre of the crowd.

'Can't find her mummy,' said the store assistant who was kneeling beside the chair on which the little girl was sitting.

The child looked up and viewed her through red-rimmed, frightened eyes. Tear tracks stained her cheeks, but Kim still breathed a sigh of relief. Better to have the child than the parent.

'How long?' she asked. Normally parents and children were reunited in a matter of minutes.

'Almost a quarter of an hour.'

'Got a description?' she asked.

'Jeans and blue jacket,' she answered as the child hugged the bear closer to her tear-stained cheeks. An occasional sob broke free from the small body.

Another store assistant appeared with a bag of sweets.

The child shook her head and tried to hide her face in the side of the bear. Kim stepped back and motioned for Bryant to do the same. Too many people crowding the little girl.

'Jimmy's gone to check the CCTV now,' one of the shop assistants said, looking behind Kim.

Her face appeared to relax. Kim turned to see two uniformed officers approaching as Bryant answered his phone.

The male officer offered her a quizzical look: what was CID doing attending a lone-child incident?

'Just passing,' she explained as a second pair of officers turned up.

Bryant ended his call.

'Woody wants you back at the station now.'

Kim realised that her boss rarely rang her personally any more to summon her back and rang her steadying colleague instead. Perhaps he'd realised that there was a certain fluidity to her interpretation of 'right now', whereas Bryant attached a higher degree of urgency to the request.

She turned to the shop assistant closest to her. 'Move some of these folks away. The poor kid must be—'

'Guv…' he urged, proving her point.

She stepped away from the crowd of shop assistants, security officers and police. There were more than enough people to deal with a displaced parent.

She nodded her agreement to her conscientious colleague and headed for the door.

This was a minor incident that really had nothing to do with her at all.

# CHAPTER TWO

Kim stared back at DCI Woodward for a full minute, waiting for the punchline that would follow her boss's opening statement.

There was only silence behind his own unflinching gaze.

'With all due respect, sir, are you having a fu... I mean, are you kidding me?'

'No, Stone, I'm not kidding you. The Emergency Planning Team is meeting today, at four o'clock, and I need you to be there.'

Kim knew the EPT group, or as she preferred to call it the INEPT group, who met in preparation of any forthcoming major event that could impact on the general public. She'd known them meet for proposed English Defence League demonstrations, discussion of raising the terror threat level and other major incidents, but meeting for the imminent visit of a bloody glamour model signing a few books told her they really did not have enough to do.

'I understand as CID we don't normally get involved, but there's no one else available.'

'Sir, my desk is full of—'

'Nothing that can't wait for an hour. And talking of desks, you need to start giving this one a bit of thought,' he said, tapping the edge of his work space. 'I'm not at retirement age quite yet, but the day will come...'

'No offence, sir, but that desk fits you perfectly; I prefer my desk to be a bit more mobile while I'm out catching bad people doing bad things, not attending—'

'And I think it's time you started to learn how to play nice with people outside your immediate team.'

Kim laughed out loud. 'While I appreciate your faith in me, sir, I'm barely able to play nice with my own dog and he's my best friend. Is there no way you can send Bryant to the INEPT meeting? He's so much better with people than I am.'

'That's not exactly news, Stone, but it needs to be an inspector. My understanding is that the handover plans from West Mercia to us are in place and this meeting is to finalise details before a walk-through later in the week.'

'It really needs this level of planning to get an ex-glamour model into the shop to?…'

'She has her fair share of haters, Stone. Many see her as a homewrecker, and there were a couple of scuffles in Leamington Spa. No one wants to see anything happen on their watch. Once West Mercia hand her over to us, her safety is our problem.'

As ever, Kim was stunned by the double standard. It was the footballer who had been unfaithful, but it was the woman being subjected to the vitriolic attacks. She wasn't the one who had committed to monogamy.

'If it has to be an inspector, we could temporarily promote Bryant for the rest of the day,' she offered hopefully. 'I'll even call him boss if you want,' she added desperately. She did not do well at these meetings.

He shook his head as boredom started to shape his features.

It was over.

The battle had been fought and she'd lost.

# CHAPTER THREE

'Okay, guys, what're we up to?' Kim asked once she'd placed the canteen drinks on the spare desk. She was hoping they'd revive her team from the early afternoon slump they appeared to have fallen into.

'Filing,' DS Penn said.

'Shuffle files,' Stacey answered.

'Life pondering,' Bryant replied, twiddling his thumbs.

Good to see her team so hard at work. There'd been an unusual lull for the last few days. A serious assault on Hollytree had been passed to Brierley Hill, as it was one of their informants. A sexual assault had been discontinued when the woman admitted she'd been drunk and had probably consented, and a fight over cannabis had been handed to the drugs team.

A part of her didn't mind the lighter workload right now, she thought, glancing over at Penn as he formed piles of paperwork on his desk. The man had buried his mother last week and had insisted on returning to work the day after the funeral.

Much as she accepted that her team were high-functioning adults, she couldn't help the frisson of concern that breathed on the back of her neck when she glanced in his direction. She had detected no change in his emotional state whatsoever. She understood that both he and his brother had been expecting it; their mother had been diagnosed with terminal lung cancer months earlier. The woman had bravely hung on to life for much longer than the doctors had given her credit for. The brothers might have been able to prepare themselves, but there was something not quite right about Penn's reaction to her death. She noted that there was no Tupperware bowl bridging the gap between his desk and Stacey's work space. Clearly, Jasper had not yet found his way back to the kitchen. The fifteen-year-old boy with Down's syndrome lived to cook and provided the whole team with tasty treats on a daily basis. The absence of the Tupperware dish saddened her.

Paradoxically, Stacey Wood, Penn's colleague and the person sitting opposite, was a ball of contained excitement and nerves in preparation for her upcoming nuptials at the end of the month. Kim knew the detective constable was holding her excitement in check out of respect for her colleague's loss.

She glanced to her right. And Bryant was once again Bryant. After making some tough decisions regarding an old case, he'd been forced into a grey area of justice that hadn't sat well on his shoulders. He had gradually returned to his normal self and just a few days ago, he had beckoned them down to the car park to show off his new car. He had written off his old one crashing through a metal fence on their last major case.

Expectantly, the three of them had followed him down to his new, prized possession and had then stood in silence, stealing underwhelmed glances at each other.

'Err… it's an Astra Estate,' Kim had stated, breaking the silence. 'Exactly the same as the last one.'

Bryant had shaken his head. 'Nah, this one is the 1.5 litre three-cylinder model with turbo—'

Kim had cut him off by laughing out loud. 'You had a turbo? When you barely crack fifty on the motorway. Yeah, good call, Bryant, but it's still an Astra Estate and it's even the same colour.'

'Aah, not quite, that one is gunmetal…'

Kim hadn't heard the rest, as she'd turned and headed back into the station. Although a few years younger, it was essentially the same car. The only person who had been impressed had been himself.

Kim turned her attention to Stacey.

'Anything in the shuffles?'

The shuffle was an annual initiative that had been implemented by Woody three years earlier. Each team in the Dudley borough passed on a few unsolved cases to another team so that fresh eyes could track the case from the beginning, to see if they could offer a new perspective on the investigation. Of the twenty-seven cases shuffled, nine had been solved by a different team, proving value in her boss's initiative. However much she hated her team raking over the work of other detectives, she supported anything that caught bad folks.

'Okay, Penn, keep filing; Stace, carry on shuffling and, to give your thumbs a rest, Bryant, you can take me to this meeting.'

She grabbed her jacket and headed for the door.

'Hey, guv,' Bryant said once they were out of earshot of the squad room, 'you reckon Penn's okay?'

'If he says he is, we've got to respect that,' she said as they reached the bottom of the stairs, running into Jack, the desk sergeant, with an armful of sweet packets from the vending machine.

'Bloody hell, Jack, low blood sugar?' Kim asked.

'Got a little visitor with PC Monaghan. Girl got separated from her mum earlier at—'

'Still not reunited?' Kim asked, meeting the concerned gaze of her colleague.

Jack shook his head.

Kim paused. She was tempted to go back there and see if the little girl was okay, but she forced herself out of the building.

It really didn't have anything to do with her.

# CHAPTER FOUR

Stacey regarded her colleague for a minute before speaking.

'Hey, Penn, listen if you want—'

'I'm fine, Stace,' he said without looking up from the neat piles of paperwork he was forming on his desk.

It was the same response she'd received every time she'd asked.

From what she knew, he had few friends, probably due to moving forces a couple of times coupled with using up the majority of his free time looking after Jasper, though one of his old colleagues, Lynne, from West Mercia, had attended his mother's funeral. She just hoped he'd opened up to her about his grief more than he had to any of them.

'How's Jasper?' she asked, looking longingly at the empty space where the cookies or muffins normally sat.

'Fine.'

'I could pop round and—'

'So, what you got in the shuffles?' he asked, cutting her off in more ways than one.

Stacey already knew her colleague kept his emotions close; his terse replies told her he was getting annoyed but didn't want to snap at her.

She took the hint.

'Okay, listen up; I've got an armed robbery from Wolverhampton, happened two years ago. The team suspected it was gang-related due to a known gang member being spotted in the area half an hour before the incident. It was their typical MO, but the team couldn't find any eyewitnesses.'

Penn shook his head. 'Don't waste your time on that one. Wolvo knows their gang culture better than you, so if their informants gave them nothing you've got no chance.'

She'd already read the file and come to the same conclusion herself. If Wolvo officers with their local knowledge couldn't get anyone to point the finger, she was stuffed before she'd even started. No one had been physically hurt, and the service station was still in business, so there was no burning desire in her stomach to get involved. She closed the file and put it to one side.

'Okay, next one. Almost two years ago, an eighteen-year-old lad was jumped outside a chip shop by three unknown assailants. Cuts and bruises but no broken bones, and the offenders were never caught.' She flicked back to the front of the file. 'And this one is from Dudley.'

'What was the final action logged?'

Stacey leafed to the end of the file and read the last few activity entries.

'A visit and phone call from the mother asking for an update.'

Penn shook his head. 'You'd be wasting your—'

'You can't write them all off cos they might be hard work. If they were easy, they'd be solved already,' Stacey protested. There was a simmering heat in her stomach for this one. The boy had been hurt quite badly.

'Agreed, but the lad is now twenty. Two years to a teenager is half a lifetime. If it's his parents doing the chasing instead of him, he's likely moved on and he's your best source of information.'

Stacey could see his point. Reopening any cold investigation in the hope of unearthing information that would solve the case, she would not only be reliant on the victim's memory but also their commitment and enthusiasm.

She put the file aside and reached for another from two years ago. 'Okay, this one is a sexual assault. Similar to another sexual assault case which brought a conviction, but Brierley Hill couldn't get enough for the CPS to charge the second victim.'

'Yep, that one,' Penn said, finally lifting his head.

'I haven't told you anything about it yet,' she replied, pleased to see his face instead of the top of his head.

He shrugged. 'It's rape and no rapist should go unpunished.'

She had to agree, and her initial perusal of the files confirmed it was the case she wanted to solve first. But on closer inspection, she could see that the case for the second victim had never even been put to the Crown Prosecution Service. She read the details again.

Lesley Skipton had been raped on her way home after a party in the park at Himley Hall, organised by Dudley Council. The event had finished at 1 a.m. The twenty-two-year-old had been rendered unconscious from a strike to the back of the head. When she'd come to, a male had been on top of her, sexually assaulting her from behind with a foreign object. Her face had been pushed into the ground, and he had not spoken a word to her.

Stacey took a moment to appreciate just how terrified the girl must have been.

The Brierley Hill team had suspected a local builder whom they'd been investigating for a sexual assault a few days earlier, but they had been unable to find any physical evidence against him.

The first assault had made it to court: Sean Fellows had been convicted of the rape of Gemma Hornley. Lesley Skipton was still waiting for justice.

On paper, there was no question that Sean Fellows had also attacked Lesley. The investigating team had thought so and so did Stacey.

The only question remaining in her mind was: could she prove it and give Lesley Skipton the justice she deserved?

# CHAPTER FIVE

Bryant pulled up at the front door of the Copthorne Hotel at two minutes to four.

'You know, Bryant, for once you could have taken your time,' she moaned, freeing herself from the seatbelt. His notoriously steady driving style frustrated the life out of her when travelling to a crime scene or to interview a key witness. Every second counted. But she wouldn't have minded being a bit late for this.

'Have fun and be nice to the other kiddies,' he said, smirking.

She slammed the car door on his words and headed towards the entrance.

The hotel had been built at the edge of The Waterfront complex in the eighties. Then, it had been all shiny and new, with its indoor pool and conference facilities.

But after three decades, its fatigue was beginning to show. The foyer seemed dimmer than it once had, the magnolia paint chipped and darkened with age that no level of cleaning could prevent.

A middle-aged woman at the concierge desk glanced up expectantly.

Kim held up her ID. 'EPT meeting.'

The woman pointed towards a set of double glass and wood doors. Kim nodded. She'd used the conference facilities many times before.

The Hackett Suite was the smallest of the nine meeting rooms, and the door was wide open when she reached it.

A few people stood around the room, self-consciously holding small white cups from the stack beside the silver tea urn. A couple of people smiled or nodded in her direction as her eyes rested on the hastily written place cards folded in front of chairs at the table. Beside the name cards were briefing packs.

She decided to forgo the coffee, already tasting the cheap bitterness that couldn't be saved by any amount of milk or sugar.

She took a seat at the card marked 'WM Police'. They hadn't known who was coming so had been unable to state her name.

She counted six cards excluding her own. She took a moment to match the people standing to their designated seats.

Nikita Jackson, a severe woman with a crew cut, was obvious as the representative from West Midlands Ambulance Service. She had gravitated to an overweight man Kim knew to be Clive Young from the Fire Service. Both were called in for any event where crowds were expected and injury or incident was a possibility. They would decide the level of manpower that would be committed to the event.

Bill Platt, the events manager for Dudley Council, was busying himself pouring a refill from the hot-water urn. He paused every few seconds to push his glasses back on to the bridge of his nose.

She'd never met the two other people in the room. The man leaning against the wall, scrolling through something on his mobile phone, she guessed was Christopher Manley, founder of TSS, otherwise known as Total Security Systems. The private company provided remote CCTV services, commercial and residential key-holding services, manned guarding and event support. Three years ago, they had won the contract to provide event security to Dudley Council. She had assumed the owner of the company would be older, but he looked to be late-thirties.

One more name: by the process of elimination, she guessed the woman with a shock of natural blonde curls falling all over her face was Kate Sewell, agent of Tyra Brooks, the celebrity.

That left one person; they had been seated opposite her at the rectangular conference table.

And every head turned towards the door as West Mercia Superintendent Lena Wiley entered the room.

Kim wasn't surprised to see that the woman's commanding demeanour was no less evident in person than it had been on the small screen she'd been watching in the café an hour earlier.

Similar to herself in height, Lena Wiley possessed a presence that demanded attention. While not overweight, there was a solidity to her physicality that offered a reassurance. It wasn't masculine, but it was assured, confident.

Kim knew little about the woman except for a couple of rumours she'd heard. Apparently, there was a standing joke that her personal assistant was only ever issued a weekly pass for the car park, as Lena hadn't kept anyone in the position beyond that period of time since taking the job. Having held the record of staff turnover rates for West Mids until a few years ago, Kim knew better than to judge her for that alone. She'd also heard the superintendent got results and wasn't afraid of authority. Not bad qualities as far as Kim was concerned. Ultimately, she had risen to a decent rank when the odds of doing so were not on her side. Kim respected that.

Superintendent Wiley offered a nod that encompassed every-one in the room before disregarding the place tags and taking a seat at the head of the table.

Kim noted the irritation on the face of the council events planner, whose job it was to coordinate both the event and the meeting.

'Sorry I'm late,' Lena said as everyone else just took the seat closest to them. The security company owner was now sitting directly opposite Kim.

Councilman Platt coughed.

'Thank you all for coming. As you already know, we have an event this Thursday—'

'Unless the details have changed since the last meeting, I'm sure we can forgo the waffle,' Lena Wiley interrupted. 'And the people not present can refresh with the briefing packs.'

All eyes in the room were on the visiting police officer. Kim. Platt reddened. 'Of course, but—'

'I suggest we run through the plan of action as already noted and any questions can be raised at the end.'

Although her following pause indicated she was awaiting his agreement, the room already knew who was running this meeting.

Kim guessed that Lena Wiley hadn't got to where she had by being a pushover, and if the woman's direct approach got her out of this meeting and back to her real job sooner, she'd happily cheer Wiley on.

'Okay,' Lena said, tapping her finger on the briefing pack but not opening it, 'Ms Brooks will be handed over to us at one p.m. on Thursday. We will escort her to Kingfisher Shopping Centre at Redditch, where she will sign for an hour and—'

'Or until the crowd has gone,' Kate Sewell interjected. 'Tyra will sign every last book.'

Lena glared at her but said nothing about the interruption.

'Followed by a meet and greet which—'

'No meet and greet,' Kate again interrupted.

Lena glared harder before making a show of leafing through the briefing pack.

'And this was changed when?'

Kate shrugged nonchalantly. 'We've decided that the meet and greets are not a good idea. Just for security reasons.'

'Has there been some kind of direct threat?' Lena asked, narrowing her eyes.

Everyone knew this type of personality attracted the lovers and the haters. Many young girls idolised the glamour model who had more than two million Instagram followers, but there were some people less than happy about her breaking up the family of a local footballing legend.

'No direct threat,' Kate answered quickly.

Both Kim and Christopher Manley appeared to notice the speed of her response.

'It's just not going to sell more books.'

Lena appeared to accept her answer and continued.

'We will then follow behind her driver as she is transported from Worcestershire to Halesowen. I will hand over to Inspector Plant at the entrance to the building in the service yard of the shopping centre.'

Lena looked Kim's way to see if there was anything she wanted to contribute.

She shook her head. This was not her circus. She was doing what she'd been asked and had brought only her ears to the meeting.

Lena stifled a mild look of irritation as she opened the briefing pack. She looked to Bill Platt, who tipped his head in a 'You wanted the meeting. You've got it' kind of way.

Lena's eyes scanned the pages.

'It is my understanding that from the handover point, to avoid unnecessary contact with the public, Inspector Plant will escort Tyra Brooks through the service corridors to the rear of the bookshop.' She glanced at Christopher Manley, making no effort to hide her disdain. 'Key points will be manned by TSS guards who—'

'Officers,' he interrupted with a low growl.

Kim knew many security bosses who bristled at the term 'guards'. Nowadays security personnel had to take exams, study and pass tests. Many were trained in First Aid and CPR and the use of a defib machine. Gone were the days of putting someone in a uniform and stationing them on a door.

'How many guards have you committed to the event?' Lena asked, ignoring his correction.

'Seven,' he said without looking at her.

Kim knew that many police officers looked down on security companies; saw all their staff as being wannabe police officers. Many disagreed with their involvement at public events, but Kim saw their contribution as being able to free up police officers to do what they were paid to do. West Midlands Police Force had denied Dudley Council that level of manpower to the event, so the councilman had little choice but to outsource. No one wanted anything to happen to this celebrity on their watch.

Christopher Manley began to outline his staff positions as she felt her phone vibrate in her pocket.

Lena Wiley stifled a yawn. Kim listened to his plans. She didn't need to consult the plan of the shopping centre with little marked crosses on it. She knew the area well and had been called to many an incident during her time as a constable.

Her phone stopped vibrating. *Just give me a minute*, she thought.

'Well, thank you for that, Mr Manley. We're all enlightened to know exactly where each of your *guards* will be standing and—'

'What about staircase nine?' Kim asked, cutting her off and speaking for the first time.

Lena now turned her annoyance Kim's way.

Kim ignored her and continued her focus on Christopher Manley, who stifled a smile.

He consulted his plans again. 'We don't have a staircase nine on the drawings.'

'Umm… excuse me,' Lena said, 'might this be something the two of you could discuss outside this—'

'Right there,' Kim said, ignoring the superintendent and leaning across the table. She stabbed an area of the plan that appeared to be a brick wall. 'It was a service stairway to the upper level before the renovations. There's still a door there that leads to an abandoned set of store rooms and a corridor that leads back to the new section.'

Kim knew because she'd got lost in that area when a suspect she'd been chasing for an ABH offence had suddenly disappeared from view.

Christopher smiled his thanks and placed a cross at the location. He looked to the councilman. 'I guess that's eight then.'

Bill Platt shook his head, indicating there would be no budget increase.

Christopher looked back at her as the phone once more vibrated in her pocket.

'It'll be covered,' he assured.

'As scintillating as that was,' Lena said, 'if we could move on to…'

Kim tuned out as she reached into her pocket for her phone. The people whose calls mattered the most knew she wasn't to be disturbed. Woody had sent her, and Bryant was waiting outside.

That could only mean one person and he never rang to shoot the breeze.

Lena looked straight at her and stopped speaking for a second. Everyone looked her way.

Two missed calls from Keats.

'Umm… officer, if you wouldn't mind putting away your phone.'

Kim ignored her and pushed back her chair.

Lena Wiley's face was colouring with rage. 'Is there somewhere you need to be?'

Kim made no apology as she headed for the door, throwing the words back over her shoulder.

'Oh yes, it appears there's somewhere I'm needed way more than I'm needed here.'

# CHAPTER SIX

Stacey drummed her fingers on the desk as she waited for DS Michaels to answer the phone and tried to quieten her second thoughts. Maybe this wasn't the case for her to get her teeth into if the team dealing with it had never even put the case to the CPS.

'Michaels,' said a low rumble of a voice at the other end.

'DC Wood from Halesowen,' she offered.

'Sorry for the wait, love, I was taking a dump.'

Stacey shook her head. Some things never changed, and she didn't have time to react to every old-school misogynistic officer on the force.

'Yeah, thanks for that. Got a minute to talk about the sexual assault of Lesley Skipton?'

Silence.

'You headed the case against—'

'I know who she is, love. I'm wondering why you want to talk about her.'

But sometimes she did have time to react. 'The name is Stacey, not love. I ain't your daughter or your niece. I got the case in the shuffle.'

'They sent you that one?' he asked, so surprised that he didn't even respond to her rebuke.

Now *she* was surprised that he was surprised.

Stacey knew that individual officers who had worked the cases didn't choose which ones to shuffle. The decisions were made by the DCI or higher.

'Why the surprise?'

'I thought they only shuffled cases with a chance of changing the stats.'

Stacey felt that was a jaded view of the process. Of course the force wanted more solved cases on their books. It didn't hurt when national statistics compared force against force like a score card, but she liked to think the priority was still about solving cases, finding bad people and protecting victims.

'You don't think the case is solvable?'

'Oh, I think it's solvable. I think we solved it. But it'll never get to court.'

Stacey could feel her irritation growing. She hated defeatists. Her own earlier doubts dissolved. She was working this case regardless of what Michaels had to say.

'So you're convinced Sean Fellows raped Lesley Skipton?' she asked.

'Oh yeah. We're sure he's the person responsible for the attack on Lesley and thank God we got him for the rape of Gemma Hornley or the bastard would still be out there.'

'I'm not getting it,' Stacey said, trying to understand what he seemed to be unwilling to say.

'Look, you know as well as I do that for a rape trial you need the victim. Doesn't matter what else you've got cos, to a jury, unless you can show them a traumatised victim, any physical evidence is just sex.'

'So?'

'We couldn't put Lesley on the stand.'

Stacey was shocked. She'd seen nothing in the files to say that Lesley had refused to testify.

'She changed her mind?'

'You're not getting it, love. We couldn't let her near the courtroom because of what she might say.'

'Like what?'

He paused for a few seconds.

'Go see her, Stacey,' he said, using her actual name. 'Talk through the assault with her and then you'll get why we couldn't put her on the stand.'

# CHAPTER SEVEN

The first things Kim noticed once she arrived at the crime scene were the blue jacket and jeans: the only description given for the woman separated from her daughter earlier.

Once she'd escaped the INEPT meeting, she'd listened to the voicemail left by Keats on his second time of calling. The message had simply stated that he had a body and the location.

Fielder Road was a side street that branched off Brierley Hill High Street. It had once held a couple of butchers and greengrocer stores before the Asda Superstore had moved in. Six of the shops had been boarded up, and the end two had been demolished, and that's where Keats had directed her to come.

It had taken her brain less than a second to calculate that the crime scene was under a hundred metres from the Shop N Save she'd been in earlier.

And right now, she was looking down at a fair-haired woman who bore a striking resemblance to the little girl whose mother had now been found.

A wave of sadness washed over her as she remembered the child clutching the teddy bear given to her by the shop staff, clinging to it in the absence of her mother who would never hold her tightly again. Just this morning, that little girl had been leading a normal life, out shopping with her mother like thousands of others. Kim was always amazed that such a normal day could turn into the worst day of your life. Where was the klaxon? Where was the warning that this day would, in the future, hold significance against all others?

'Has she been moved?' Kim asked the pathologist.

Keats shook his head as he motioned towards the plain black handbag lying by her side.

'Opened the flap to find ID. Her name is Katrina Nock, and this is her address,' he said, handing a small piece of paper to Bryant. 'Twenty-five years old.'

Kim was guessing he'd got the information from the driving licence, which would now be packaged up with the handbag and all its contents and sent off to the lab.

Kim walked around the body noting the position.

The woman's torso was face forward; her front was pressing into the ground. Her legs were bent at the knee and the right side of her face flat against the earth amongst half-house bricks and clumps of grey plaster. Nail and screw debris littered the area. Kim felt the anger begin to build in her stomach; the woman had been killed and left amongst decay and rubbish – the guts of a building that no one wanted – in an area now abandoned and unused. That fact alone told her plenty about the person who had killed her.

'Obvious injuries?' she asked, pushing the thoughts away. They would not help her victim now. There were no stab wounds or pools of blood and no trauma that she could see. The woman looked as though she'd just lain down for a nap amongst the strewn building materials.

Keats shook his head. 'I think her neck has been broken. I'll be able to confirm once I get her back to the morgue.'

Kim looked again at the position of the body and visualised the woman kneeling, the murderer behind. One good, strong twist. Immediate death and then her lifeless form falling to the ground.

A quick, functional kill that lacked the frenzy of a crime of passion. There was no presence of multiple stab wounds or cuts and bruises. There was no evidence of sexual assault. The woman's clothes appeared all in order.

Where was the feeling? Where was the emotion? Where was the motive for killing a young mother out shopping with her child?

'I'd estimate two to five hours,' Keats offered even though she hadn't asked. She'd been able to work that out for herself.

As it was late afternoon, Kim guessed the post-mortem would take place the following day.

'First thing,' he said, reading her thoughts.

'Oh, Jesus, I know that frown,' Bryant said as they headed towards the car. 'What's up?'

'She didn't need to die,' Kim said, and then wondered where those exact words had come from.

'Well, someone wanted her dead cos she didn't break her own—'

'I can't explain it,' she said, turning to look back at the scene. 'It's all so throwaway, Bryant. There was no passion, no hate, no frenzy, no message, no statement and she was just left amongst all this shit. Unless Katrina Nock was leading some kind of double life away from being a wife and mother, I really have the feeling that this woman didn't need to die.'

Kim's thoughts returned once more to the small child whose life was now changed for ever. It was down to her to deliver the bad news.

# CHAPTER EIGHT

Kate Sewell closed the car door and glanced at her Hermes handbag, bought courtesy of her commission on the book deal brokered between her client and one of the big five publishing houses.

Tyra Brooks was not her normal type of client, and the back of beyond in the Black Country was not where she'd seen herself in her late thirties, but needs must, she told herself.

The two of them had needed each other.

At twenty-eight years of age, Tyra's glamour modelling days had been numbered. Waning interest in her physical attributes had led to her being dropped by the agency that had represented her for ten years. Right at the time Kate had lost her last high-paying client, who had been poached by a swanky agency, promising to take his mediocre acting talent to another level and make him a household name. *Good luck with that*, she thought. Ryan Hardwick was a handsome, arrogant man whose delusions far outweighed his ability. He was also a self-sabotager, scared of success and increased his alcohol intake at the first sign of a decent role. It hadn't been her holding him back, it had been himself, but she'd let them discover that on their own.

Regardless of his shortcomings, Ryan's piecemeal work had kept her business going, along with the other half-dozen clients she had left, and her hands were still full because Tyra was almost as delusional as Ryan had been.

The only person who hadn't known Tyra's career was on the decline was Tyra herself. Even though fuller lips and bigger boobs hadn't reignited the interest, she still felt that it was only a matter of time before she was back on top. A blip. A dry spell. What Tyra hadn't realised was that each surgery was making her look less like herself, and that the gigantic boobs had turned her into a novelty fixture. When approaching Tyra to represent her interests, Kate had envisaged a year or two of minor bookings, eking out the last dregs of the woman's career, to help pay her mortgage until she secured a couple of high-paying clients.

That was until Tyra had revealed she'd accidentally slept with a well-known footballer after a drunken night in a Birmingham club. Kate had been unsure about the accidental part. How did one accidentally sleep with someone else, she had wondered, but she'd seen the financial opportunities straight away.

Together they'd devised a plan to maximise exposure and had started a marketing campaign of teasing out the information, dropping hints via social media and her YouTube channel. With the sniff of scandal in the air, Tyra's followers on all platforms had tripled, and Kate had chosen the perfect moment for the identity of the footballer to be revealed. His denial had been met with photos from Tyra's phone of the two of them, and social media had exploded. Hashtags placed carefully had kept the story trending for days. The offers had started rolling in: TV appearances, radio interviews, podcasts. An interview with a national newspaper had been followed by three publishing houses bidding for her tell-all, especially once Tyra alluded to the fact he wasn't the only celebrity who had graced her bed. The deal had been secured, and Tyra's memories had been turned into a book by a ghost writer Kate had used before.

It had been hard going. She'd worked seventeen-hour days for months. She'd spent many hours of that time massaging the ever-inflating ego of her client, who was relishing the limelight and eager to wring every last bit of drama from the situation.

But the tide had begun to turn. Kate could feel it. The dignified silence of the wife who had been wronged was damaging the campaign. An all-out bitch fight would have been better.

Oblivious to the change in tone to some of the messages, Tyra was milking the situation for every hour it had left in it, but more and more trolls were coming out of the woodwork and the name-calling had turned meaner. The idle death threats from the keyboard warriors were met with the same response: ignored and blocked. They were vague, vitriolic, violent and forgotten by the sender minutes later. It was par for the course. Anyone in the public eye was a magnet for the haters.

It wasn't a situation she hadn't been in before, but human nature dictated that hateful characters made more money.

In the meeting, she'd been asked if there was any direct threat to Tyra Brooks and she had said no.

She glanced towards her mobile phone sitting in the hands-free cradle.

She had lied.

# CHAPTER NINE

Stacey paused before knocking on Lesley Skipton's door. Was she really being fair to the woman raking it all up again if everyone felt there was no real hope of closure?

As a victim of rape, Lesley had already been subjected to enough. Not least the physical attack, but everything else that came afterwards.

Rape investigation had moved on in the last twenty years, but women still had to fight through the disbelief and doubt that came into the eyes of everyone to whom they told the story: police officers, medical staff, solicitors, a jury, in some cases even friends and family.

It was the only crime Stacey knew where everyone immediately looked for a loophole. Was she drunk? Was she being provocative? Was her skirt short? Did she invite it? No one accused a mugging victim of waving their wallet in the air or a burglary victim of advertising their worldly goods in the window. Only in cases of sexual assault was the victim made to feel like they had invited the crime. Stacey was yet to imagine any action at all that a woman could do to invite the horror of a sexual assault.

No, Stacey decided as she knocked on the door, she wasn't making a mistake in trying to get justice for a rape victim. And so what if the original investigating team thought it was a done deal? If she'd learned anything from her boss over the years, it was that you didn't give up on something just because it was hard.

The door was opened a fraction by a fair-haired girl with the majority of her hair tied back in a ponytail. A few wisps had broken free and framed a pretty face reddened by activity. The sportswear indicated she'd been doing some kind of physical activity.

Stacey held up her ID above the second chain fixed to the door. 'May I come in?'

Lesley frowned. 'For what?'

Stacey would have liked to explain inside, but she could understand the woman's reticence in allowing a stranger into her home.

'I'm from Halesowen station and I'm taking another look at your case.'

'It was handled by Brierley Hill,' she said, narrowing her eyes as though she'd caught her out in a lie.

'Please, ring Halesowen and check. I'll wait,' Stacey said, taking a step away from the door.

Lesley closed the door and locked it.

Stacey took another step back and noted the small CCTV camera looking down at her. The green wheelie bin to the left of the front door overflowed with broken-up delivery boxes. In front of that were two empty glass milk bottles.

Stacey heard the locks slide before the door opened for a second time, but wider.

'Okay, you're legit but I still don't see why you're here.'

'May I come in and explain?'

Lesley sighed and stood aside.

Stacey entered the ground-floor flat and almost tripped over a box from 'Jane's Kitchen', a local health food supplier.

'Sorry, it's just come,' Lesley said, picking it up and taking it through to the kitchen before pointing Stacey to the lounge.

Stacey immediately noticed there were few hard furnishings in the room. One oversized armchair and a few beanbags strewn around the place. An exercise bike with a laptop attached to the handlebars stood in front of the window.

'Please, take the chair,' Lesley said, disconnecting the laptop from the bike. 'Daily Peloton class,' she explained.

Stacey had seen the remote exercise workouts advertised on the television; just the thought had made her sweat. She'd considered joining a gym a month ago, during her disastrous attempt to lose weight in time for her wedding, but had decided she wasn't going to fork out a monthly payment for something that she didn't enjoy and was unlikely to ever use.

Lesley sat on a beanbag as Stacey took the seat she'd been offered.

'I've been asked to take another look at your case,' Stacey said, and then took a moment to explain the shuffle process.

As she spoke, she saw a range of emotions flit across the woman's face. Not least of which was fear.

'Why did you choose my case?' Lesley asked, picking at a loose piece of cotton on the bean bag.

'Because I want a conviction. I want the person responsible to pay for what he did to you.'

Lesley lowered her head for a moment and then lifted it. In that time Stacey could see that the mask had dropped. The Lesley who kept her emotions closely guarded and well hidden had moved aside to reveal the real Lesley hiding behind the screen.

She shook her head. 'I'm sorry but I don't think I can go through that again. You can't even begin to understand.'

'Talk to me,' Stacey said, trying to figure out what the officers at Brierley Hill had seen to stop them putting her on the stand. How could putting Lesley before a jury have held the potential to weaken the case against Sean Fellows? Surely two victims presented a stronger case than one.

Right now, she was looking at a presentable, eloquent young woman who would have been authentic and believable in the courtroom.

'It's too much,' Lesley said, shaking her head. 'The questions, the doubt in people's eyes when you're telling them the most horrific thing that's ever happened to you; the shame that it ever happened at all. I'm sorry but no, I can't go through it again. The attack was almost two years ago. Please choose another case. I've managed to put it behind me. I've moved on with my—'

'Well, that's not totally true, is it?' Stacey asked gently. 'You have two dead bolts on your front door, a CCTV camera so you can see who is approaching. You have your meals delivered and just about everything else you buy comes from Amazon. The milkman keeps you topped up with basics, and you exercise via an internet site.' Stacey paused. 'So when exactly did you last leave your home?'

Lesley stared at her for a moment and then burst into tears.

Stacey wondered if the presentation of just how much her life had changed beyond normal had somehow held a mirror up to what she'd allowed her life to become. Had it been a gradual process as she'd retreated behind the safety of her front door, or had she never addressed the fear of leaving the house directly after the attack?

Stacey tried to comprehend that basic right of free movement being taken away from her.

For some reason, a memory played in her head. She remembered when she was thirteen years old and the school netball team had played another local school. Her team had won, and Stacey had netted the winning shot from her position as Goal Attack. Three girls from the other team had followed her home, chanting and calling her names. As she'd turned into her front gate, the lanky, redheaded one had told her they were going to wait until she came back out and beat her up. She remembered running upstairs and looking out the window every few minutes for the next two hours to see if they were still there. Eventually they'd grown bored and left and she'd never seen them again, but for those couple of hours she had felt helpless, scared and trapped, and yet no one had even laid a finger on her.

Stacey reached out a hand and touched the woman gently on the arm.

'Please, Lesley, I really would like to try and help.'

# CHAPTER TEN

'Hey, guv, you're not gonna question the little girl yet, are you?' Bryant asked as he pulled up outside the narrow townhouse at the edge of Merry Hill Shopping Centre.

She'd been considering it, but the warning note in his voice convinced her otherwise.

'Bloody hell, Bryant, what kind of monster do you think I am?'

He glanced sideways. 'You were going to, weren't you?'

She huffed in response as she got out the car. Sometimes he just knew her far too well.

It was almost six thirty, and the sun was setting on what had been a grey and humourless day. In the time since they'd left the squad room, Andrew Nock had called the station, identified his daughter and collected her. Jack, the desk sergeant, had overseen the collection, checked the man's identification and, more importantly, witnessed the response of the little girl upon seeing her father. Without knowing the full details, Jack had informed the man that an officer would be along to speak with him later.

The man had left the station with no clue as to what had happened to his wife and was opening the front door before they'd reached it.

'Have you found her?' he asked hopefully.

Kim offered no answer to his question as she asked if they could come inside.

'Please, come into the kitchen,' he said quietly.

As she followed, she caught a glimpse of the little girl curled up asleep on the sofa, still clutching the teddy bear from the store.

'Mia's exhausted,' he explained, pulling the door closed.

'Oh, hello,' Kim said to the woman, who was using kitchen towel to wipe down the work surface.

'Ella, my sister,' he explained. 'I called to ask if she'd seen Kat, and she came straight over.'

Kim would not have needed the explanation of their relationship had the woman turned to face her a few seconds earlier.

The siblings had the same straw-blonde hair and square jaw. She guessed Ella to be maybe ten years older than her brother's twenty-nine years.

'Is Kat okay?' Ella asked, but Kim could see in her clear blue eyes that she already knew she was not, whereas her brother's expression was full of nervous hope.

'Mr Nock, please, sit down,' Kim said. All four of them standing in the cramped kitchen was overpowering.

'Just tell me—'

'Mr Nock, if you'll just—'

'Sit down, Andy,' his sister said as though she knew what was coming.

He sat and Kim did the same. Bryant moved to the doorway to offer a little more space.

Ella dried her hands on a tartan tea towel.

'Mr Nock, I'm sorry to have to tell you that your wife is not okay. She's—'

'I knew I should have said no,' he claimed, running his hand through his hair. 'I could tell by her mood that she wasn't quite with it, but we did the usual checks and—'

'What checks?' Kim asked. She'd been about to tell him his wife was dead, and she knew that anything she could learn at this point may not be accessible after he received the news.

'My wife has problems, officer. She suffers from anxiety and depression. She refuses to take medication and normally she's fine and handles it well, but this morning I watched her take dirty plates out of the dishwasher for breakfast.'

'And the checks?' Kim asked, not sure she hadn't accidentally done the same thing herself on occasion. It didn't mean that she was depressed or anxious. More likely distracted by some problem she was having with her current motorcycle restoration project or a case she was working.

'She tells me exactly where she's going, and I call her every couple of hours.'

As though knowing her next question, Bryant took out his pocket notebook.

'And where exactly was your wife going today?'

'She had a doctor's appointment at ten, and then she was going to Brierley Hill to pick up some things from Asda and Shop N Save. Then she was taking Mia to the Ball Factory play centre.'

'And you called her?'

'Probably three times during the morning, and then I couldn't get her after lunch. I called Ella and then I went out looking for her, just in and out of shops, and couldn't see her anywhere, so made some calls – the hospital and then the station – to see if there had been any accidents.'

'Is she in trouble, officer?' Andrew asked, linking his hands together. 'Has she done something wrong?'

*In a minute, you're going to wish she had*, Kim thought, taking a deep breath.

'Mr Nock, I am so sorry to tell you that your wife is dead.'

No matter what words she used to lead up to it, that last word still had to come out of her mouth and there was no way of softening it up.

The only movement in the room was the tartan tea towel falling from Ella's hands to the ground.

Andrew Nock simply stared at her and began to shake his head involuntarily. His gaze moved to the door across the hallway where his daughter lay sleeping.

She watched as a range of emotions crossed his face.

The truth of the news registered with his sister first.

'How?… I mean…'

Kim guessed Ella was thinking that Katrina had harmed herself in some way. Kim hated the fact that it was all going to get worse when she delivered the rest of the news. She'd seen many methods of suicide but breaking one's own neck wasn't one of them.

'I'm afraid I have to inform you that Katrina was murdered.'

'No… no… no…' Andrew cried out.

Kim understood his pain. The first bombshell had barely landed before she'd ripped the pin out of a second grenade.

Disbelief shaped his features as he continued to shake his head. As yet there were no tears. She knew they would come with acceptance.

'This is some kind of mistake. I'm in a nightmare. There's something wrong. It makes no sense. Why would anyone want to kill Kat?'

He looked to her as though she had the answer when, in fact, she was hoping to learn that from him.

'That's exactly what we intend to find out,' she said, looking from one to the other. 'Is there anyone you can think of who had any kind of grudge against Katrina, or anything strange that might have happened to her recently?'

Both shook their heads as though they were humouring her until she told them the truth.

A light cough from Bryant told her what she was already thinking: they both needed space and time for the news to sink in.

'We're going to leave you alone for now, but a family liaison officer is on the way. They'll answer any questions you have, and we'll be back to talk again.'

Kim stood.

Andrew Nock continued to stare forward as though she hadn't spoken. Kim wished she had words of comfort to ease his suffering, but there was nothing. As the hours grew, he would understand that the nightmare was real. There would be tears and heartache and more tears as he considered how to tell his little girl that her mummy wasn't coming home.

'I'll see you out,' Ella said.

Kim passed the door to the lounge where the little girl slept. Kim's heart ached. When she woke, Mia's life would never be the same again.

'Does the body need to be identified, officer?' Ella asked, taking a deep breath.

Kim could sense that the woman before her was a coper: one of those people that came into their own in the face of tragedy. The sort of person one needed in times like this.

'Yes, when your brother is—'

'I can take care of it,' she stated.

Kim hesitated. 'It may be something your brother needs to do for acceptance,' she said, looking back into the house and noting that the man still hadn't moved an inch.

'I'll decide later if he's up to it,' Ella said in a parental tone.

Kim didn't show her surprise at the woman's take-charge attitude. Sometimes it was what people needed at times like this.

'Oh, and Inspector,' she said with her hand on the door handle, 'please cancel that liaison officer. My brother has me. He doesn't need anyone else.'

# CHAPTER ELEVEN

'It was around one thirty in the morning,' Lesley began with a faraway look in her eyes.

Stacey guessed that was the last memory she had of being carefree and unafraid.

'The last act had finished a while before and security were ushering us out the gates. Taxis and parents' cars lined the road, even at that time. I lived less than a mile away, so hadn't asked anyone to pick me up. I said good night to my friends, and they piled into different cars and carried on up the road. I could still hear the beat of the band in my ears, which is probably why I didn't hear anyone behind me.'

Lesley paused as a dozen 'if onlys' appeared to surge through her mind.

'I was about halfway home when I felt a searing pain to the back of my head,' she said as her right hand touched the spot. 'I didn't know I'd been hit. I didn't know anything until I regained consciousness and, even then, the blinding pain came second to the smell.'

'The smell?' Stacey queried.

Lesley nodded. 'I was face down in someone's front garden. My head was being held against the dirt amongst a bed of geraniums; it's a smell I'll never forget. I can't smell it now without wanting to burst into tears.'

Stacey knew that some victims retained triggers from their attacks that brought the memories flooding back, even if the attack was not at the forefront of the mind. It could be the sound of traffic, a car horn, certain words or phrases used by the attacker. For Lesley, it would be the cloying scent of geraniums.

'I felt the suffocation of the smell before the thundering pain in my head or the realisation of what was happening. His hand was holding me down exactly where I'd been struck, and he was assaulting me from behind. Any movement and the pain brought nausea up to my throat. I thought I was going to choke on my own vomit. I thought I was going to die,' she whispered, blinking back the tears.

Stacey nodded but said nothing. She didn't want to rush her along. The story had to be told at her own pace, in her own way.

'It was only then that I became aware of what was being done to me. I could feel something cold and hard being pushed in and out of my vagina. My shorts and underwear were around my ankles, and he was positioned on my left side, one hand on my head and one… well…'

Stacey nodded, trying to keep her face expressionless in spite of her growing rage. She didn't need the girl to keep repeating it. The ordeal was horrific enough the first time.

'I tried to scream, but my mouth was face down in the dirt. I tried to struggle, but my body was beyond exhausted, as though every limb was being held down by lead weights. It carried on for a few more minutes and then it was over. I could still smell the flowers, but the weight disappeared from my head. I still couldn't lift it. I didn't even know I'd been crying; the tears had mixed with the dirt. Suddenly, the silence was overwhelming.'

Stacey waited.

'Eventually, I managed to crawl to the front door of the house and hit the front door. At first, the elderly man who lived there thought I was drunk and threatened to call the police. I just croaked out that I'd been raped. He called the police, and then sat beside me, careful not to touch me but just telling me he wasn't leaving me and that the police were coming. Ten minutes later they did.'

She opened her hands expressively as if to say, 'that's it'.

Stacey had been forming a list of questions in her mind as Lesley had been speaking. Right now, she was at a loss to understand why this woman had been denied the opportunity to testify on the stand. She was clear, concise, had a good memory of events which she recited calmly.

Stacey knew her questions had already been asked at the time of the attack, but maybe the retelling of the event had brought up some forgotten detail.

'Did he say anything to you at all?'

Lesley shook her head. 'Not one word.'

'Was there any obvious smell, other than the flowers?'

Lesley sighed heavily, as though she wished she had more to offer. 'None.'

'And you saw nothing at all?'

Again, she shook her head. 'Once he was gone, I didn't move for ages in case he came back to kill me. I thought I was going to die, so I was too frightened to look.'

'Do you have any idea what he used to assault you?'

'I'm sorry but I don't. It was hard and smooth, but not cold like glass.'

Stacey knew nothing had been found at the scene.

'It said in the report that there was minimal damage and bruising to the vagina.' A fact that had thrown doubt over her story at the beginning of the investigation.

'He wasn't rough.'

'I'm sorry?' Stacey said, taken aback. The attack had sounded horrific.

'He wasn't brutal. Don't get me wrong, I was humiliated, angry, hurt, shamed and undeniably changed for the rest of my life because of what that bastard did to me. I'll likely never trust a man again, but you haven't asked me if there was anything I sensed.'

'Was there?'

She nodded.

'I got the impression that he wasn't in control, that he didn't really want to do what he was doing.'

Stacey sat back, careful to keep the surprise from her face. But, finally, she understood why Lesley Skipton could never have been put on the stand.

# CHAPTER TWELVE

*I did it. I killed her, and there was a satisfaction to the twist of the neck that was morbidly gratifying for me. A slight thing, she didn't put up much of a fight, but it wouldn't have mattered if she had. She was going to die regardless.*

*There were so many stages of the killing process to enjoy. The planning, the how and the where and eventually, the who. There is a power that comes with deciding whose life I'm going to take. I relish that anticipation, enjoy the dominance I have. I imagine their life and the grief it will cause. I want to inflict the maximum amount of pain on the victim and their family.*

*The act itself is almost the best part. I had visualised the manner of death way before I touched her. In truth, there was a little disappointment. It was much harder to twist the neck than I'd thought. Even with one hand on the chin and one hand on the top of the head, there was no definite crack of the neck as the spinal cord snapped, making a sound like it does in the films. I would have liked to hear a sound. Instead, she just fell limply against me, her eyes staring up in an anticlimactic kind of way.*

*I must try not to think about such things; my enjoyment pales against the practicality and prefers to remember it how I saw it in my mind's eye. And anyway, it was quick, it was clean, and I will not get caught. That's what matters the most.*

*I saw your face again. I see it every time I take a life. I pretend that I'm killing you instead of the victim, and that's okay because I can continue to kill you a million times – over and over again.*

*Yes, every single part of murder is enjoyable to me. But nothing compares to my favourite part.*

*The best is yet to come, I think to myself as I take out my phone.*

# CHAPTER THIRTEEN

'Run that by me again,' Kim said once Stacey had updated her on the shuffle case.

'She has some kind of sympathy for her attacker,' Stacey repeated. 'She was even grateful that he pulled her shorts up and covered her once he'd finished. I get why they couldn't use her,' she admitted.

Kim got it. 'She'd have been more like a witness for the defence. His barrister would have gone to town and twisted the whole thing so it would have appeared consensual.'

'Exactly, boss, which would have weakened the case for the first victim, Gemma Hornley. It's likely he'd have walked and paid for neither crime.'

Kim agreed. 'Well, given that we've got a murder investigation to—'

'Can I stay on it, boss?' Stacey asked. 'She's still a victim and she's being denied justice for telling the truth.'

Kim opened her mouth to refuse until the irony of Stacey's words hit home. Truth and justice didn't always go hand in hand, but they had to give it their best shot.

'Okay, but if I need to pull you off while Bryant and I—'

'Err… present and fit for duty, boss,' Penn said, throwing his hand in the air to indicate he could pick up any slack on Stacey's behalf.

'Noted,' Kim said.

Despite his offer, she was not prepared to let him spread himself too thinly. She couldn't help going a bit easier on Penn given his recent loss, even though he didn't request it. He was now sole carer for his brother, which would include a period of adjustment for both of them.

'Okay, guys, there's little more we can do tonight on Katrina's murder, so go home, sleep well and be back at seven o'clock sharp.'

It was almost eight now, so that gave them all a good eleven-hour turnaround.

Not so much for her. She had yet to brief Woody on the INEPT meeting, but once she'd done that her involvement with the event at the end of the week would be well and truly over.

# CHAPTER FOURTEEN

Penn opened the door of his home and took a good long sniff.

He swallowed his disappointment. He'd hoped to be greeted by the delicious aromas of baking that filled the house when Jasper was cooking. Jasper hadn't been allowed to cook alone since the time he'd allowed a pan of melting butter to burn when his best friend, Billy, had sent him a link to some YouTube videos. The pan had caught fire, and Jasper had had the sense to run next door for help.

Lily, a retired schoolteacher, had put out the fire and told Jasper that any time he wanted to cook without Penn she'd come round and be chief taster.

Every night when he phoned to say he was going to be late, he hoped his brother had taken Lily up on her kind offer and returned to what he loved to do.

Looked like Stacey was going to be disappointed again tomorrow. His brother hadn't set foot in the kitchen since their mother's funeral. In fact, he'd barely left his room at all.

Penn headed up the stairs and knocked gently on a door that was now permanently closed.

He received a grunt in response.

Penn fixed a smile to his face before he entered the room.

'Hey, bud, fancy trying out a new recipe I found for cheese scones?' he asked, ruffling his brother's hair.

Jasper pulled away and shook his head.

Penn tried not to let the gesture hurt him. His brother was in pain and it was up to him to keep things as normal as he could.

'Come on, mate, I'll even let you grate the cheese.'

Jasper shook his head and continued to focus on the game.

'Okay, what if I let you?…'

'No, Ozzy,' he said testily.

Anger was not a natural state for his brother, so Penn knew when not to push.

'Okay, what do you want to eat?'

'Not hungry.'

'Mate, you gotta eat something,' Penn insisted.

He could already see that his brother had dropped a few pounds, offering Penn the proof he'd been right that Jasper had eaten as much as he'd baked.

'You want beans on toast?'

Hardly a balanced meal, but it was his favourite and it was hot and right now he'd take it.

Jasper shook his head.

'Mate…'

'Had a noodle.'

Penn opened his mouth to argue and thought better of it. One of Jasper's biggest frustrations was being treated like a small child when he was almost sixteen years of age. He knew his own mind and Penn sometimes had to respect his right to choose.

'Okay, bud, I'll be downstairs if you want me,' he said, leaving the door slightly ajar.

He was halfway down the stairs when he heard it close completely.

Penn switched on the kettle for a cuppa and checked the bin. Sure enough on top was a half-empty pot noodle container. It wasn't enough, but he couldn't force-feed the kid.

If he was honest, he felt he was in uncharted territory. He missed his mum every day. The months they'd known she was dying hadn't prepared him for the eventual loss.

Between the three of them they'd stumbled along. His mum had been the firm but gentle parent with Jasper, always able to reach him, and Penn had been the older brother, making Jasper laugh, encouraging him to try new things while protecting him from the harsher elements in the world. Both he and his mum had held a place in Jasper's life, fulfilled a role in his development. But what was his role now? Was he fun-loving brother or firm parent? If he was both, how did he juggle the two? All he knew was that his brother needed him to be strong and that's what he intended to be.

He poured the water into the cup as his phone began to ring.

He smiled when he saw the caller's name.

'Hey, Lynne,' he answered.

'Yo, comrade,' she responded. It was how she had greeted him when they'd worked together at West Mercia.

He had been grateful for her support at his mum's funeral, and she'd called to check on him a couple of times since.

'What you up to?' he asked, enjoying hearing the sound of her voice.

'Just finished a long shift and wondered if you two guys wanted to help me eat my own body weight in pizza?'

'Where's Simon?' he asked. Lynne had been engaged to the accountant for almost five years.

'Oh, err… squash practice. Not sure what he's practising for, but hey ho with all this practice he's gotta be getting better.'

Penn laughed out loud. It was a good feeling. Lynne had always been able to make him laugh.

'So how about it, homey?'

The thought of sharing a meal and some light conversation with his old colleague was tempting. Chatting had always been easy between them. They shared similar taste in films, and Lynne's own music collection was as eclectic as his own. Yet as much as he appreciated her sympathy mission, he didn't feel that either he or Jasper would be very good company this evening.

'Thanks for the offer, Lynne, but maybe another time, eh?'

'No probs, matey. Just give me a shout when you're up to it. I'll be waiting for your call.'

'Cheers, buddy,' he said, ending the conversation.

As soon as the line went dead, the brief light that had shone into his mind was gone. Her company was something he could have used, but a part of him recoiled at being the guest of honour at anyone's pity party.

He knew people felt sorry for his lot in life. He didn't have the same freedom as most guys his age. In the wake of his mother's death, Jasper was his number one responsibility and would always be his top priority.

# CHAPTER FIFTEEN

Lynne fought the disappointment that rested heavily in her stomach as the phone went dead in her ear. All day she'd been looking forward to spending a couple of hours with her old colleague.

She'd known she was going to miss him when he transferred out of West Mercia. Their easy working relationship had grown into a firm friendship she valued and intended to maintain. Her working day was so much longer without her partner in crime.

She smiled sadly as she remembered their years working together. For a damn good police officer, he didn't notice some things that were staring him in the face.

Over the years she had watched him wrestle with the decision to leave his old team to move back home to his ailing mother. She'd watched his commitment to his younger brother, for which he wanted no comment or praise.

She had taken him out for a drink on some of his tougher days.

It was only once he'd left that she'd realised she looked forward to going to work more than she looked forward to going home, and that Penn was a big part of that feeling.

She had wanted to see him tonight in the hope that he'd finally start to take notice.

She wanted him to see that she didn't seek his company out of pity, that she genuinely wanted to spend time with him. She'd wanted him to notice her new hairstyle and the touch of make-up that she rarely applied for work.

But mostly she had wanted him to notice the absence of the engagement ring on her finger. Yes, there was a part of her that wanted to wave her left hand in front of his face, but what if he didn't feel the same way? Did she want to risk ruining a genuine friendship and lose him altogether? For her that wasn't an option. If he did feel the same, she would just have to wait for him to wake up to his own emotions in his own time.

But that wouldn't be tonight, she thought as she saw the light illuminate in the front bedroom.

She started the car, glanced at the pizza boxes on the passenger seat and slowly pulled away from the kerb.

# CHAPTER SIXTEEN

It was after eleven when Kim let herself into her home.

'Hey, boy,' she said, reaching down and stroking Barney's head.

Charlie from down the road had dropped him off around 7 p.m., said his text message, followed by an emoji of a panting dog. There was something surreal about a man in his early seventies discovering emojis.

'Did you have a good day, buddy?' she asked as he followed her to the kitchen.

His day had started at 6 a.m. with a run around the park before another soul appeared. Barney had never reacted well to other dogs, and she had never forced the issue. She didn't play well with others either, and efforts to force her to do so were met with hostility and aggression, just like Barney. He was far more interested in human interaction, and she wouldn't lose his trust by forcing him to be anything else.

'Had a good afternoon with Charlie?'

Worryingly, she could swear he nodded.

It was a great arrangement that worked well for everyone. Charlie had lost his own beloved dog a few years earlier and missed the company, but no longer wished for the responsibility of vet visits and illness. What had started as Charlie popping in to let Barney out for a bit had developed into him collecting Barney for an afternoon walk around the block, taking him back to his home and spoiling him for a few hours before bringing him back. It was how she envisaged treating nephews and nieces if she'd had them. Get all the good bits but none of the responsibility. Luckily, Charlie was not against the occasional overnight stay if the need arose.

And she'd considered that tonight, but the thought of returning to an empty house had stopped her from making the call.

'Oh, come here, you big doofus,' she said, lowering herself to the floor. The day had been long and hard, and she needed just a few minutes' break from her own head.

Barney ran into the kitchen and returned with the carcass of a stuffed toy he'd ripped open and gutted a couple of days earlier. The scraggy piece of material was now his new best friend.

'Give it here,' she said, tugging on what might have been a tail or an ear.

He pulled back, wagging his tail, his eyes bright and alive.

'Mine,' she said, feeling the stresses of the day lift as she played tug-of-war with the dog.

After a few minutes, he dropped the toy and nestled into her body.

'Aah, this is what you want, eh?' she asked, scratching at the skin beneath the dense fur.

'Time for Aunty Dawn to come get you, my boy.'

Barney had developed a tolerance for the groomer. She came and collected him at the end of the day to keep him separate from her other clients.

He nuzzled Kim and looked up at the counter top. The place she always deposited his leash.

'Okay, boy, let's get the coffee on first,' she said, getting to her feet. She opened the back door in case he was desperate to pee.

He knew the routine. Coffee pot went on before their late-night walk, whatever the time.

Sleep experts would be shaking their heads at her right now. She knew that counting down the hours until she was back at work did her no good. Neither did making a fresh pot of coffee before bed or taking a brisk walk with her dog around midnight, but she'd tried it their way and that hadn't worked for her either. The relaxation tapes had annoyed the hell out of her, and sleep hygiene was a set of rules she just couldn't follow.

Only one thing had the power to fully relax her, she thought, opening the door that led from the kitchen to the garage.

The last motorcycle she'd restored had been sold a week ago to a Japanese collector. The money she'd received was already in the account of Enterprise Electronics, ready to update the communication equipment used by Lucy Payne, a smart, courageous teenager with muscular dystrophy she'd met during one of the team's first big cases. The girl and her father didn't know the source of the anonymous donations, and that was fine by her.

But the working area of her garage was now empty. Her tools were clean, tidy and in their rightful place. A thin layer of dust covered the iPod full of classical music, and she'd never seen anything so depressing in her life.

She closed the door, stepped back into the kitchen and took out her phone.

The call was answered on the fourth ring by a voice thick with sleep.

'What the fuck?…'

'You got that frame for me yet, Dobbie?' she asked. He was the local scrap merchant and the provider of many of her bike frames.

'Fuck me. Do yer know what fucking time it is?'

'Yeah, but I'm your best customer. So, have you got it yet?'

She'd asked him to source the frame for a Vincent Black Shadow, which she planned to rebuild from scratch.

'Bloody hell. This is police harassment, yer know.'

'Not yet but it could be. So…'

'They're like rockin' horse shit, but I might have summat for yer tomorra. I'll shout yer some time reasonable.'

'Three hundred quid, right?' she said, confirming the price they'd agreed.

'Yeah, yeah, now f—'

Kim ended the call before he could swear at her again.

She smiled hopefully as she reached for Barney's leash. Having a restoration project kept her sane. It kept her occupied. It channelled her thoughts. It was where she directed her stress at the end of the day. It helped keep her bad temper and natural aggression at bay.

She hoped Dobbie came through for her soon.

Everyone preferred it when she had a project.

# CHAPTER SEVENTEEN

'Okay, kiddies, let's get to it,' Kim said, placing her coffee beside her as she took her spot on the edge of the spare desk.

She was pleased to see that Katrina's details had made it onto the wipe board. Her team knew how she felt about victim identification. This time yesterday, Katrina Nock had been a stranger to them all, but now she was their top priority. Their relationship with her was now paramount. They knew where she lived, they knew her family and by the time they were finished they would know her killer. Every victim had an identity and a story.

'Thanks, Bryant, but why have you put the little circle above the "i" in Katrina's name?' she asked.

He smirked. 'I was trying to do Stacey's writing to confuse you.'

Kim raised an eyebrow. 'If I'm that easily deceived, we're all fucked! So, anyone had any thoughts on our victim's murder or murderer?' she asked, crossing her arms.

'Not getting it, boss,' Stacey said, shaking her head. 'She was a young mother out shopping with her kid. She wasn't showy or part of any bad crowd. She had no enemies we know of and the method was clean.'

Kim agreed. The absence of blood or rage or obvious violence was puzzling.

'It's almost like it wasn't personal,' Penn observed.

'But why her, then?' Bryant asked. 'If the object was only to kill, there were easier subjects out and about in Brierley Hill yesterday lunchtime.'

'And what about that?' Kim asked. 'Time of day she was murdered?' In her experience most murders happened in the dark.

'Strange time to kill someone,' Stacey offered. 'Busy time of day, shoppers around, potential witnesses. Maybe a thrill-seeker?'

Kim shook her head. 'The murder wasn't ostentatious enough for that.'

'So maybe it was about Katrina,' Penn answered. 'Perhaps it was just about her, and all the murderer wanted was this particular woman gone.'

'Maybe,' Kim answered.

Between them her team had put into words the thoughts and confusion that had been swirling around her head all night. Why take the unnecessary risk of luring away a young mother in the middle of the day if that wasn't the specific person you wanted?

'Okay, Penn, you're on post-mortem duty, which is first thing.'

'Yay,' he said, rubbing his hands.

Kim had long ago become used to Penn's enthusiasm for the grisliest part of their work. It wasn't a thirst for macabre entertainment. He genuinely enjoyed the science behind the process. He relished a puzzle and seeing what the body could reveal.

'Stace, check on Katrina's health records. She suffered with depression. We need to know if she's spent any time away and how bad her problems were. Also liaise with Inspector Plant on witness statements.'

A team of PCs had been tasked with talking to the stores and potential witnesses.

Both of those jobs Stacey could do while still working on the rape case from the day before. She was confident the constable knew how to prioritise her work.

'And us?' Bryant asked.

There was still so much about the events of the murder that she didn't understand.

'We, Bryant, are going back to the scene of the crime.'

# CHAPTER EIGHTEEN

Stacey set about completing the tasks issued by the boss before continuing her investigation into the rape of Lesley Skipton, who had been on her mind for most of the night.

She couldn't get her head around Lesley's feelings towards her rapist. She'd read enough about Stockholm syndrome to understand the psychology of how a victim can grow attached to their captor.

Famous cases of the syndrome had been documented, most notably the infamous Patty Hearst, granddaughter of American publishing magnate, William Randolph Hearst. Patty had been kidnapped by the Symbionese Liberation Army in 1974. After nineteen months in captivity, the woman was arrested for committing serious crimes along with her captors.

Even more startling had been the case of Colleen Stan, who was abducted by a husband and wife, Cameron and Janice Hooker, while hitch-hiking in 1977. The woman had been kept as a domestic/sex slave in a box beneath the couple's bed for seven years and did not attempt to escape. When freed by Janice, Colleen remained silent about the abuse, as requested by her captors.

But any case of Stockholm syndrome that Stacey knew of involved the victim spending time with their captor, and the attachment growing over a period of years, months, even weeks. She'd never heard of it with a rape victim.

She put the thoughts aside as a constable appeared at the door.

'First statements will be up in a couple of hours,' he said, throwing the post on the spare desk.

'Cheers, John,' she said as he went out of view.

She typed up an email to Katrina's doctor and hit the send button. Gone were the days she could get medical information over the phone.

Okay, jobs done, she reached for the file of Lesley Skipton, and yet what she really wanted was the file of Gemma Hornley. That hadn't been sent to her, as the case was solved and Sean Fellows was doing the time.

She searched for the case electronically. If Sean Fellows had raped both of them, why hadn't his first victim had similar feelings to Lesley?

She read through the initial statement given by Gemma on the night of the attack.

She had been leaving a pub in Hagley, again with only a short walk home. Just like Lesley, she'd been hit on the back of the head, rendered unconscious and dragged into someone's property. She'd regained consciousness to find her head being held into the dirt by a hand and a foreign object being inserted savagely into her vagina.

Stacey skipped forward to the medical report which bore out Gemma's description. The bruising and cuts to her vagina and thighs had indeed been the result of a brutal attack.

There had been no words spoken, just like Lesley's attack, but there was one significant difference. After the sexual assault, Sean Fellows had taken a knife and cut into the flesh of Gemma's buttock. The wound was only an inch or so, made up of a few small cut marks. Why had Sean Fellows not done the same to Lesley?

The more she read about Gemma's attack, the more confused she became. The cases were so similar yet different.

Sean Fellows had been identified by Gemma Hornley herself. She'd had sex with him earlier in the evening in the club toilet.

He'd approached her as she was leaving, asking for a repeat performance. She'd refused, and he'd got angry. CCTV had shown a heated argument between them, Gemma storming off, and him heading away in the same direction.

Gemma had been convinced it was him, so had the police and so had the jury.

Stacey suddenly had a ridiculous thought that Brierley Hill didn't even appear to have considered: what if Sean Fellows wasn't responsible for the attack on Lesley Skipton? What if they'd been chasing the wrong man for it all along?

Stacey knew she needed to talk to Gemma, his first victim. Having already spoken to Lesley, she would then be in a position to compare the attacks on both women.

She reminded herself that Gemma was a solved case and that Brierley Hill wouldn't be thrilled to have her sniffing round, asking questions of one of their victims.

But whether it made her popular or not, it was something she was just going to have to do.

# CHAPTER NINETEEN

'There she is,' Kim said, stabbing the screen with her finger.

The store detective at the Shop N Save had kindly burned the relevant CCTV footage to disc, which they were viewing right now.

They watched as Katrina Nock and her child entered the store. Mia immediately began pulling at her mother's hand to go in the direction of the toys located at the back of the shop. Katrina appeared to protest for just a few seconds as she looked towards the card stand located at the entrance, but then gave in and followed her daughter out of camera shot.

The CCTV operator had had no cause to follow them on camera, so they disappeared from view within seconds.

The screen went blank as the computer jumped to the next snatch of footage on the disc. This was a visual of both mother and daughter looking around the toys in the background of the main shot. The camera was focused on a teenage male wearing a hoody and loose jeans.

'Fair play,' Bryant said, and she knew what he meant.

The CCTV operator had pored over every bit of footage they'd recorded to find any instance where Katrina or Mia had appeared on camera. His efforts had saved Stacey or Penn hours of work.

The camera moved away from the mother and child as the operator had followed the known shoplifter out the door.

The camera rested there for a moment, and Kim could visualise the store detective putting out a radio message to other stores warning them of his presence.

The camera then swept the length of the store to return to its resting position close to the tills.

'Play that bit again,' Kim said.

Bryant rewound and slowed the footage. On its journey back, the camera's gaze had caught Katrina perusing the toiletry aisle and Mia still hovering around the toys.

Kim took a good look. Katrina was interacting with no one and no one appeared to be showing her any undue attention.

The screen went blank again before the final piece of footage filled the screen. The angle was back to the fixed camera at the entrance. Katrina was picking out and reading greetings cards at a stand just inside the door. A basket of small purchases was at her feet. She placed a card back before looking over the top of the stand to the rear of the store.

'Checking on Mia,' Bryant observed. Obviously satisfied that her child was safe, she reached to pick out another card, but paused and turned her head to look out of the shop.

'Slow it,' Kim said.

In slow motion they watched as she appeared to listen to someone on the outside of the shop.

She nodded and began using her hands to point.

Kim had the urge to try and turn the camera to capture who had been outside the store, but of course it wasn't live time: it was an historic piece of footage that couldn't be altered. 'Directions,' Kim said, watching Katrina's mannerisms. 'Someone was asking for directions.'

Kim watched as Katrina glanced back up towards the toys before taking a step towards the exit of the shop.

Kim had the urge to shout out not to do it, not to take those last few steps that were going to end her life.

Her mind screamed the words as Katrina continued to move towards the door.

She stepped over the threshold and out of sight.

Kim knew she had just witnessed the last time that Katrina Nock had been seen alive.

# CHAPTER TWENTY

'Err… mind stepping back a little, Penn,' Keats said, moving towards the weighing scales with a kidney in his hands.

'Oh, sure,' Penn said, moving away from the body of Katrina Nock.

'I can honestly say I'm flattered by your diligent interest in my work, but very few observers want to get this close to the process.'

Penn shrugged and waited. If that was the pathologist's indirect way of calling him weird, it wasn't the first time the observation had been thrown his way. And it didn't bother him one little bit.

His analytical brain was interested in the mechanics, the detail of a subject: how the sum of the parts made something work. He remembered one of his friends in school falling from a tree while on a school trip. Kids and teachers had gathered around out of concern, and Penn had gathered too. Once the screaming from Jimmy had assured Penn his friend was alive, he had focused on the angles of the broken limbs, captivated by the picture of flesh ripped open by splintering bones, picturing the twisted muscle and sinews hidden from view. So engrossed, he'd been disappointed when the paramedics had whisked Jimmy away to hospital.

It wasn't that he didn't feel empathy for the victims, but he'd never been one to dwell on things he couldn't change.

If he could have prevented Jimmy Ryland from falling out of the tree, he would have done so. If it was in his power to resurrect Katrina Nock and send her home to her family, he would do so in a heartbeat, but he couldn't and so it was best to learn all that he could so they could catch the person who'd killed her and offer some comfort to her loved ones.

Luckily, he'd never been squeamish and was able to dispassionately view the sight before him and see the body for the complex and miraculous sequence of parts that had once worked together to form a life.

Keats noted a measurement before carefully placing the organ back into the body. Had there been any doubt as to the cause of death, Keats would have taken samples from each organ and sent them to the lab for testing.

'Normal,' Keats said out loud.

*Just like everything else*, Penn thought. So far, there had been nothing not normal about Katrina Nock. She'd been in decent physical shape and all major organs had been functioning correctly. She'd never smoked, had no broken bones, good teeth and had eaten a bowl of cereal for breakfast.

Samples of blood and urine had been taken for toxicology to determine drugs, medicines and other natural body chemicals, but Penn didn't expect anything out of the ordinary there.

Clean was the word that kept going through his mind. Everything about it was clean. The murder itself had been clean: confirmed by Keats as a broken neck. He had explained that when the neck breaks near the skull, three things happen – you can't move, you stop breathing and your body loses the ability to control your heart – resulting in instant death.

'But it's not as easy as they portray it in the films,' Keats had explained. 'The neck bones and muscles offer some resistance, so we're talking considerable physical strength to execute this method of murder, if you'll excuse the pun.'

Penn had seen the fatal injury before in traffic collisions, but never as a result of murder.

There was no blood, no messy wounds, no bruises, no suffering, no emotion. It was almost like a different class of murder:

polite, well-mannered, genteel. Without excessive violence. There was no mess.

'Okay, Penn, I'm going to close her up now,' Keats said, disturbing his thoughts.

Penn reached around to remove his face mask.

'Okay, Keats, thanks…'

'Didn't say I was finished with you yet, did I?' he asked, expertly bringing the flesh back together with the sailmaker's needle and the heavy twine, which was much coarser than normal stitches. The end result always reminded Penn of a baseball.

'Eager beaver,' Keats said, glancing his way.

Oh, how Penn loved the cat-and-mouse games they played.

'I'm a bit pushed for—'

'It's this I'm not sure about,' Keats said, laying the needle onto the flesh that covered the rib cage. He went back to the scratches he'd noted on the left wrist close to Katrina's watch.

'I thought you said they were probably marks left by the watch,' Penn questioned. It was the first thing he'd noted during the procedure, and Penn had written off their relevance.

'It was definitely my first thought that at some point this girl was grabbed around the wrist, but I'd like to take another look.'

Penn watched as the pathologist took out a hand-held magnifying glass and peered closely at the scratches, even though they were obvious to the naked eye.

'Hmm…' he said, viewing the flesh at every conceivable angle.

Penn knew better than to prompt the man until he was finished, and so looked over his shoulder. He had agreed that the few small sticks and arcs had come from rough handling of the watch and had attached no further significance to the finding.

'Hmm…' Keats repeated. 'I appear to have been mistaken.'

'I'll be sure to let the boss know,' Penn quipped.

Keats peered over his glasses before continuing.

'It's no longer my opinion that these scratches were caused by the watch.'

Penn waited.

'I believe these scratches were inflicted post-mortem.'

Penn considered his words. Scratches or marks received before the attack meant nothing. Wounds suffered during the attack spoke volumes about the struggle, physicality, physical ability and positioning. Wounds inflicted *after* the crime meant something else entirely. They were a message to someone.

Finally, with a strange sense of relief, he began to remove the protective garments Keats had forced upon him.

The murder was not so tidy after all.

# CHAPTER TWENTY-ONE

Kim stood in the exact same position that Katrina had stood when she'd been gesticulating. Bryant was standing outside, where Katrina had been looking to from the card stand.

She moved towards the door, just as Katrina had, and looked around, watching people go in and out of shops: looking down, looking at where they were heading, looking at phones. *Why here? Why Katrina?* Kim wondered for the hundredth time.

She stood in the middle of the pavement and did a 360-degree turn and saw what she hadn't noted yesterday: between the Shop N Save and the chemist next door was a gap, joined together by an old white gate. Right now, the gate was closed.

'Come on, Bryant,' she said as she opened the gate and peered up the alley. In the distance, she could see the back of a white van she knew well. A forensics van.

'Shit.'

Bryant moved towards her to follow. She held up her hand to stop him.

'Wait a minute. Let's act it out,' she said, taking Bryant's position just outside the door. 'You be Katrina,' she instructed. She was the killer and knew what she was going to do. Bryant was the victim and had no idea what was in her mind.

Bryant stepped out of the shop and took a couple of strides towards her, moving his arms around as Katrina had been doing.

The second he was out the door, she grabbed his elbow, guided him forcefully to the alleyway and kicked the gate shut behind her.

'Guv, what the?… aah,' he said as he followed her gaze to where Mitch was taking something from his van.

Bryant had not known what she was going to do and had had little time to act in the three strides it had taken her to remove him from view. Despite the physical differences between them, the element of surprise had been on her side.

'No clue this was here,' Bryant said as they headed towards Mitch, who appeared surprised at their direction of travel.

'Neither did he,' Kim noted as he tapped a techie on the arm and pointed.

The techie grabbed a roll of incident tape and nodded as he passed.

'For all the good it'll do,' Mitch said, stroking his freshly trimmed beard.

'Play with that too much and it'll drop off,' Kim said.

'My mum told me that once when I was a little boy. Actually, now I come to think of it that had nothing to do with my beard.'

Bryant groaned and shook his head.

'Hope you didn't make a special journey,' Mitch continued, pointing to the clear plastic evidence boxes. 'Empty. Absolutely nothing of interest so far.'

Kim could hear the frustration in his voice. Given that the hint of a partial fingerprint or a rogue fibre had the power to electrify the man, she was not hopeful for anything of forensic value. If he said they had nothing, they had absolutely nothing.

'Our guy was very careful to leave no clues behind,' he said miserably.

They all knew about the theory of transference and so knew that his statement wasn't true. But you had to have a starting point.

Many things helped to find forensic evidence on a body. The duration of time the killer spent with the victim, the amount of physical contact, the passion involved in the crime. All of these things offered a better chance of the killer leaving something of himself at the scene.

Kim looked back to the gate through which they'd come. In her estimation, killer and victim may have been together for less than two minutes. Grab, walk, snap and dead. To Kim, it was like the speed-dating version of murder.

Everything about this case so far was random. A victim chosen God only knew why. The risks involved with choosing a young mother out shopping with her child, yet carefully planned so that the murder was seen by no one.

Parts of this case indicated that Katrina had been chosen as a means to an end, yet Kim knew that statistically that was unlikely.

Studies indicated that approximately eighty per cent of murder victims were killed by someone they knew.

*But what had Katrina done?* Kim asked herself as her thoughts continued to chase their own tails.

Before she could make a judgement on whether Katrina was the intended victim or not, she needed to know more about the woman herself.

And for an honest opinion, she knew where she wanted to start.

# CHAPTER TWENTY-TWO

Penn had just about managed to grasp Stacey's hurried instructions before she'd darted out the door, mumbling something about interviewing a second rape victim.

He'd heard the words 'medical records' and 'CCTV' and 'chasing the shops'.

He knew that Stacey had already established that Katrina had attended the morning appointment with her GP, as stated by her husband, and that she'd requested Katrina's medical records. He was guessing she wanted him to do a follow-up, so he quickly tore off an email to the surgery. Both he and Stacey tended to copy each other in on most things in case they needed to jump in and job share.

Next he sent a group email to all the stores on the high street partner scheme, requesting any CCTV footage of Katrina Nock from inside their premises.

Satisfied he'd covered two of Stacey's three requests, he readied himself for the final instruction. Following Stacey's email requests and parameters, they'd received relevant footage from both Asda in Brierley Hill and the Ball Factory. The boss had already viewed the footage at Shop N Save, but there was a copy of everything she'd viewed, and he would look at it again, to see if he could spot anyone appearing in more than one place that would indicate that she'd been followed.

It was a long job ahead, so he'd already visited the canteen, wolfed down a plate of chips and gravy and brought a muffin back for energy later. Just a coffee to pour from the machine and he was set for the long haul.

He placed his mug on his desk and took the headphones from his drawer as he did when he wanted to be totally focused.

He glanced over at the spare desk where the post had been deposited. Usually, either he or Stacey had opened it by lunchtime.

He placed the headphones over his ears and loaded the first file of footage.

He was sure there was nothing there that couldn't wait.

# CHAPTER TWENTY-THREE

One of the first things Kim noticed about the Victorian terrace was its tidiness. The properties either side had hanging baskets still holding onto trailing fuchsias that were bending towards the last rays of sunshine. Most of the small spaces in front of the houses had been decorated in some way to personalise the area. The front of Ella's house was slabbed with no plant pot in sight or hanging basket in front of the plain front door that opened before they had a chance to knock.

Ella was dressed in jeans, a cream jumper and held two carrier bags in her hand.

'Oh…' she said, looking from one to the other.

'May we have a word?' Kim asked.

'I'm just on my way to—'

'We'll just take a minute,' Kim said, standing right in front of her.

She hesitated and placed the bags on the floor. Kim guessed they were emergency supplies en route to her brother's house, although she could think of nothing she could have in those bags that would tempt him right now.

Ella stepped aside for Kim to enter the small reception room, which gave way to an open-plan diner that brought in the light from the back garden.

Kim took a seat at a small, round dining table that seemed familiar. 'Doesn't your brother have this exact same table?'

Ella smiled. 'Mine is solid oak. His is a knock-off from Argos.'

'Oh, okay,' Kim said, receiving more information than she'd needed.

Ella pointedly looked at her watch. The gesture annoyed Kim. Her brother wasn't going anywhere, and neither was his grief.

'We're trying to bother your brother as little as possible and were hoping you could tell us more about Katrina. How would you describe her?'

'Flaky. She was often distracted, glazed, as though she was only half there. I'm not the slightest bit surprised that she wandered off leaving Mia—'

'We have no reason to believe that Katrina did anything wrong. Mia was never in any danger,' Kim said, feeling the need to defend the woman.

Ella shrugged as though it mattered not.

'She suffered from depression?'

Ella rolled her eyes. 'Yes, different medicines over the last few years, but she wasn't on anything at the minute. She'd weaned herself off the last lot of pills because of side effects and was trying to manage without the drugs. I thought it was the right decision: all that muck in her system just making stuff worse. I told her to snap out of it, get herself a hobby.'

Yeah, Kim was sure that a bit of knitting would fight the chemical imbalance in her brain.

'And what was your brother's view on her illness?' Kim asked, using the word pointedly.

'Urghh, he coddled her too much in my opinion. Taking time off work on her worst days, phoning her countless times a day to check on her.'

Sounded perfectly reasonable for a loving husband living with a person suffering from depression.

'Sounds like a happy marriage?' Kim stated as a question.

'To them, perhaps.'

'Sorry?'

'I think happy and healthy are two totally separate things. So yes, they were probably happy despite it being a totally unequal and dysfunctional relationship.'

Kim was quickly realising that Ella viewed her own opinion as a gift she was happy to give over and over again.

She needed no prompt to continue.

'Andrew showed her unqualified levels of patience. They had few friends, as Katrina struggled to maintain relationships outside of her marriage. They didn't mix socially with many people at all.'

'They preferred each other's company?' Kim clarified, not finding the picture dysfunctional if it worked for them.

'I suppose that's one way of putting it,' she said with the slightest hint of huff in her voice. Clearly, once shared her opinion was to be accepted by all.

'He didn't get frustrated with her?' Kim asked. Andrew Nock was beginning to sound like a saint.

'Of course. Who wouldn't? The constant care-taking was getting him down, wearing away at him: always worrying about her and then about Mia. He never showed her though.'

'Did he confide in you?'

She frowned. 'Of course. I'm his sister. He told me everything. I told him to put her away for a bit. Give her and him a rest, but he wouldn't hear of it.'

She was growing to like Andrew Nock more and Ella Nock less every time this woman opened her mouth.

'You wanted him to have her sectioned?' Kim clarified.

'Yes, but he was convinced they could get through it. Things seemed to improve a little after Mia came along, although I still think she was hugely irresponsible in getting pregnant. The child wasn't planned. I mean, who needs a child to look after when you can barely get dressed in a morning?'

Kim wondered if there was anything for which Katrina didn't get the blame because, of course, Andrew hadn't contributed to the pregnancy one little bit.

'But like I said, she improved after Mia came along, which only proved my point that she'd needed more to do.'

Kim swallowed down her irritation. She was pretty sure that wasn't how it worked. It was her understanding that busy people suffered from depression too.

'When Mia turned two, it started up again: new medication, days spent in bed. I don't know how Andy kept his patience.'

'And yesterday he called you when he couldn't find her?'

'Of course. He was beside himself. He was terrified she'd done something stupid and—'

'Done something stupid? Had she ever tried to harm herself before?'

Ella hesitated before nodding. 'Not what I'd call serious attempts. More like cries for attention, but still Andy wouldn't put her away.'

That phrase was starting to grate on Kim's nerves. The woman had not been an embarrassing inconvenience to be shoved out of sight while she came to her senses.

'So she was never hospitalised?'

Ella shook her head. 'I've told you—'

'Andrew wouldn't hear of it,' Kim finished as Ella once again held up her left arm for an obvious look at her watch.

'You must have been quite frustrated on your brother's behalf?' Kim asked, ignoring the gesture. It was clear to Kim the siblings were close.

'Obviously, but he wouldn't listen, so I had no choice but to just put up with it.'

'Can you think of anyone who might have wanted to hurt your sister-in-law?'

Ella shook her head. 'Officer, I have no idea and I don't really care.'

Kim allowed her surprise to show. 'Excuse me?'

Ella shrugged, unconcerned.

'My priority is and always will be my brother and my niece, with whom I must now visit,' she said, moving towards the door.

'Well, thank you for your time,' Kim said sarcastically, although Ella didn't seem to notice as she picked up the bags and locked the door behind them.

'What're your thoughts?' Bryant asked as they watched the woman drive away.

Kim didn't have an answer, but she knew that Ella had not asked about the murderer or murder once.

# CHAPTER TWENTY-FOUR

Stacey knocked hard on the door of the narrow townhouse on a small development in Wordsley. She was unsure whether the sound would be heard above the deep bass music coming from the other side.

She was about to knock again when the door was opened by a woman in her mid-twenties with a mane of deep red hair, wearing a crop top and jeans.

In her left hand was a tumbler of gold liquid and a cigarette. As the smile died on her face, it became clear she had been expecting someone else.

'Gemma Hornley?'

'I am she, her, I mean, yes that's me,' she said, and then laughed out loud. 'No, honestly, I'm Gemma.'

Stacey held up her ID. 'Can I have a word?'

Gemma leaned across her, poking her head out the door.

'Bertram Jennings you're a fucking wanker,' she shouted to the rest of the street. 'Always fucking complaining. I swear they're deader than… well dead folks. Can't stand a bit of fun, but we'll turn it down as soon—'

'I don't know who Bertram Jennings is,' Stacey clarified. 'And this isn't about your music.'

'Oh, okay,' she said, sobering slightly.

'I'm here to talk about Sean Fellows.'

'He getting out?' she asked, frowning.

'Not yet, but if I could just…'

'Come in, come in,' she said, opening the door wider. She held up her tumbler. 'Can I get you something to drink?'

'Err, no, thanks,' Stacey said. It was barely two o'clock.

'Okay, give me a sec,' she said, ducking into the lounge.

'Keep it down, you noisy fuckers,' she shouted.

In response to her request, the music increased a few decibels.

'Dicks,' she said, closing the door on the noise.

She nodded towards the kitchen. Stacey stepped in. The work surface was littered with cans of cheap cider and a couple of bottles of spirits.

Gemma closed the door, but even with the double barrier the music was thudding through loud and clear.

'Celebrating something?' Stacey asked.

'Nah, got a big night out later, so just getting warmed up. A few of us are off into town and the booze is bloody expensive.'

Stacey guessed town meant Birmingham, and she wondered just how warmed up this lot needed to be. She was grateful she wasn't sharing a train or bus with them later.

Stacey couldn't help but draw comparisons between the woman she'd visited the previous day and the woman in front of her. Same attacker, same type of sexual assault. But different outcomes. One who was frightened to leave the house and one who didn't want to stay in. One who seemingly had few friends and one who appeared to have a houseful. Someone lacking in confidence and someone with more than enough. She wondered if that was the difference in justice: that day in court, closure and the ability to move on. Maybe if she could somehow get justice for Lesley, she could also move on with her life like Gemma.

'Do you mind if I ask you a few questions about your attack?'

'Why?' Gemma asked, meeting her gaze. Any evidence she'd been drinking appeared to have gone.

'There's just something to do with another victim that I'm trying to understand.'

'But he's not getting out?'

Stacey shook her head. 'There are no early release plans. It's the attack itself I'd like to discuss, if that's not going to be too painful.'

Gemma dropped the cigarette, which had appeared to burn itself out, in the overflowing ashtray. She reached for the pack on the table and lit another one.

Any hint of the inebriated girl was long gone as her trembling hand put the lighter back down. Gone was the confident young woman drinking herself into a party mood. Now Stacey was seeing the victim of a sexual assault.

'Where do you want me to start?'

'At the beginning. From the minute you were grabbed,' Stacey prompted. She wanted the girl's own words.

'Okay, I'd just left the club heading for home. Not here, I moved from that place. I didn't want to live there any more. Anyway, I'd done the walk loads of times. Never any bugger about. It's through an estate, no fields, alleys or dark corners. Just rows of houses. I was about halfway when I just felt this fucking pain from behind. That's all I remember. I passed out and when I came to he was lying against me. I was face down with the taste of soil in my mouth. I tried to cough it out before it went down my throat. His hand was pressing hard on the huge fucking lump on my head. I blacked out again. When I came to for the second time he was—'

The kitchen door opened, surprising them both. 'Hey, Gem, got any?…'

'Fuck off,' Gemma shouted to the girl who had put her head round the door.

The girl slid away quickly.

Gemma took a long draw on the cigarette and blew out the smoke slowly.

As though sensing the seriousness of the situation in the kitchen, the music miraculously dropped to a reasonable level.

Stacey felt sure that Bertram Jennings, whoever he was, was relieved.

'Please continue when you're ready,' Stacey urged.

Gemma took a deep breath. 'He was ramming something up and down inside me. It was thick and hard, cold. I felt like it was gonna come out my mouth. The pain blinded me. It was worse than the bang to the head. My mind was screaming for it to stop. I thought it was gonna split me open.'

With Gemma he'd been rough.

With Lesley he had not been.

Yet the crimes had been too similar not to have been committed by the same person.

'And what happened next?'

'I wasn't sure if I'd died cos the pain stopped. I could still feel my insides pulsing and throbbing and the soreness of the cuts, but the blinding pain had gone.'

Gemma's genitals had been injured.

Lesley's had not.

'Then I felt something on my bare arse cheek. Something sharp, but nothing compared to the other pain. I didn't even realise I'd been cut. Bastard decided to carve me up into the bargain. Couldn't sit down right for fucking weeks.'

Gemma had been cut.

Lesley had not.

It was the thing that had bothered Stacey most when she'd first read the file: so many similarities but discrepancies too.

'And then?'

'He was gone. I was lying in some fucker's flowerbed trying to find the strength to move.'

The second cigarette, barely smoked, was ground into the ashtray.

Stacey hated prolonging the woman's pain, but she had to be sure.

'Was he tender with you at any time?' Stacey asked, hating the words as they came out her mouth, but needing to say them anyway.

Gemma's eyes widened. 'You are fucking joking?'

Stacey shook her head.

'Did anything I just say sound as though he was being tender? Five stitches down there and a game of noughts and crosses on my arse?'

Stacey could feel the woman's rage rising, and she was sorry she was the cause of it, but she didn't want to leave with questions still in her mind.

'I'm really sorry to push you, Gemma, but was there anything at all that he did to suggest that he didn't want to do what he was doing?'

Gemma stood. 'Bitch; I don't care who you are, you can get the fuck—'

'Gemma, I'm not doubting your story. I know you were sexually assaulted and scarred for life and—'

'And you're trying to turn the bastard into some kind of poor, misguided soul. Not off the back of me you're not. He was brutal, he was sadistic and appeared to enjoy every fucking minute of it. Now get the fuck out of my house.'

Stacey obliged, the nausea at the harm she'd caused swirling around her stomach, aggravating the pit that lived there and growing by the hour.

# CHAPTER TWENTY-FIVE

Kim was pleased to see that Stacey was in her seat by the time she returned from briefing Woody. Kim could also see the tension hunching her shoulders and decided to give her a minute to settle down.

'Okay, Penn?' Kim asked as Bryant handed out the drinks from the canteen. 'Learn anything at the post-mortem?'

'Keats is a knob.'

'Anything I didn't already know?' she asked. This was not news to anyone.

'But a bloody good pathologist,' Bryant defended, seeing as he'd been in a bromance with the guy for years.

'Also, true,' Kim admitted. The latter being the reason he got away with the former.

'Nothing we weren't expecting about the cause or manner of death. But…'

'Go on,' Kim urged.

'There were scratches on her wrist.'

'Caused during the struggle?' Kim asked. She could certainly see how that could happen.

Penn shook his head.

'Inflicted after death. I've enlarged the photo and put it up,' he said, pointing to the wipe board. 'No evidence of bleeding, so the heart had stopped.'

Kim took a closer look. It wasn't a symbol or anything legible, just a collection of scratches.

'Hmm… okay,' she said, stepping back to the spare desk. She picked up the post as Penn continued.

'Been through the CCTV and there is nothing out of the ordinary. Katrina changed things up a bit and went to the ball park first, but she went everywhere she told her husband she was going. Boss, I just want to say one thing.'

'Go on,' she said, opening the first envelope.

'I saw absolutely no evidence of Katrina being forgetful, confused or disoriented. She always knew where her child was, so…'

Kim nodded her understanding. She'd thought the same herself. Katrina's death was not linked in any way to her being a negligent or even forgetful mother.

'Anything on the statements?'

Penn shook his head, and, knowing now what she did about the alley to the side of the building and how quickly one could be shepherded towards it, she was not surprised.

'Stace, what you been up to?' she asked, taking the single sheet of paper from the envelope.

'Getting different stories from the rape victims, boss. If it's all right with you, I'd like…'

Kim was no longer listening as she read the first line of the note.

She tried to hold her rage, but the words thundered into the air as she looked around at her team.

'How fucking long have we had this?'

# CHAPTER TWENTY-SIX

'Bryant, get me an evidence bag. Stacey, call Mitch and get him over here. Now.'

Both sprang into action as Kim held the single sheet of paper up by the top left-hand corner. She took out her phone with the other hand and snapped a photo of the text.

The sheet itself appeared to be simple copier paper with no watermark or obvious means to discern it from any other plain sheet of paper. The text was handwritten in what looked like blue biro ink. Without moving her thumb or forefinger, she slowly turned the page around for anything on the back that might help. There was nothing obvious to the naked eye, but who knew what forensics might find?

She dropped the letter into the evidence bag being held open by her colleague. She turned and took a photo of the envelope before dropping it into the bag with the letter.

'Mitch is on his way,' Stacey said, ending her call.

'How the hell long was this just sitting there?' Kim asked, looking around the room.

'Since about twelvish,' Stacey said. 'I was here when the post was—'

'And I just glanced over it,' Penn said interrupting.

There was a part of her that wanted to let loose on both of them. A letter that appeared to be a direct communication from their killer had been sitting on the desk for four hours.

She swallowed down her anger. Chewing them out for ignoring the post may make her feel better, but in truth the post rarely held anything interesting.

'Is it from him?' Penn asked as she emailed both photos to Stacey.

'Print them off,' she said, moving towards the printer. It sparked into life, and Kim took the top sheet.

She leaned back against the table and read the contents.

*DI Stone*

> *You have to stop me from hurting anyone else. I don't want to do these horrible things. I don't want to kill anyone, but I have no choice. You have to understand that I have no power to stop. I'm sorry that she's dead, but I couldn't stop it. But you have to stop me. You're the only one who can end this. You have to be the one who listens. Help me before I'm forced to do it again. And I will do it again because I have no choice. I've never had a choice.*

*Noah*

Kim then read the letter aloud to the rest of her colleagues. She passed the page to Bryant as she took a look at the envelope. 'Posted somewhere in Dudley, last collection last night.'

'After he'd killed Katrina Nock,' Penn observed.

Kim shrugged. 'Why would the killer try to communicate with us directly?'

'Correction, guv, he's trying to communicate with *you* directly,' Bryant pointed out, glancing again at the envelope.

Another reason she hated giving press conferences. It caused all the crazies to look in her direction. She'd given a brief statement with no names at teatime after briefing Woody and now she was the focus of attention. She had to consider all options, and the letter could easily be from someone messing about.

'You think it's really from him?' Penn asked, as though reading her thoughts.

'There are no specifics, so it's hard to say and I'd bet Bryant's new car's name isn't Noah, but…' she turned towards Stacey.

'Already started looking, boss,' she answered.

Kim read the letter again. 'If it is him, he really wants us to stop him from…'

Kim stopped speaking as her phone rang.

It was Keats.

It appeared they were already too late.

# CHAPTER TWENTY-SEVEN

'You know she's pissed off with us, don't you?' Stacey asked once Mitch had zoomed in and collected the letter. She'd taken time to wave in his direction, even though she was on an urgent call from her mother, who never rang her during the day.

'What do you mean Aunt Abebi can't make the cake?' Stacey had asked in response to her mother's panic-stricken words.

Aunt Abebi was her father's sister; she had come to the UK at the same time as her parents thirty-four years ago. She'd forged a place making authentic African cakes for the local Nigerian community. Over time, she had developed new recipes and tried them out on friends and neighbours. Now, few events took place in the Dudley Nigerian community without one of Aunt Abebi's cakes. There had never been any question that Aunt Abebi would make her wedding cake.

'She has to leave for Lagos tomorrow. Uncle Egbo is very poorly. She is in tears for letting you down.'

Stacey immediately felt sorry for her selfish response to the news.

'Mum, please ring her and tell her it's fine. She can't leave feeling bad, but what are we going to do?' she'd asked, hoping her mum would magically have the answer.

'I could try…'

'No, Mum, that's not going to work,' she cut in quickly. By her own admission, her mother was not a good baker. She was a demon with jollof rice and pounded yam, but cakes were not her forte.

'We'll sort something out, sweetie,' her mother had soothed before Stacey had ended the call.

And that was exactly what she needed to be thinking about when her priority had to be making up ground with the boss.

Stacey had printed off more copies of the letter and put them on every desk.

'Yeah, I can see her point. It was just sitting there for hours,' Penn said.

'But to be fair to us both,' Stacey defended, 'nothing interesting ever comes into the office by post.'

'Agreed, but in future…'

'We'll open the bloody post earlier,' Stacey finished for him. She paused and then caught his eye.

'Does this mean we're officially on the naughty step?'

Penn laughed out loud and it was a good sound to hear.

'Yeah, stop pulling my pigtails,' he said.

'You think the letter really is from our killer?' Stacey asked.

'Hard to say,' Penn said. 'But some killers really do want to make contact with the investigators. Worked a case about six or seven years back with Travis at West Mercia when he first became a DI. Lynne had just joined the team as a DC, and she started getting these weird emails. They were sexual in nature, but there was something else about them that bothered her. The first murder was a brutal stabbing of a thirty-three-year-old exotic dancer but with additional wounds to the thighs. The emailer made references to Lynne's thighs, but Travis wrote off the messages as being from an attention seeker.'

'And?' Stacey asked, noting that he'd said 'first murder'.

'Lynne went behind his back and had tech try and trace the sender. There was no rerouting of email addresses or attempts to hide his identity. His name was Nicholas Brewin, from Droitwich Spa.'

'Stop making me beg here, Penn. What the hell happened?'

'Travis hesitated in taking Lynne's concerns seriously and it cost another girl her life. Brewin was brought in for questioning no more than an hour after killing his second victim.'

'Bloody hell.'

'Yeah, Lynne struggled with it for a while, felt she should have pushed harder, made Travis listen sooner, but the guy was just begging to be found.' He shrugged. 'Might be the same with this guy.'

'You think his real name is Noah?' she asked doubtfully.

Penn shook his head. 'No, but we need to check it out.'

'Found four on the system so far and none were arrested for violent crimes,' Stacey offered.

'So we know Noah was famous for arks and animals. That's a start. We should have his identity locked down by teatime.'

'Yeah, piece of cake,' Stacey agreed, turning back to her computer. Immediately she turned back again and had to voice the words that were running through her mind.

'Penn, the boss has been summoned by Keats. Got to be a second body.' She glanced at the A4 sheets she'd put on everyone's desk. 'You don't think it's something we could have stopped if we'd just opened the…'

'I hope not,' Penn said, reaching for his headphones.

Damn it. That wasn't the answer she'd wanted to hear.

# CHAPTER TWENTY-EIGHT

'You know they did nothing wrong, right?' Bryant asked as they headed out of the car park. 'If this is his second victim, then it wouldn't have mattered what time they'd opened the post.'

Kim knew he was right, but she had a vision of that letter on the desk, crying out for help, and the two of them sitting there with their fingers in their ears.

'You think it's even from him?' Bryant asked. 'I mean, you do attract the crazies. Especially when you're on the six o'clock news and there are even more of them watching.'

'I'm not sure, Bryant, but we've got to treat it like it is.'

'Why use the name Noah and why can't he stop himself?'

'Ask me one on sport, Bryant,' she said. She'd had the letter ten minutes and those same questions were running around her own mind.

'Who won the gold medal for the one hundred metres in the 1994 Olympics?'

'Linford Christie,' she snapped back.

He glanced her way. 'You knew that?'

She rolled her eyes. 'Only you would ask me a question to which you don't know the answer. I could have said anything,' she replied as Bryant turned off the Thorns Road on to Stevens Park; the place Keats had instructed them to attend.

The park itself was approximately seven hectares and boasted areas that were open flat grass and those that were in shade. In recent years, a skate park had been added to the two tennis courts, outdoor gym and children's play area. For as long as Kim could remember, the park had had a football pitch where many local schools came to play.

Bryant pulled up beside a squad car just as Mitch pulled up behind them in his white van.

'You got the letter?' she asked as they all got out of their vehicles together.

He nodded back towards the van. 'It's in there. I was just leaving the station when I got the call. Tried to get here quickly but got stuck behind a slow-assed driver in an Astra Estate who was heading for a picnic instead of a crime scene.'

Both she and Mitch looked towards the offending driver of the Astra Estate.

'Keeping it legal, folks,' he said without remorse.

Kim headed towards the activity at the far end of the playing fields as Mitch began to get suited up.

As she walked the width of the park, she couldn't help but think how big the space had seemed when she was a child. Keith and Erica, her foster parents from the age of ten to thirteen, had brought her to both a bonfire and the travelling fairground before both events had been stopped. Back then it had felt as though the glowing fire had been miles away from the refreshment kiosks and side stalls. Now, with her long stride she could traverse the whole area in minutes.

As she neared the far edge of the park, she saw the park ranger sitting on the grass. A constable was by his side.

'On it, guv,' Bryant said, following her gaze.

She continued towards Keats and the figure she could see on the ground.

She nodded in Keats's direction, took a closer look and immediately saw from the angle of her head, like an owl caught mid-turn, that she'd been killed in the same way as Katrina.

She guessed the woman to be late twenties, early thirties. She wore bootleg jeans, black boots and a thick cardigan buttoned up to the breastbone. Her dark hair was held up in a single ponytail and she wore little make-up. Her dark brown eyes stared unseeing up to the sky. A white gold wedding ring was the only jewellery she could see. Another wife. Possibly another family robbed of a young, vital woman.

'Same as yesterday?' she asked, completing her journey around the body. Again, there seemed to be no signs of sexual interference.

Mitch appeared just in time to hear the answer.

'Definitely looks that way,' Keats said as Mitch nodded to his colleague to begin taking photos. More vehicles had arrived on the car park and additional forensic techies were headed their way.

'Clearly the neck has been broken and I can see no other injuries.'

*Exactly like Katrina Nock, then*, she thought, remembering the letter that had been on the spare desk. This was a murder he hadn't wanted to commit but had done so anyway. And so soon after the first.

'No more than an hour,' Keats said, nodding towards the man beside Bryant. 'Park ranger doing his final check of the park before closing it.'

The body was about as far away from the entrance as it could be.

Kim walked a few paces to the edge of the park. The area was bordered by trees that had been allowed to grow together and form a dense hedge, but recent pruning had left gaps between brittle bare branches. Kim could easily see through to the housing estate on the other side.

'Mitch, I think he went this way,' she said, stepping away to ensure she destroyed no potential evidence.

There would be far less risk in parking outside the grounds and would explain the location of the body so close to the perimeter edge for a fast getaway after the deed was done.

'Anything obvious missing?' Kim asked, nodding towards the handbag on the ground to her left.

Keats shook his head. 'Phone, purse, a few receipts and a half-empty juice bottle.'

Nothing taken. Same as Katrina. Robbery was not the motive; but the phone puzzled her, unless the killer knew there was no link at all back to them through her call logs or contacts. Maybe this murder was not about the victim at all.

'Ranger found her after the game finished. Always does a full perimeter once the kids are gone,' Bryant said, coming to stand beside her.

'Game?'

'After school football, guv. Two local kiddy teams.'

'Ah, anything else?'

'Nothing, except he's been looking after this park for thirteen years but he ain't coming back tomorrow.'

'Mitch,' she said, nodding towards the handbag.

He knelt on the floor with the evidence bags to his right.

He opened the purse and took out the driving licence as Bryant took out his notebook.

'Louise Webb-Harvey, 44 Charleston Way, Wollescote.'

'Thanks,' she said, turning to Keats who answered before she opened her mouth.

'In the morning. Nine sharp. Will I be seeing you or the strange fellow?'

'Aww, Keats, are you missing me?' she asked, glancing sideways.

'Emphatically, no. Please, send Penn; I like him much more than I like you.'

'Keats, you like everyone more than you like me,' she said, turning away.

'Well, maybe you should take yourself into a corner for a good, hard look at yourself.'

'If only I cared,' she threw back over her shoulder.

Bryant walked beside her and, as ever, he seemed to know when she needed silence and, right now, she wanted a minute or two with her own thoughts.

Two young, married women killed in as many days. The method and manner exactly the same. Nothing taken and nothing interfered with. No passion or rage. Just death.

There were cases that were more about the killer than they were about the victim. Had either Katrina or Louise done anything wrong?

But then her mind wondered: if the crime had nothing to do with the victim, why were they so similar? Why not a male, younger or older? Had both women just been in the wrong place at the wrong time? Had he watched them and chosen them for a reason she did not yet know?

And if the letter was from him, why was he begging her to catch him before he killed again if he knew he was going to take another life so soon? Despite her irritation at Stacey and Penn, she knew there was no way they could have prevented this even if they'd ripped the letter out the postman's hand.

And if she didn't catch him soon, how the hell did she know who was going to die next?

# CHAPTER TWENTY-NINE

Stacey replaced the receiver as Penn entered the room with a handful of snacks.

Although it was after five, the call from the boss naming the second victim had meant no one was leaving the office for a while yet.

'Monster Munch and Twix, please,' she said, eyeing his booty.

After the call from the boss, he'd made a quick call to Jasper before offering to grab whatever he could from the vending machine to keep them going.

He threw her requested items across the desk and reached for his headphones.

'Jasper okay?' she asked, opening the packet of crisps first. Even as a poor substitute for an evening meal, it was savoury before sweet.

'He's fine,' Penn answered, wrinkling his nose as she crunched on a pickled onion flavoured giant claw.

'How the hell do you eat those?' he asked, shaking his head.

Pickled onion was her favourite flavour even though the smell stayed with her for hours.

'Devon won't come near me if I've eaten these and, seeing as I'm stuck here for now, I'll make the most of it. She went on an overnight course last week, so guess what I binged on?'

'Stace, you kill me.' He chuckled.

'What?'

'Your partner is away overnight and your idea of living it up is stinky Monster Munch?'

She laughed with him. Yes, he had a point.

Again, he'd refused her given opportunity to talk. It was clear to her that Jasper had been offering one-word responses to his questions, and even though he'd said more, it was so unlike the usual banter that would lift Penn's mouth without him even realising.

But she could do no more than offer her shoulder or her ear.

'Just keep doing what you're doing, Stace. Normal helps.'

He placed his headphones over his ears and focused on the screen. Even if she responded, he wouldn't hear.

*Okay, normal she could do*, she thought, turning back to her computer.

Penn had taken over the witness statements from Katrina's murder, and she'd been tasked with finding background on victim number two: Louise Webb-Harvey.

Despite the events of the day, the sexual assault case was still playing on her mind. After interviewing both witnesses, she knew the only thing she could do to resolve the questions in her mind was to speak to the rapist himself; however, the double murder they were working had to take priority in her normal working hours.

Which was why an appointment to question him at 6 a.m. the next morning had already been made.

# CHAPTER THIRTY

Charleston Avenue was a cul-de-sac at the edge of the Wollescote conurbation that bordered a strip of green belt. Now classed as a residential area of Stourbridge, it was located two miles east of the town centre and bordered with Halesowen. The area had been predominantly rural until the 1920s when it was developed as a dense residential area of private and council-owned dwellings. It wasn't known as a high-crime area and residents lived in reasonable harmony.

Within the avenue itself, Kim counted five sets of Mucklow-style semi-detached properties with garages attached to the side of the house. Each property was separated from its twin by a waist-high wooden fence that ran down the middle of a shared lawn. The houses were identical with double driveways in front of the garage. From memory, houses around here went for around a quarter of a million, and if there was a picture in the dictionary to describe middle-class suburbia this would have been it. A place where both parents went out to work and nothing out of the ordinary ever happened.

Until now, Kim thought as Bryant pulled up outside the houses smack bang in the middle of the curve.

A newish Toyota Corolla sat on the drive awaiting the arrival of a second car.

'Guv, you want me to?…'

'No,' she said, refusing his offer of breaking the news. Whoever was on the other side of that front door was not going to care from whose mouth the devastating news came. It's not what they'd remember for the rest of their lives.

She took a deep breath and knocked.

'Have you forgotten your?…' a female voice said as the door began to open. The tolerant smile died on the woman's face as she realised they were not who she was expecting.

Kim held up her identification.

'Is this the home of Louise Webb-Harvey?'

The woman nodded, looking from her to Bryant.

'Yes, she's my wife but she's not here right—'

'May we come in?…'

'Robyn,' she said, offering her name and standing aside.

Kim passed the stairs leading out of the hallway and headed into a light and airy kitchen formed of shiny white units and an island in the middle. A saucepan simmered on the hob and the smell of a freshly made pot of coffee mingled with the aroma of some kind of bolognaise. A half-drunk glass of wine stood beside the chopping board, an empty glass beside the bottle. Everything in this kitchen was waiting for someone to come home.

'Please, take a seat, Ms Webb-Harvey.'

'Robyn, and please don't tell me to sit down in my own home. Has something happened?'

Kim took a seat at the dining table, hoping the woman would follow her lead.

She didn't and leaned against the island instead. She crossed her arms and Kim could see her hands grabbing the bare flesh of her upper arms.

'Robyn, I'm afraid we have some bad news about Louise. There's been an incident.'

Robyn looked around the room and reached for her handbag. 'Where is she? I'll go to her.'

Kim remained seated and shook her head.

'It's the car, isn't it? I told her to get something more practical, more sensible but—'

'It's not the car,' Kim said. 'But I'm sorry to tell you that Louise is dead.'

That Godforsaken word again.

No response.

Kim knew she had heard, but right now her mind was trying to compute those words against the normality of cooking dinner with a glass of wine, waiting for her partner to return home.

'I'm sorry but I think you should leave,' Robyn said as the colour started to seep from her face. The woman thought she could get them, along with their bad news, out of the house. And then it wouldn't be real.

'She's not coming, Robyn. I'm sorry but your wife has been murdered.'

Her mouth fell open as her legs buckled. Bryant had been moving closer and was there to offer a steadying hand so that she didn't fall.

'M… murdered.'

'I'm afraid so,' Kim said as Bryant guided Robyn to a chair.

The sound of something bubbling over and hissing on the hob drew Bryant's attention.

He reached over and turned the knobs off.

Kim continued. 'She was found by a ranger at Stevens Park in—'

'I know where it is,' she said as her eyes came alight with a sudden urgency, as though there was something she'd completely forgotten.

'Where's Archie?'

Kim's head snapped towards Bryant.

'Who is Archie?' she asked as a boulder began to form in the pit of her stomach.

'Archie is our six-year-old son.'

# CHAPTER THIRTY-ONE

*I am startled awake from my dream.*

*I can feel the breath building in my body. I feel like an over-inflated balloon. I am full of air and it has no way to escape.*

*I try to let out a breath, but there is something heavy across my face bearing down hard; my nose feels as though I've inhaled a hundred feathers and my mouth is blocked.*

*In response, my eyes try to open, to see the threat against me, but my eyelids meet the fabric of something that feels like a pillow and offers only more darkness.*

*My legs begin to thrash but the force is immovable. My lower half convulses as the panic and fear runs through my veins, but my upper half is held rigid.*

*My mouth opens and I am gasping for air, trying to draw breath from or through the fabric.*

*Please, help me, someone, my mind screams as a drop of urine escapes and runs down my leg.*

*My shame is quickly swallowed by the knowledge that I am about to die. My head begins to swim, and fireworks are popping in my head.*

*There is no time left. I am dying.*

*And then it is gone. The weight is lifted from my face. I gulp in fresh air, forcing it down into my lungs. I cough and I splutter into the darkness that surrounds me. Stars twinkle in my head. Fireworks are popping behind my eyes.*

*The beating of my heart is deafening in my ears. The silence beyond it is terrifying.*

*I lie still. Not daring to open my eyes in case it comes back. In case I cannot breathe again.*

*Eventually, as my heart returns to normal, I open my eyes, one at a time and take a good look around.*

*No one is there.*

# CHAPTER THIRTY-TWO

'Sir, there's a child,' Kim said once Woody answered the phone.

'Sorry?' he said. The faint noise of the talk radio station he liked to listen to in the background told her he was already at home.

'Our second victim, Louise Webb-Harvey, was at the park with her six-year-old son for a football match. He's nowhere to be found.'

'Immediate area searched?'

'Yes.'

'He's not gone back to the car?' he asked, echoing instructions most parents gave to their children; it was the first area she'd asked the officers to look.

'Checked and no,' she answered.

She had made the call to the site and spoken to the sergeant at the scene the moment Robyn had mentioned the boy's name. Even the techies had stopped working to conduct a search of the immediate area for the little boy, while the sarge had sprinted to check the car.

Kim had stayed on the phone, crossing her fingers the whole time.

The words 'nothing marm' had inflated a balloon of fear in her stomach.

The sergeant had called in to his inspector and an extensive foot search of the area was now being organised.

'Is there someone at the home with the family?'

'Yes, sir, Robyn's brother was five minutes away and a FLO will be there within the hour.'

'Okay, Stone, I'll make the necessary arrangements for a press conference, and you need to get yourself back to the station. I'll meet you there.'

She ended the call as Bryant pulled away from the house. The case had taken a sinister turn that threw even more questions into the air. There had been a child with Katrina the day before. Mia had been only feet away, but she had been left alone. Untouched.

So why the hell had he now taken a six-year-old boy?

# CHAPTER THIRTY-THREE

It was 9.30 p.m. when Kim finally got the call from the family liaison officer at the Webb-Harvey home. All Louise's family members had been informed and just in the nick of time.

'Sir, we're up,' Kim said, calling her boss on his internal phone.

The local media had been assembled by the press communication team and were waiting outside.

'I see Frost is front and centre,' Bryant observed, glancing out the window as Kim grabbed her jacket.

She headed for the door then turned to the rest of her team.

'Guys, get off home. I need you back fresh in the morning.'

They all nodded their agreement.

Bryant followed her down the stairs.

'You too,' she said. 'Get out while you can.'

'Are you new, guv? I go when you go.'

She shook her head as Woody appeared. The man could be stubborn sometimes.

'Okay, Stone, remember what I said?' her boss asked as they met at the bottom of the stairs.

She nodded. Woody was going to speak, and she was to stand silently by his side. They could not afford for her to get rattled and bite, which would detract from the script and the singularity of what they were trying to achieve with this impromptu gathering.

Everything had been timed so that none of Louise's family were going to get a devastating shock by watching the local news bulletin. They couldn't appeal to the public and show Archie's photo without revealing the identity of the mother.

And they needed the story to run as soon as possible.

'Phones off?' Woody asked as they reached the door.

Both she and Bryant switched to silent and followed Woody outside.

In the few short minutes it had taken them to get downstairs, a television camera from Central News had arrived and set up right next to Tracy Frost, who wouldn't have shifted from her position even if a hurricane had moved into town.

'I'll do props,' Bryant said, positioning himself behind Woody to the right.

It was always good to have professional-looking people in camera view. Although after fourteen hours he didn't look as fresh and crisp as he had at the beginning of the day, his presence was still calming and offered reassurance.

Kim stood beside her boss and set her face to neutral: an expression that rested easily on her face.

Much as she hated doing press conferences, she was sure she would have handled this one just as Woody was about to.

'Thank you for coming,' he said pleasantly, taking in all of the reporters with his gaze.

Okay, she would probably have forgotten to say that. And she wouldn't have made eye contact with them all either.

'From the outset, I'd like to clarify that there will be no questions at the end, as I'm sure you'll understand the urgency of sharing the information we have as quickly as possible.'

Nice. Let them know before you even start. Manage expectations. If she had a notepad, she'd be writing these guidelines down.

'The body of a female was found earlier today at the Stevens Park in Quarry Bank. We can confirm that she was thirty-one years of age and her name was Louise Webb-Harvey. Our deepest condolences go out to her family at this time.'

Yes, she'd done the major incident press training and under-stood the importance of communicating the condolence message, but she knew that Woody genuinely meant it.

She also remembered being told to form your poker face before leaving the building. A few years earlier, a high-profile police inspector in Birmingham had been caught chuckling at a col-league's comment seconds before speaking about the bludgeoning of an elderly male. The appeal for witnesses had been lost beneath every article's focus on the callousness of the police inspector. He had been forced to resign his position.

She noticed the reporters glancing sideways at each other. The news of the body had got out a few hours ago and they were clearly wondering at the reason for the early identification of the victim.

Woody continued, quickly reaching the point of the impromptu press conference.

'We will be working day and night to bring Louise's murderer to justice, but our current priority is locating Louise's six-year-old son, Archie, who is so far unaccounted for. We know that the boy was with his mother at the park playing football, so we would appeal for any witnesses to make contact with us immediately.'

Woody held up the photo of a blond-haired boy who was smiling widely as he stroked his pet rabbit.

Frost nudged forward. 'Is the murder linked to?…'

'A full search of the area has been initiated,' Woody continued as though Frost had never spoken. Woody held up the photo long enough for everyone to get a good shot of it with either the cameras around their necks or their phones. The press office had been poised to flood social media with the photo once Woody started speaking.

Kim caught the knowing frown on Frost's face as she realised that the sole purpose of the briefing was to get Archie's photo out there and not to answer any questions she was going to pose. But that wasn't going to stop her from trying.

'DCI Woodward, do we have a serial?…'

'Obviously, we are all concerned for the safety of Archie and would like to return him to his family at the earliest opportunity. Anyone with any information as to Archie's whereabouts should contact us here at the station or call…'

Kim tuned out as he read off the number. Her boss had done a good job in using Archie's first name as many times as possible. If his captor was watching, it was designed for him to see the little boy as a person.

As Woody finished the appeal and was clearly summing up, Kim could see the rage building in the face of the *Dudley Star* reporter at being continually ignored, despite the fact Woody had advised accordingly at the outset.

'One last question,' she shouted up as Woody finished thanking the press for their attendance. Kim's stomach did a roll. Tracey's eyes were hard and cold and fixed only on Woody. 'Is it true that the killer had already communicated directly with?—'

'Again, thank you all for your time and let's bring Archie home quickly,' he said, turning away. Only because she knew the man did she understand that the tension in his shoulders was due to the curveball from Frost.

*Damn it*, Kim thought. Frost had very nearly derailed the press conference and taken the attention away from a missing boy to something being withheld, and how the hell did Frost know about the letter?

She used every ounce of the willpower she possessed to keep her face in neutral as she followed her boss into the station. Once away from the glare of the press, he turned to face her, his expression thunderous, and she understood why. If they didn't shut her up, that would become the story instead of a missing child.

'What the f… bloody hell was that about? How does she know about the letter?'

Kim took a step back from a level of rage rarely shown by the man. It was the closest she'd known him to use foul language.

'Sir, I have no idea how she could have known.'

'Well, Stone, you'd better find out whose police career just died on local television,' he growled, storming up the stairs.

'On it, sir,' she called after him before turning and heading back out of the station. There was no way she was going to allow her boss to be blindsided by a local reporter because her nose was out of joint. Kim fully intended to put that nose right back where it belonged.

Instead of heading towards Frost, who was now beside her Audi TT, she moved to the side of the building out of sight and took out her phone.

The call was answered immediately. 'What?'

'Frost, round the back, now,' she barked.

It would do no good for the other press personnel to see her confronting Frost openly, giving credence to her question.

Kim heard the high heels tottering on the slabs before the woman came into view. The woman's ponytail of long blonde hair whooshed behind her as she moved with uncharacteristic speed.

'What the fuck were you doing back there?' Kim growled.

'My job, Stone,' she barked back.

'At the expense of finding a little boy?'

'Getting a bit fed up of getting used,' she said, crossing her arms.

Kim narrowed her gaze. 'Since when has it been a two-way street, Frost? Name the date we were supposed to consider the delicate feelings of the press while trying to bring criminals—'

'Yeah, that's the bloody problem. We get information when it suits you lot to just dangle a carrot, when there's something *you* want but not when we need stuff.'

'Not our problem. More importantly, you could be putting a little boy at risk if you mention anything about communication in your report. If anything happens to Archie, I swear—'

'Oh, give me a break, Stone. I was pissed at your boss for cutting me off for trying to do my job.' She paused and tapped her chin. 'You should know that some people are more accommodating than your lot and are happy to share, but rest assured no mention of it will go in my report.'

In spite of her boss's request, Kim swallowed down the urge to demand Frost's source. There was no way she could just come right out and ask where the reporter had got her information. To do so would be to confirm that she was on to something and they'd never hear the end of it. She'd explore other avenues to find the leak given the hint that Frost had just unknowingly given her.

'Then you were misinformed, Frost.'

'Oh, so that's how we're going to—'

'Good chat,' Kim said, walking away. Frost had confirmed that no mention of the communication would be made in her report and that's what she'd been after.

'Stone, you should know by now that I make a much better friend than enemy.'

'So do I, Frost, so do I,' she said as her phone began to ring.

# CHAPTER THIRTY-FOUR

Jasper stood in the kitchen and counted off the ingredients as he put them back in the cupboard. He found reassurance in numbers. They were firm and unyielding. They didn't change. They were solid and dependable.

*Not like cookie dough*, he thought.

'One flour. Two butter. Three eggs. Four raisins. Five sugar. Six baking powder. Seven chocolate bar,' he said aloud as they all went back.

He hadn't known what he was going to bake. He had been going to let Ozzy choose, seeing as Ozzy had been so keen for him to get back in the kitchen. He didn't really feel like it, but Ozzy was being strong, so he had to be strong too.

He closed his eyes and listened as the theme tune to *EastEnders* played out. He put the telly on just to hear the sounds of the soaps. Some nights when a few of them had been on, his mum would just sit and swap channels, moving from one soap to the next while he and Ozzy baked in the kitchen. And then she would come in to make a cup of tea and talk about the characters as though they were real people. He would glance at Ozzy, who would wink and then mix up storylines deliberately.

'But I thought Sharon was seeing Tommy and that Gail was married to a Mitchell brother.'

His mum would raise her hands in despair and explain how he was getting his soaps mixed up, and Jasper would try not to laugh as she patiently talked Ozzy through the plot lines until he had it straight. Until the next time.

He clapped his hands and laughed out loud at the memory. Ozzy was so funny. He always made him laugh.

His hand raised to his cheek and he was surprised to find it wet. He hadn't even realised a tear had escaped. He brushed it away roughly.

He couldn't cry. He was being strong for Ozzy.

He headed upstairs. It was eight o'clock and Billy would be on the Xbox. They could carry on playing the game they'd started last night.

He paused at the door to his mum's bedroom. Everything still looked the same. They hadn't moved anything when she was taken to the place that was like a hospital but different. They had both pretended that she was coming back. He didn't think Ozzy had been in the room once since the funeral, but he came in every night before Ozzy came back from work.

He touched the reading glasses sitting on the bedside table. He stroked the cover of the last book she'd been reading before the pain got too bad. He could still see her lying there with the glasses on her nose and the book on her chest when she'd fallen asleep. He could still see her in his memories, but he wanted more.

He moved across the bedroom and opened her wardrobe door. The smell of his mum reached out to him immediately: a mixture of the lavender fabric conditioner and the summery perfume that she'd worn all year.

His vision blurred at the memories that played through his mind: the trips they'd taken; the games they'd played; the nights they'd spent watching his favourite films.

He leaned into the wardrobe, drinking in the familiar smells. He closed his eyes and imagined her nearby, asking about his day, leaning across and gently moving a lock of hair from around his eyes.

He opened his arms and enclosed them around a clump of her clothes. He took them from the rail and placed them on the bed.

He knew the tears were coming. He could feel them closing up his throat, but it was okay. Ozzy wasn't here, so for just a little while he didn't need to be strong.

He pulled the arm of one of her winter jackets across his torso, lay amongst her clothes and allowed the tears to run free.

# CHAPTER THIRTY-FIVE

'You sure you're not gonna tell me why we're heading back to the morgue at ten o'clock at night?' Bryant asked once they were in the car.

'Are you scared of it in the dark?' she asked as the conversation with Frost played over in her mind.

'Place freaks me out any time of the day to be fair,' he admitted.

'Maybe I should partner with Penn. He sees the place as a fun day out.'

'Ooh, guv, just the thought of you wanting to partner with someone else cuts me deeply. I could even think you don't like me now you've made some new buddies at your EPT meeting,' he offered in a deliberately whiney voice.

'Yeah, cos they're as much fun as a heart attack, so you ain't got much competition.'

'It's okay. I'll take it.' He smirked. 'But seriously, why are we going?'

Kim shrugged. 'You know Keats likes to keep me in suspense until I get there.'

Probing after his summons to the morgue had prompted only that there was something she should see. Just as concerning to her right now was the conversation with Frost.

'Hang on a minute,' she said, taking out her phone.

'Me?' Bryant asked.

'Nah, you keep driving as though you're stuck in traffic,' she replied. There were few vehicles on the road as they headed through Dudley, but steady Eddie kept just below the speed limit the whole way. The empty roads, to her, were a tantalising invitation to press the accelerator, just a little bit.

She scrolled through her contacts and pressed the button, not caring if he'd finished work.

'Stone?'

'Mitch, you've got a leak. Find it and plug it. The press know we've got a letter and—'

'Just a minute. I'm in the—' he said as Bryant pulled into the car park of Russells Hall Hospital.

'It's not my lot, Mitch,' she insisted.

'Look, just—'

'I know no one wants a leak in their department but quit arguing with me and—'

'Bloody hell, Stone, I'm trying to tell you I'm parking right behind you. Put your bloody phone down.'

'Oh,' she said, looking behind to see his white van at their rear for the second time that day.

Bryant pulled into a space close to the entrance, and Mitch pulled up two spaces away.

'You're gonna need to find out who it is,' Kim said, continuing their conversation in person as they both got out of their vehicles.

'Why do you assume it's one of my guys?' he asked as the three of them began to walk towards the morgue.

'Frost said something about not getting the information from "my lot", which to her means police as a whole. The only other folks that know about the letter are Keats and your guys.'

'Damn it,' he said, stroking his beard.

Kim struggled to remember sometimes that the forensic technicians were not police officers, so integral to an investigation was their expertise. But they were civilians who sometimes didn't understand how necessary it was not to speak to the press or, in some cases, realise they actually were speaking to the press. Tracy

Frost was ruthless when it came to getting a story and buying someone a few drinks to get information wasn't even close to the depths she'd sink for a good headline.

'Keats called you in too?' she asked as they echoed along the empty corridors.

Mitch had a small lab next to Keats's office, but the majority of his work was done at the Ridgewood House facility in Birmingham. He was rarely here by choice at ten o'clock.

'Yeah, cryptic message as usual,' he said, rolling his eyes.

Kim was even more intrigued. Bringing Mitch in had to mean he'd found something of evidentiary value, but the post-mortem wasn't due until the following morning.

She opened the door that led into the morgue corridor, and the lighting dimmed just a little from the brightly lit hospital corridors. Kim always felt it was like a warning that you'd taken a wrong turn. Leave now while you still can.

Mitch stepped through first, followed by Bryant. She closed the door gently behind her. Her boots made little sound as she snuck up behind her colleague.

'Boo,' she shouted, tapping him in the back.

He jumped forward as though she'd electrified him.

'Bloody hell, guv, that was not funny.'

Well, Mitch was hiding a smile in his beard and it was killing her not to laugh, so she begged to differ. It really had been a long day.

'Okay, Keats, your audience has arrived,' she said, stepping into the lab.

She was surprised to see there was no body on the table or evidence of recent activity. The place was gleaming, and no decaying smells lingered in the air. It had been a while since he'd put his last customer back into the chiller drawers.

She noted Bryant shift uncomfortably beside her after shaking hands with the pathologist.

She was amused at his reaction to their late-night morgue visit, but even she had to admit that there was an eeriness without Keats's assistants milling around in the background or the sound of the cleaning staff mopping and wiping every surface.

'Relax, Bryant, they don't come out to play until after midnight,' Keats said, nodding to the fridges across the corridor.

Much as Kim would have loved to enjoy Keats prodding her colleague instead of her, both of them had been at work for almost fifteen hours.

'Come on, Keats, show and tell.'

'Oh, Inspector, I remember when you were so much more fun.'

'Grow up, Keats, I've never been any fun.'

He looked up and to the left. 'Yes, actually, you're right.'

He stepped over to the desk and picked up an evidence bag. 'This fell out of her trousers as we were putting her to bed.'

Kim's stomach lurched.

In the bag was a single sheet of paper.

The killer had written to her again.

# CHAPTER THIRTY-SIX

Kim leaned against the kitchen counter and took out her phone.

On the journey back from the hospital, she'd checked in with the search co-ordinator who had officers already combing the immediate area and was working up a grid system ready for first light.

There was something that felt inherently wrong in being at home when there was a child unaccounted for, and if staying in the office would have made Archie reappear safe and sound in his bed, she'd be there with her sleeping bag right now.

*Find the killer, find the child*, was the phrase that kept going around in her mind.

A ground search was being carried out, but in her mind the child was not going to be found hiding in a bush somewhere. The dual part of the search was to look for clues: anything the killer might have left behind.

Kim's heart went out to Robyn Webb-Harvey who had not only lost her partner but whose child was nowhere to be found either.

A quick call to the FLO had confirmed that Robyn alternated between grief and restless pacing as her varying emotions all demanded space in her mind. The grief wanted to close her body down, but the fear for her son kept it on high alert. She just prayed the woman would manage to get some kind of rest.

The FLO had also informed her that every neighbour in the cul-de-sac was out searching the immediate area, checking garages and gardens, even though they were a few miles away from where Archie had last been seen. But that was what people did. Friends and neighbours had to do something, had to feel as though they were contributing and trying to help.

Kim closed the back door behind Barney, who now sat before her waiting patiently for his late-night walk.

'Just a sec, boy,' she said, scrolling to the top email on her phone.

She opened the attachment from Keats, which was the letter he had photographed and sent to them all.

She had read it at the morgue, but now she wanted to study the words. Before she had a chance to, though, her phone switched to display an incoming call.

'Hope you've got good news, Dobbie.' *For both me and my colleagues*, she thought to herself.

'Well, yeah and no,' he said.

'Explain.'

'Well, there's bin an err... development on yer request.'

Kim's radar reacted to two things: Dobbie trying to sound like a businessman and the note of coyness in his voice telling her the problem was for her but not him.

'Go on,' she said, narrowing her eyes.

'I've got the frame and...'

'You've got my frame,' she corrected.

'Aah, well that's the rub, see. I day know just how rare these frames was. Had two calls already from folks offering to pay more for it than yer offer.'

'It wasn't an offer, Dobbie. We had a deal.'

She could imagine him shrugging cagily. 'Yeah, but a man's gorra ate.'

The man was twenty-four stone. He didn't miss many meals from bad deals. 'You do all right, Dobbie. It's my frame and I'll be round to collect it at—'

'Hmmm... not sure that's gonna work for me any more. But I'll tell yer what I'm prepared to do to help yer out.'

Help her out. It was her bloody frame.

'Oh do tell me, Dobbie,' she said, grinding her teeth.

'I'm gonna hang on to the frame until seven tomorrow night, and whoever comes and offers me the most money is gonna get it. See, gives yer a fighting chance just cos I like you and I cor be fairer than that.'

'You're gonna fucking auction it back to me?' she asked.

'Fairest way, I reckon,' he said, and she could hear the smirk in his voice. Her back was aching from the barrel over which he was bending her.

She pictured the thousands of pounds that had made it into his till from her back pocket over the years, and opened her mouth to tell him so, but stopped herself.

She didn't doubt that there was a higher demand for the frame than he'd thought. The Vincent Black Shadow, with a top speed of 125 mph, had been produced by Vincent HRD at their factory in Stevenage, Hertfordshire from 1948 to 1955 over three Series. Official records said that only 1,774 were ever made alongside the fifteen White Shadow models built to the same mechanical spec, but with an engine that was polished rather than enamelled.

He took her hesitation as an opportunity to drive home his point.

'Hey, these things are fetching hundreds of thousands at auction. I gotta look after—'

'Not for just the frame, Dobbie,' she said, rolling her eyes. 'And not restored models either. The ones getting silly money are original models that have been kept wrapped in tissue paper and bubble wrap for fifty years.'

'Yeah, but—'

'I'll be there, Dobbie,' she said, knowing she had little choice. He had possession of the frame and, as she knew, that was nine-tenths of the law.

'Fanbloodytastic,' he said.

She could hear him smacking his lips as he salivated in anticipation.

She held the phone away from her ear.

'And don't you dare sell it before I get there,' she shouted before ending the call.

She swallowed down her rage. She'd deal with Dobbie tomorrow. Right now, she had to study the second letter that was addressed to her.

She reloaded it to her phone and the words lit up the screen.

*DI Stone*

*I told you that you needed to stop me. I begged you. I told you this would happen. I had no fucking choice. Do you not understand that? You have failed me, and you have failed the woman who is now dead. Her blood is on your hands. She is dead because of you, and you have to live with yourself just like me.*

*Well, DI Stone, I'm afraid I can't help you any further. You fucked up. You didn't catch me. I asked you to fucking listen to me. I thought you were different. I thought you got it, but I was wrong. I pinned my hopes on you to make this end and I should have known better. You're just like everyone else. You didn't fucking listen.*

*I cannot tell you what I am going to do next, as I do not even know that myself.*

*But you can be sure that more people are going to die.*

*Noah*

Even she could see the difference in tone from the first letter. She had a murderer who had set his sights on her personally and now that murderer was very pissed off.

# CHAPTER THIRTY-SEVEN

Stacey leaned over and kissed Devon on the cheek. 'Thanks, love.'

'Want me to wait?'

Stacey shook her head. An immigration officer, Devon had been on a late-night raid. She'd walked in the door at 4 a.m., too wired to go straight to sleep, and had offered to drive Stacey to the prison. Stacey knew she should think about learning to drive, but in truth, the longer she left it the more frightening it became.

She yawned. 'I could just pop my head down here for a…'

'It's not a sign, is it, D?' Stacey asked.

'Is what not a sign of what?' she asked with a look that asked if she'd said that right.

'The cake?' Stacey asked.

Despite her fatigue, Devon opened her eyes widely.

'Babe, we've booked a photographer, flowers, ushers, a DJ and catering without a hitch, but you wanna call it off because Aunt Abebi can't make our cake?'

The smile behind her eyes spoke volumes of Devon's tolerance levels when Stacey's thoughts were carrying her away.

Truth was, there were still times she couldn't believe that the gorgeous, intelligent, funny woman by her side had chosen her to spend the rest of her life with.

Devon reached across and squeezed her arm. 'Babe, I'll marry you in the high street with a bouquet of daisies, my camera phone, a supper from the chippy and a jam doughnut if it means you'll become my wife, so…'

'I bloody love you, woman, now go home and get some rest,' Stacey said, leaning across and kissing her on the cheek. Devon wasn't due into work until 2 p.m., so she could get some quality sleep in bed.

'Yeah, yeah,' Devon said as Stacey got out of the car.

She approached the entrance to the prison and looked back. She was not surprised to note that the engine on the Clio had been switched off and the driver's seat reclined.

Devon was waiting for her.

She shook her head as that familiar glow ignited inside her again. She was a very lucky girl.

The entrance to the prison looked pretty standard to her, even though Stacey was not a frequent visitor to male prisons.

Featherstone was a category C prison housing approximately seven hundred inmates. Stacey remembered reading that in the early 1980s inmates of the prison were caught making forgeries of the work of Bernard Leach. At the turn of the millennium, the place was revealed to have the highest number of drug-using prisoners in the UK, with a whopping thirty-four per cent getting high on something, even if it was the beer they made using Marmite, fruit and vegetables. Stacey often wondered how such industriousness could be used for the purpose of good if channelled in the right direction.

Stacey stepped inside and introduced herself to a security officer named Nathan who looked to be around eighteen years old. Whatever his age, she couldn't imagine that his youthful appearance elicited a compliant response to his instruction.

Stacey understood that the profession of a prison officer had probably altered over the years in line with diversity directives. Muscles, aggression and fear were not the tools needed to deal with every situation or every prisoner. And yet, a small part of her couldn't help thinking he wouldn't be the first officer to whom you'd be handing out riot gear.

The same could be said for her, she supposed, as Nathan began explaining the rules of engagement.

'Obviously, this was a special request due to an ongoing investigation. There will be no other visitors in the room, but Daisy will remain with you at all times.'

On command, the least-looking Daisy she'd ever seen appeared and towered over Stacey. The smile took the sting out of the six-foot height and gym-honed body that Stacey would have to step left or right to see around. *Now, she would be getting riot gear*, Stacey thought.

'Ready?' Daisy asked pleasantly.

Stacey nodded as Nathan locked away her possessions.

'So what's he like?' Stacey asked, falling into step beside the prison officer who notably slowed down to accommodate her.

'Not bad, bit cocky, gets frustrated now and again like some of them, swears he didn't do it. Like all of 'em.'

Stacey smiled at the exaggerated eye roll that accompanied the words.

'I swear there ain't so many innocent folks at a Sunday morning church service.'

Daisy opened the door to the visitors' centre and stepped inside.

Sean Fellows was already sitting at a table smack bang in the centre of the room, wearing a pale grey sweatshirt and jogging bottoms.

Stacey wasn't exactly sure of the protocol when greeting a convicted rapist. When meeting someone for the first time, she normally offered her hand. Certainly not an appropriate action.

He turned to look at her as she approached. He undertook a swift appraisal of her before dismissing her. Stacey was not offended. Maybe it was the extra few pounds she carried; maybe it was her black skin. Either way, she wasn't upset about not being to the visual taste of a rapist.

And anyway, she pretty much did the same to him, but for different reasons.

She wasn't sure how she'd expected him to look in person after seeing only his face, but somehow she had expected more. There were no rippling muscles, visible tattoos. His brown hair was cut short and tidy, and she'd have guessed his full height to be around five feet seven. She would have passed him in a crowd without a second glance, which she supposed was half the problem.

'Thank you for agreeing to see me,' Stacey said, taking a seat opposite.

Her skin crawled at the thought of what he'd done to two innocent women, but she knew that allowing her personal feelings to show would not help her get a confession to the rape of Lesley Skipton. And, ultimately, that's what she was here for.

He shrugged. 'Curious is all. Hoping someone has realised there's been a fuck up.'

'Fuck up?' she asked.

'Yeah, that I'm innocent and that Gemma Hornley is a slut and a lying bitch.'

Stacey bit down on her lip to prevent her true feelings from coming out. This was going to be more difficult than she'd thought if he still wasn't admitting to the one he'd been convicted of. What chance did she have of getting justice for Lesley?

She decided to let him talk about Gemma. Maybe he'd slip up and say something she could seize upon.

'Wanna tell me about it?'

'Sure, but don't get comfy, this ain't no love story. Saw her in a club, fancied her, danced with her and fucked her round the back of the building.'

He shrugged, as though that was the end of the story, which she already knew it wasn't.

'And then?'

'Went back inside, danced some more, saw her as we were leaving and asked if she wanted to go again.'

Absolute charmer, Stacey thought as she nodded for him to continue.

'She said no, we had a few words and she stormed off.'

All accounts said they were openly shouting and that he'd been angry.

'How exactly did she refuse?' Stacey asked. 'Did she just say "no thanks, I'm good"?'

'Nah, the bitch told me I'd been fucking useless the first time.'

'She insulted your manhood?'

'Let's just say it took a while to get it up.'

Stacey tried not to react to his crudeness.

'Well, you asked, love.'

'Did that piss you off?'

'Course it did. I was pissed and she wound me up.'

'So you followed her?'

'No.'

'You were seen going in the same direction.'

'As were fifty other folks who were leaving at kicking-out time. At the end of the road, I turned right not left like they said in court.'

'And you were carrying a beer bottle?'

'I ain't wasting beer,' he offered, as though it was a criminal offence.

'The bottle was never found?'

'Fucked if I know where I lobbed it.'

'So you insist you didn't follow Gemma and assault her with the beer bottle?'

'What would be the fucking point in that? That's some weird fucking shit right there. I ain't no freak.'

'But the—'

'What's this all about, love?' he asked, narrowing his gaze. 'This is old news. I didn't do it, jury says I did and now I'm here doing time for somebody else. Good for them and shit for me.'

'And you've never met Lesley Skipton?'

He stared at her for twenty seconds as realisation began to dawn.

'Ah, I see what this is all about and you can fuck right off. I never met her, and I never shagged her. Not with my dick or anything else.'

'The similarities between the two—'

'Yeah, yeah, I know. Coppers asked me all about her, but do you all assume that because I swear a lot I'm a dumb fuck?'

Stacey shook her head.

'Good, cos I ain't stupid enough to take that kind of risk.'

'What risk?'

He pushed back his chair and signalled to Daisy that he wanted to leave.

'I'm done cos it's breakfast time and I ain't missing it for this bollocks, so if you wanna know what I mean, check the fucking dates, love, check the fucking dates.'

# CHAPTER THIRTY-EIGHT

'Okay, guys, let's get started,' Kim said as Stacey slid into her seat. The constable looked pensive after her early meeting at the prison. With such a troubled expression, Kim guessed the sexual assault of Lesley Skipton wasn't getting solved any time soon.

'You've all seen the second letter. Thoughts?' she asked.

'He's pissed off,' Penn offered.

'Why?'

Penn shrugged. 'Cos we didn't stop him?'

Kim folded her arms. 'That was my first thought too, but now I'm not so sure.'

'He knows we couldn't stop him,' Bryant offered. 'So I'm not sure he's pissed off because of that.'

'Agreed,' Kim said.

'Still using the name Noah,' Penn said.

'Yep, great observations, folks, but what are these letters telling us about the killer?'

Silence.

'Okay, we'll come back to that in a minute. Penn, gonna give you a break on the post-mortems, which Bryant and I will attend. I want you over at the search area. If they find anything at all, I want to be the first to know.'

'On it, boss.'

'Stace, I want you doing background checks on all family members of both victims.'

'Got it, boss,' Stacey said, making a note.

'Okay, back to the letters. We don't know for sure if they're definitely from him, but we're gonna take a bet they are. Given that, we now need to extract any detail we can find, which includes the handwriting itself as well as the content. Stace, find me someone who can help with the handwriting.'

'Won't forensics have an expert at the lab in Birmingham?' Penn asked.

'I want as little involvement over there as possible until Mitch finds his leak.'

'No probs, boss.'

'Now to the actual content,' she said, focusing on Stacey.

It took the constable just three seconds to catch up with where she was heading and start shaking her head.

'She won't do it, boss. She hasn't worked an active case since that last one with us. She's writing her book.'

Alison Lowe was a profiler, or behaviourist as she liked to be called, who had consulted for them on a couple of major cases, until a year ago when her own life had been put in jeopardy by a killer who was focused on Kim.

'She's still writing it?' Kim asked.

Stacey nodded.

During the investigation, the two of them had become friends and still kept in touch.

'A lot of research, apparently.'

'You mean, she's hiding behind writing a book?'

'Maybe,' Stacey said, 'but she still won't do it.'

Because Alison had removed herself from the force's list of available consultants, Kim couldn't ask Woody to bring her in, but she needed the woman's insight.

'Get her on the phone,' Kim said.

Stacey took her phone from her satchel. 'I'm telling you, boss, she won't do it.'

'Put the call on speaker,' Kim said. She wanted to hear the excuses herself.

Everyone stared at the phone as the ringing sounded out loud.

'Yo,' Alison answered.

'Hey, Alison. How are?…'

'No,' the profiler said straight away.

'You don't even know what I'm ringing for and I said a total of four words,' Stacey protested.

'Yeah I do, and those four words are all I need. You never use my name when you call. You never sound so serious when you call. The echo of your voice tells me I'm on loudspeaker. It's the beginning of the day and you're at work, so I'm guessing that right now I'm talking to all four of you. Morning, folks.'

Kim couldn't help the smile that turned up the corners of her mouth.

She motioned for Stacey to continue.

'Ali, I swear this is something you are going to want to have a look at. We have two letters—'

'Nice sales pitch, Stace, but it's not happening. You could have Hannibal Lecter in a holding cell requesting a one on one and I still—'

Stacey cut her off, persisting. 'We just need some insight into the mind of—'

'Nope, unless you've forgotten last time I worked with you guys I almost died, so there's nothing you can say that will change my mind. I'm not on active duty.'

Kim understood her fear and sympathised. Her ordeal had been traumatic, and she needed gentle persuasion to get back on the horse. She probably needed patience, understanding and an empathetic approach.

Kim grabbed the phone. 'Hey, Alison, we've got two dead women and a missing six-year-old boy, so do me a favour, put your big girl pants on and come help us find the bastard responsible.'

# CHAPTER THIRTY-NINE

Once the office was empty, Stacey tried Alison's number again. It rang and eventually clicked to voicemail. She could imagine Alison staring at the screen, seething with anger. She tried again, but this time there was no ringing as voicemail kicked straight in.

'Great,' she said, throwing her phone down onto the desk. She'd done a fantastic job of letting her friend down. But she couldn't have known what the boss was going to say to her, and even if she had she wasn't sure she'd have disagreed.

It was true that the two of them had become close during that investigation. They spoke a couple of times a week and met for coffee at least once a month. Initially, Stacey had understood Alison's need to take a step back from her profession and had thought that writing a book would be good for her. At first, Alison's enthusiasm for the research had kept her animated and alert, buzzing with the challenge. The last two times they'd met, Alison had barely mentioned the project at all.

Stacey agreed that she needed to be back consulting. She just wasn't sure she'd have phrased it the same way. She resolved to try her friend again later, once she'd had chance to calm down.

She turned back to her computer to begin the background checks the boss had mentioned, but her meeting with Sean Fellows was still at the front of her mind.

What exactly had he meant about the dates?

The meeting had left her more confused than before. She'd been hoping to move her investigation into the assault of Lesley

Skipton forward, prayed he'd say something that would give her a place to start. She'd expected to feel repulsion being in his presence, but she hadn't felt anything at all.

She reached for the file and a plain piece of paper and began noting the events sequentially.

*3rd May – Gemma Hornley assaulted.*
*3rd May – Sean Fellows questioned.*
*4th May – Lesley Skipton assaulted.*
*7th May – Sean Fellows questioned.*
*11th May – Sean Fellows arrested.*
*12th May – Sean Fellows charged.*
*13th May – Sean Fellows questioned about Lesley Skipton.*
*15th May – Lesley Skipton's file marked as no further action.*

Stacey sat back and looked at the key dates.

*How stupid do you think I am?* Sean Fellows had asked her and seeing the dates spelled out she understood what he meant.

Would he really have raped again so soon when he'd already been questioned by the police?

# CHAPTER FORTY

'Okay, Keats, time's a wasting,' she said, stepping through the automatic doors to the morgue for the second time in less than twelve hours. And every hour that passed was an hour that six-year-old Archie was in danger.

Kim and her colleague had spoken little in the car, after he had succeeded in pissing her off before they were even out of the station car park.

'Well, that was a sensitive way to speak to Alison,' Bryant had said once they were in the car.

'It was what she needed to hear.'

'You really think she's gonna help us out after that?'

Kim had shrugged. If she was the woman Kim thought she was, she'd put her ego to one side and get involved. Whatever Alison told herself, her passion lay in analysing events and people. It reminded her of former athletes turning to coaching. There were few who didn't wish they were still competing.

'Pretty sure you've pissed Stacey off too.'

'Jesus, Bryant, are you the feelings police this morning?' she snapped, turning slightly in her seat.

'You working on any project at the minute?' he asked, shooting her a sideways glance.

'None of your damn business.'

Bryant had got the message and focused on his driving.

Truth was she did care about people's feelings. Up to a point. There was a six-year-old boy missing and they needed all the help they could get, but she wasn't going to explain that to her colleague, who appeared much calmer walking into the morgue in full daylight.

'Aah, as I suspected and I was right,' Keats said, turning from the sink with a triumphant smile on his face. She wasn't sure who he had been in a secret battle with, but she was pleased he'd won.

'I thought it might be you instead of Penn this morning, so I took the liberty of getting it done early. It's not the same with you peering over my shoulder. At least when Penn is breathing down my ear it's because he appreciates the artistry.'

'Of what?' Kim asked, leaning against the spotless stainless-steel counter.

He thought for a moment. 'It's the difference between a seven-course tasting menu and a sandwich.'

She turned to her colleague. 'Hear that, Bryant, Keats is calling me a—'

'You're the sandwich,' he clarified. 'Penn observes the process, asks questions, learns from the expertise. You, on the other hand, like to grab and go.'

'Hey, I ask questions too.'

'Not about the process, only about the results.'

It was on the tip of her tongue to add that knowing the process did not aid her in finding the killer, but she kept her mouth closed. Keats was clearly testy, and she was pleased she didn't have to sit through the post-mortem.

She rubbed her hands. 'Okay, what we got?'

'Absolutely nothing,' he said, reaching for his clipboard, 'that is going to help you.'

'Someone's glass is half-empty, isn't it?' she asked.

'You already know the cause of death. Her neck was broken just like Katrina. There was no sexual assault and she appeared to be in reasonably good health.'

'Toxicology?'

'Has been sent off, but I don't expect anything earth-shattering to come back on that score.'

Kim crossed her arms and waited.

Keats raised an eyebrow. 'What are you waiting for?'

'The reveal, Keats. You're like a good crime novel: you always save something for the end.'

'Inspector, I have nothing interesting to offer.'

'Well, I know that, Keats, but what about the body?' she quipped.

'There is nothing more to add. My official report is already in your inbox, so I'll thank you to leave me in peace until circumstances dictate that we shall meet again.'

Kim glanced at Bryant, who shrugged in response.

There really was nothing else.

She moved towards the door, feeling as though there were questions she needed to ask.

Keats had listed all the similarities between the murders of Katrina and Louise. Her mind's eye travelled back to the bullet-point list on the wipe board.

She stopped walking as the automatic doors opened to let her out.

'Scratches?' she asked, turning. 'You noted deliberate scratch marks on Katrina's skin?'

Keats shook his head. 'None on Louise. Clean as a whistle.'

Kim frowned as she left the morgue.

A subtle difference to the first murder was the absence of something. What did that mean?

So had she learned something after all?

# CHAPTER FORTY-ONE

Penn knew Stevens Park well. It wasn't a huge expanse of space. There were no undulating hills to climb or hidden lakes and beauty spots. The entire length of it was fringed by a dual carriageway that ran from Quarry Bank to the border of Lye.

The rest of its exterior was hemmed in by industrial buildings and a housing estate that adjoined every other perimeter.

This was not a country park where one went for a peaceful stroll amongst a stolen patch of nature. It had few facilities and was popular with local dog walkers, which was how Penn knew it.

When Jasper had been a toddler, they'd had a small dog, some kind of mixed-breed terrier. His parents had assumed that Jasper would be a lonely child and wanted him to have something to love. And love it he had. They all had until the day Mutley had gone off his legs and died due to kidney failure. Jasper had been inconsolable and had learned about death quite early for a little boy. Once he understood that Mutley wasn't coming back, Jasper took to pulling the dog's bed out of the utility and sleeping in it. There had been tears and tantrums for weeks, over a dog. And that was what was bothering Penn now. He'd seen his brother's grief. He knew what it looked like when allowed to break free. He had seen the all-consuming effect and it hadn't looked anything like what he was witnessing right now.

*It's just time*, he told himself as he approached an officer he recognised.

'Planty,' he called out to the white-haired officer.

'That's Inspector Planty to you, my boy,' he said, offering his hand.

Penn took it and shook it warmly. Before joining CID and moving to West Mercia, he'd worked as a constable with the man as his sergeant many times.

'You here to keep us plods in line?' he asked with a smile.

'Nah, expedite communication,' he explained. 'Boss's orders.'

'Yeah. I'd do what she told me as well.'

Penn knew there was no malice in his words. From what he understood, they had worked together multiple times with co-operation and respect.

'Anything to report so far?'

Inspector Plant shook his head.

'Had a fair few volunteers this morning,' he said with a frustrated look.

Penn knew that volunteers always turned up to help search, especially if there was a child involved. It was both a blessing and a curse. More bodies in the mix meant greater co-ordination and constant instruction.

'How many?' Penn asked, moving towards the open boot of Plant's squad car, which was currently serving as an on-site command point.

'Had forty-eight so far, but the day is young,' he said, tapping the list where the names had been recorded. 'All been tasked in pairs outside of the park area, and trained techies and police officers all over the park and the immediate area beyond the boundary.'

Penn picked up the sheets detailing the names and the location they'd been tasked to search.

His gaze rested on a name halfway down the page.

It was a name he already knew.

# CHAPTER FORTY-TWO

'Well, he's not done too badly out of it, has he?' Kim asked as Bryant turned on to a tree-lined road on the outskirts of Quinton.

Although only two miles from Halesowen, the area fell within the Edgbaston formal district bordering the suburbs of Harborne and Bartley Green and covered only two square miles. Its claim to fame was having the highest point of any building in Birmingham at the top of the Christ Church spire. The area had a few housing estates which balanced social and private housing, but as Bryant drove a mile or two from the centre Kim noted the properties they passed were around fifty metres away from their neighbours, separated by vast tree hedges and high walls. All of them were gated.

'Go on, how much?' she asked, revisiting a game they often played.

'I'd say the upper sixes or low sevens.'

That was a fair range he'd offered, and she agreed with him.

'For looking at handwriting,' she mused as they drove through the only set of open gates in the road.

The house itself was a double-fronted, Victorian home, painted pure white with blue detail added to all the windows.

The overhanging trees formed a canopy blocking the weak sunlight from above.

Kim got out of the car and took a look around.

'Stacey said he was... oh my god,' she said as a woman appeared from behind a thick tree trunk with a large pair of shears. For a moment, she looked like she'd been in some low-budget horror movie where everyone with a speaking part met a slow and horrific death.

Kim glanced again at the shears as the woman smiled pleasantly. Kim guessed her to be late sixties or early seventies; she had a tanned and healthy complexion.

'You must be the police officers,' she said, placing the shears against the tree and wiping her hands on her jeans. 'Reginald is very much looking forward to seeing you, even if he pretends otherwise,' she said with a cheeky wink that took years off her appearance. 'He's in the sunroom, if you follow me.'

Kim did as she was told and was led from the front of the house to the rear, passing one high-ceilinged room after another, all painted in light colours, harvesting as much light as possible. As they neared the rear of the property, it was like stepping into another house. The weak sunlight flooded every room and warmed the house considerably.

The woman stepped down into the sunroom that stretched half the width of the house. The space was filled with wicker furniture and plants that appeared to have been brought in from the cold.

'Mr Wilkins?' Kim said as Bryant offered his hand.

'Reg, please,' he said, putting his book aside and motioning for them to sit.

'Coffee, tea?' the woman asked from the doorway.

They both shook their heads and Bryant thanked her.

She disappeared whistling.

'You'll get it whether you want it or not,' Reg said, watching her go.

'Sorry?'

'By the time Henrietta gets to the kitchen, she'll have forgotten your answer and will make it anyway.' He glanced at the plants to his left. 'This lot don't go thirsty.'

'Is she?…'

'Early stages. We cope. Now what can I help you with? Police finally come to their senses?'

Kim hid her smile. As an institution, the force was not quick to embrace new ways of doing things, and assessing people from their handwriting was not something they openly embraced.

'It's an interesting subject. How did you get into it?' Kim asked.

Reg Wilkins laughed out loud, displaying even white teeth in a lightly stubbled face beneath a full head of grey hair.

'An innocuously innocent small-talk question hiding an interview assessment. You want to know my credentials for the job even though you came to me,' he said, meeting her gaze. 'I'm not the one with dementia, officer. Aaah, coffee, perfect,' he said as his wife carried a tray into the room. The gesture pleased Kim as his wife placed the tray on the coffee table. He chose not to remind his wife that they had all refused her offer of a beverage.

'Thank you,' she and Bryant said at the same time.

She nodded and left.

'There's no need to drink it,' he said, glancing at the plants. 'But it is good coffee.'

Bryant poured them both a cup as she met the man's gaze.

'Okay, Reg, forget the small talk, what are your credentials?'

'That's better,' he said, smiling. 'And to answer your question, I began studying graphology in the eighties when British Steel Corporation let me go. I studied at the Cambridge School of Graphology and am a member of the British Institute of Graphologists, the British Academy of Graphology and—'

'Okay, thank you,' Kim said, holding up her hand.

'I scraped a living from it through the nineties, but once the millennium hit there weren't enough hours in the day. Every business or company suddenly wanted insight into the people they were employing.'

Kim now understood the house he was living in. His newly acquired skills had put him in the right place at the right time.

'Have you ever consulted criminally?' Kim asked.

He shook his head. 'I understand that the police force remains dubious on the subject.' He paused. 'And I think we have the perfect example sitting here.'

Kim turned to her colleague, who was frowning as he listened.

'I'm sorry, I don't mean to be rude,' Bryant answered. 'But if I'm honest, I struggle to accept the science when we were all taught how to write by our primary school English teacher.'

Reg smiled. 'Gather up your classmates and see if you all write the same now.'

Bryant's nod conceded the point.

'Bear with me a second,' he said, standing and opening a drawer in a wicker side table. He brought out a piece of paper and a pen and thrust it towards Kim.

'While I speak with your colleague, just write down what you're hoping I'll be able to achieve.' He tapped his temple. 'I don't remember so well, any more.'

Kim did as he asked as the man sat and continued to talk to Bryant.

'We are all totally unique. We look, speak, act and move in different ways. The way we write is unique. It leaves a permanent trail. Your writing will change upon your mood—'

'So how can you determine anything if?...'

'Because certain components remain consistent throughout. The uses of the science are endless. It's used for people changing careers, to highlight strengths and weaknesses, compatibility. It can help guide you in how to deal effectively with people. It's been used to detect forgery for decades.'

'But it's a pretty new science, is it not?' Bryant asked.

He shook his head. 'It was used in Ancient Greece for many centuries and by the Chinese. Even the famous Swiss psychologist Carl Jung recognised the validity of handwriting analysis. In Israel it's estimated that ninety-eight per cent of job applicants have their handwriting analysed first, although Europe is still the area where most research and use of graphology remains.'

Kim handed him the note of her expectations and took the two pieces of paper from her back pocket.

'Would you take a look at these?'

He put her list to the side and reached for them. 'Aah, copies.'

'Is that a problem?' Bryant asked.

'It's better if it's the original document, but these are good copies,' he said, inspecting them both. 'Yes, I think I can do something with these.'

'What makes the original different?' Kim asked.

'You can tell a lot about a person by the force of the actual writing onto a sheet of paper; but never mind, we have a lot to work with.'

He met her gaze. 'You're not going to get anything right now. This isn't a drive-through kind of thing. There are well over a hundred basic stroke formations to be identified.'

Kim couldn't help her disappointment that there was no immediate snapshot to take away.

'I'm sorry that's not what you want to hear but the general picture of writing – such as where is it on the page, are margins wide or narrow, are they equal, is writing large or small, heavy or light, consistent or messy – all tell us something, but only in conjunction with the individual stroke formations, like where are the T bars placed, how long are the lower loops, are the circle letters open or closed.'

'But surely…'

'Okay, I'm not a party trick kind of guy,' he said, reaching for the list Kim had just written.

'Hmmm… officer,' he said, looking over the page, 'I can tell straight away that you are determined. What I can't see is whether that trait gets you in hot water.'

'It does,' Bryant said, leaning forward.

'Is your determination mixed with recklessness?...'

'Yes,' Bryant answered again.

Kim offered him a look.

'Are you determined to the degree of bloody-mindedness?'

Kim looked at Bryant who closed his mouth.

'And even without his handwriting, I can see that your colleague there just exhibited the trait of bravery coupled with self-preservation. Knowing a couple of personality traits will tell you nothing unless I can tell you how the traits work together.'

Kim accepted defeat. Yes, she wanted an answer, but she wanted it accurate.

'How long?'

'I'd normally want three to four days.'

'Shit,' Kim said, picturing bodies stacking up in that period of time.

'But given the urgency,' he continued, 'give me twenty-four hours.'

Kim knew that was the best she was going to get if she wanted a reasonable picture of their killer.

She stood, turned towards the door and then hesitated.

'You said you didn't care much for party tricks, so why did you do one?' she asked.

He nodded towards her colleague. 'Because when you come back tomorrow, I'd like you both to be receptive to what I have to say. I won't justify my findings again.'

'Touché,' Bryant said, nodding his understanding.

'Thank you for—' her words were cut off by the ringing of her phone.

'Excuse me,' she said as Reg started to pour his coffee into one of the plants.

She turned away and took out her phone.

It was Penn at the search site.

*Please God, let Archie be found*, she thought, mentally crossing her fingers.

She answered the call and listened as she worked her way back to the front of the house.

She paused at the front door to ask the question that was playing on her lips.

'What the hell is she doing there?'

# CHAPTER FORTY-THREE

It was almost eleven when Bryant pulled up at Stevens Park. A light drizzle had just started to smatter against the windscreen.

Kim headed straight for Penn, who was to the left of an open-booted squad car.

'Are you sure it's her?' Kim asked, continuing the conversation they'd started as she'd been leaving the graphologist's home.

Penn reached into the boot and took out a sheet of paper.

'Says here Ella Nock arrived at 8.55 a.m. and was paired with a woman called Dorothy Birch to search down to the traffic island, along Caledonia and back up the other side.'

'Has she been back yet?' Kim asked.

Penn shook his head as the drizzle turned to heavy rain.

'Here come a batch of volunteers now,' Penn noted, nodding towards the walkway to the main gates.

A group of four women and two men were approaching the co-ordination point at speed, driven by the rain no doubt.

Kim picked out Ella pulling up her jacket collar around her neck.

Inspector Plant appeared at the car as the group approached.

'Thank you all for coming out to help,' he said as the three sets of two offered their names and declared their area searched.

'Ella,' Kim said, stepping forward, 'I'm surprised to see you here.'

Ella shrugged as the others headed back to their cars. 'It's the least I could do, Inspector. I saw the news report that a child was missing. We were lucky. We got Mia back but...'

'And we'll get Archie back too,' Kim said with more confidence than she felt. 'I'd just have thought your brother needed you more.'

'He wanted to come, but I insisted he stay home with Mia. She's now realised that mummy isn't coming home.'

Kim wondered if Andrew Nock always did what his sister told him to do.

'And how is your brother doing?'

Ella raised an eyebrow as if there was little point offering an answer to that question.

'Well, if that's all, Inspector, I'd like to get—'

'Of course,' Kim said, noting that her hair was now flattened against her head.

She watched Ella walk away and tried to quiet the uneasy feeling in her stomach. On the face of it, she was a woman doing her civic duty and offering a helping hand. But the fact she was related to the first victim added an unusual flavour to the selfless gesture.

Kim was still watching as the woman got into her car and drove away.

Kim took out her phone. Stacey answered almost immediately.

'Those background checks on family members, Stace.'

'Yeah, boss,'

'Move Ella Nock to the top of your list.'

# CHAPTER FORTY-FOUR

Stacey turned to the page that held the list of the names of family members and put an asterisk next to the name of Ella Nock.

She turned back to her most recent page of notes and the phone number she'd just scribbled down.

She would get on to Ella Nock as a priority, but she just had one phone call to make first.

After poring through the court documents of Sean Fellows's trial, she was no more settled in her mind than she'd been before.

From the court transcripts, Stacey was sure that Gemma Hornley had been a compelling victim and after speaking to the woman herself she could see why.

Sean Fellows, on the other hand, had been aggressive and hostile and had been warned twice by the judge to mind his language and calm down.

The court record had revealed nothing that she didn't already know. There was no additional evidence, no sudden and dramatic courtroom admission, which left Stacey with one single burning question that she hoped to have answered if she dialled the number on her pad.

Getting hold of the juror's information wasn't a difficult task. Thelma Bird had chosen to speak to the press the day after the verdict. Not allowed to speak about jury deliberations, she had instead chatted about Sean Fellows's conduct in the courtroom. The woman had been noted in the article as being from the Willenhall area, so a number had not been too difficult to track down.

The phone was answered with a simple and friendly 'Hello.'

'Is that Thelma Bird?' Stacey clarified.

'Speaking,' she answered brightly.

Stacey introduced herself and added, 'I'm looking into the case of Sean Fellows, who was convicted of rape—'

'Oh, I know who he is, my dear,' she answered. 'Wait a minute.'

Stacey waited, hearing sounds of movement in the background.

'Just closed the door to the lounge. Hubby's taking a nap. How can I help?'

Stacey had thought about the many different ways to phrase this, but there wasn't really any way to dress it up.

'I'd really like to know why you convicted him.'

'I'm sorry?'

'Please, don't misunderstand me,' Stacey said, not wishing to cause the woman offence. 'I'm not saying you were wrong, but I'd just like to know what the deciding factor was. Was it the testimony of the victim?'

'Partly; she was very credible and convincing. But no, it wasn't completely that.'

'Was it because of his anger, or the fact he was seen leaving in the same direction as the victim?'

'Not really. We all understood that was circumstantial.'

Stacey was confused. That was pretty much the sum of the evidence against him.

'So…'

'It was him, his manner, his attitude. He was cocky and arrogant, as though he was just going to get away with what he'd done to that poor girl. I mean, the majority of rape cases don't even get to court, do they?' Thelma asked, finding her stride. 'I looked it all up, you see, and approximately eighty-five thousand women experience violent sexual crime every year and only fifteen per cent of those women report it to the police. Very few cases make it to court and conviction rates for rape are lower than other crimes: only around five per cent if memory serves me.'

'So the numbers swung it for you?' Stacey asked.

'Not the numbers as such – but we knew we had a rapist sitting right in front of us. It's like, well, if the victim believes he did it, the police believe he did it and the CPS as well, there must be something in it. If the case has made it this far in the process given all those negative numbers, how can we possibly let this man go?'

Stacey glanced at the jury demographic again. Seven women and five men. Was this some kind of sisterhood vote? Or had they treated the case like a civil case, on the balance of probability? Was it more likely he did it or not?

'I stand by our decision. I still think he was guilty, and you should have seen his face when the verdict was read. Knocked the cocky smile right off his face.'

Yes, she was sure it had, and Stacey had a feeling she could guess exactly why.

# CHAPTER FORTY-FIVE

'Where are you, Stone?' Woody asked when she answered the phone.

'En route back to the station for a check-in, sir,' she replied as the rain from her hair continued to drip down her neck.

She and Bryant had continued to stand in the rain for a few more minutes, getting an update of the search areas from Inspector Plant. After realising there was nothing she or her team could add, she'd instructed Penn to head back to the station after lunch. Any updates would come directly from Inspector Plant.

'Perfect. A slight detour, if you don't mind.'

She frowned. 'To where?'

'Halesowen: the shopping centre. The EPT is meeting for a walk through.'

She wondered if she'd heard correctly. 'Sir, you do know I've got—'

'Don't insult me with those next words, Stone. It's ten minutes and we need the continuity. It's just the operational staff, so it'll be brief.'

She had never known any of these meetings to be brief.

'Sir, I really think…'

'Stone, you've been requested so just do it.'

The phone went dead in her hand as another protest was forming on her lips.

'Bloody great,' she growled, putting the phone back in her pocket.

'What's up?' Bryant asked. 'You gotta go play nice with the EPT crew?'

'For that smug look on your face you're now coming with me,' she said as more rainwater seeped down her neck. She looked around. 'Jesus, Bryant, don't you have anything in this bloody car that I can use to dry myself?'

'Nah, sorry. I had the mobile spa taken out. It took up too much room.' He thought for a second. 'The dog's towel is in the back if you wanna use that.'

'Bryant, you really can be a f—'

'Think you'd better call Stace?' he asked, cutting her off.

'Good idea,' she said, taking her phone back out.

'Hey, Stace,' Kim said when she answered. 'Slight delay but should be with you in about half an hour.'

'No probs, boss.'

'So what you been doing for the last twenty minutes?' she asked, preferring to speak to the constable rather than her colleague in the car.

'Just had to finish something off on the—'

'Stace, I did tell you that our current case takes priority. If I ask you to do something I expect—'

'I know, boss, I'm sorry but this shuffle case just got complicated.'

'Why? You no longer think your guy raped the second victim?'

'To be honest, boss, it's even more complicated than that cos I no longer think he raped either one of them.'

# CHAPTER FORTY-SIX

'Well, ain't that just a whopping can of worms?' Bryant asked, pulling into the service yard of the shopping centre.

Kim's thoughts were also on Stacey's admission. She'd told the constable they'd talk more when she got back to the station, but if she was right, a lot of people were going to be pissed off, not least their colleagues at Brierley Hill. The purpose of the shuffle was to solve unsolved cases, not pry open the lid of cases that had been sealed shut. For once she was hoping her colleague was wrong.

'Looks like the show has already started,' Kim said, spotting the representatives from the ambulance and fire crew. Superintendent Lena Wiley stood between them both.

Kim tried to ruffle some life into her rain-dampened hair.

'Bloody hell, guv, you don't normally care about your appearance.' She offered him a look.

'And that didn't come out quite the way I meant it.'

'Come on, let's get to it,' she said, getting out of the car as a black BMW pulled up beside them.

Bryant paused as the man got out the car.

Christopher Manley smiled widely and immediately offered his hand. Bryant shook it warmly.

'Hey, Chris, heard you'd done well for yourself.'

The man reached into the back of the car for a hanging jacket.

'Can't complain, mate. Picking up the slack for you guys.'

Bryant laughed out loud. 'Someone's gotta do it, pal.'

Chris briefly looked from one to the other.

'Aah, partners.'

'Colleagues,' Bryant offered quickly, before taking a look around. 'Wasn't there some kind of incident down here once?'

Chris smiled. 'Oh yeah. Popular boy band turned up to perform a short gig at the record shop. Turned up pissed as farts and were kept secret down here until performance time. Except, lead singer wasn't happy there were no adoring, screaming fans, so started posting on social media to let everyone know where they were. Girls came running, broke the barriers and surrounded the tour bus.'

'What happened?' Kim asked, amused.

'Three minor injuries, event was cancelled and the tour bus sent packing.'

'Yeah, I remember hearing about it,' Bryant said.

'Yeah, you guys turned up, eventually,' Chris said with a wry smile.

He glanced over at the crew already gathered.

'Well, suppose we'd best get over there before her majesty gives us detention.'

'Nice guy,' Bryant said, nodding towards the security manager. 'Almost one of us.'

She wasn't surprised. Many security personnel had aspired to the force but had diverted for different reasons.

'Money?' she asked. Everyone knew the pay wasn't great. And he was making a decent living for himself with his own security company.

'Nope. He was doing the training. I had him for a couple of shifts then one night at the pub he stepped into a domestic. The guy got belligerent and smacked him. It all got physical and the drunk guy pressed charges. Police career over.'

'Okay, officially bored now,' Kim said, although she did think it was a shame he'd lost his career by trying to do the right thing. She hoped his company balance sheet helped to soften the blow.

'Inspector Stone, thank you for making it,' Lena said, leaving Kim in no doubt who had requested her presence.

Her failure to acknowledge Bryant demonstrated once again her disregard of people she felt were beneath her or not worth her time.

Chris and Bryant shared a look. His arrival had clearly been met with the same level of enthusiasm.

'Okay, now we'll begin,' Lena said, pointing to the barriered entrance to the service yard through which they'd all just driven. 'Deliveries will be cut off to this area one hour before Tyra's arrival. This area should be—'

'I've got a guy on it from 2 p.m.,' Chris said without looking at her.

Lena turned a complete circle.

'I'm not sure one guard is sufficient for the whole—'

'I've got two guys down here patrolling from 1.30 p.m.,' he added wearily, as though this wasn't his first rodeo.

'Splendid,' she said, turning to the ambulance rep. 'Is this a good place for you to be stationed?'

'Ain't nobody gonna get hurt down here,' Kim offered.

The point of medical assistance was for the public. In crowd situations people got crushed, they got hot and giddy, they fell over. All that would be happening on the upper level in the mall area.

'There's a fire exit right next to the shop. We'll be stationed there,' said Nikita Jackson.

'Very good,' Lena said. 'Okay, Tyra will arrive with her agent, Kate Sewell. I will be right behind. Once she is safely delivered to the rear of the store, myself and my officer will stand down.'

Kim heard the underlying message in her words: once I've done that I couldn't care less what happens.

'So if we could just walk the route from here to the rear of the store, I'll be satisfied that we've covered everything and we're ready for tomorrow.'

They continued across the service yard to the service corridor that led up the stairs in two sets of three. Lena was between the fire officer and the paramedic and Kim between Bryant and Chris.

'Why do I feel like we're the naughty kids back here?' Bryant asked.

'Shush or she'll hear you and we'll all be doing lines,' Chris said.

'Looks smaller than she does on the telly,' Bryant observed.

'You should tell her that,' Chris said, smirking.

'Yeah, sure, I've learned over the years when to keep my mouth shut around ballbrea—'

'Ahem,' Kim said.

'Strong women,' Bryant corrected himself.

'Doesn't it piss you off when she does that?' Kim asked Chris.

There was nothing wrong with strong women in powerful positions, although she preferred a more generous sprinkling of manners, which was rich coming from her.

'Does what?' Chris responded as they neared the fire exit door.

'Speaks to you like dirt or doesn't acknowledge you at all.'

'I'm used to it,' he said, shrugging.

'You've worked with her before?'

'I meant in general. There are police officers that appreciate what we do and others that don't. The good ones make up for people like her. And I like to remember that she started out in the security industry too.'

'Really?' Kim asked.

'Yeah, close protection officer, bodyguard to important people,' he said, widening his eyes.

Surely the woman should have some empathy for the thankless job Chris was trying to do.

'Any time you want to stop gassing and catch up would be fine,' Lena Wiley said, shooting daggers at Chris.

None of them were aware that she'd come to a stop just inside the door.

'That's the door I was talking about,' Kim said, ignoring her and nodding to the right as the lift from the upper level sounded and a cleaner with roller cages exited.

'Noted,' Chris said. 'There'll be an officer stationed right here.'

'I want those lifts shut down for the duration of the visit,' Lena said, even though she was absolved of all responsibility once she got Tyra to the rear of the store.

She trotted to the top of the stairs and then stopped. The sameness of windowless corridors was discombobulating and messed with your sense of direction.

'I'm not sure which…'

'Oh, please, let me help,' Chris offered smoothly, moving to the front of the group. 'I've assisted with many signings here.'

Lena's face reddened, but she said nothing.

'If we go left, it's a complete circuit to another service yard on the other side of the shopping centre. The right turn services all the shops on the upper level of this part of the site.'

He began walking and the group followed.

'Just around the bend here and the shop is on your left-hand side.'

'Well, that wasn't too difficult,' Lena offered snidely.

'Yeah, but none of us knew the way, did we?' Kim snapped, getting a little narked at the woman's dismissive attitude. He was not less of a person because he wasn't a police officer.

'Happy to help,' he said, stepping back towards where Bryant was messing with his phone.

'So if we could just finalise the timings of—'

'Oh, sorry, excuse me,' Kim said as her phone began to ring.

She turned away and answered it as Bryant's phone disappeared back into his pocket.

'Sir, yes, just at the walk through now. Shouldn't be too much longer… what, right now?… okay, sir, I'm on my way,' she said, ending her conversation with the inside of Bryant's trouser pocket.

'Sorry, gotta dash. Boss's orders.'

'Happens a lot, doesn't it?' Lena challenged.

'Yeah, murder victims got no respect for EPT meetings,' she said, pulling a face. 'But great to have met you, Superintendent Wiley,' she offered, before she turned and walked away.

'I said five minutes, Bryant, not an hour and a half.'

'It was five minutes, guv,' he answered with a smile.

'Well, it seemed longer,' she said, heading back to the car and her real job.

She'd done what she'd been asked or instructed to do. She'd attended, she'd played nice and she'd produce a briefing sheet for Woody to disseminate to whomever it would concern.

And finally, that was the end of that.

# CHAPTER FORTY-SEVEN

'Bloody hell, Stace,' Kim said once the constable had finished speaking. Part of her had wished that Stacey was overreacting to whatever she'd found out, that her emotions had overtaken her and she'd got caught up in one man's emotional protestations of innocence.

But her presentation of the facts, following interviews with all three people concerned, had been objective and without emotion.

'I mean, bloody hell,' she repeated.

God only knew how she was going to break this to Woody. His scheme had worked quite well up until now, and each station had put aside their collective pride if another team managed to progress or solve an open case. To her knowledge, no team had reopened a closed one; but Kim had to agree that her colleague was on to something. She didn't know if Sean Fellows was guilty or not, but she did know he should never have been convicted.

'Sorry, boss,' Stacey said.

'Don't be sorry for doing your job, Stace.' She stopped herself from saying *however unpopular it makes you*, and it would once the team at Brierley Hill got wind. Someone would be in the cross hairs.

'But we need to park it for now. I need you on this. We've got two victims and a missing child. Mr Fellows is just gonna have to give us a minute.'

'Got it, boss,' Stacey said, opening the door of the Bowl and heading back into the squad room.

*And I need to consider how best to proceed*, Kim thought to herself, following Stacey out.

'Good job, Bryant,' she said, glancing at the fresh pot of coffee that had miraculously appeared during her meeting with Stacey.

'Anything to make your life easier, guv,' he quipped.

'Your resignation,' she said, holding out her hand.

'You wish,' he said as she perched beside the printer at the top of the office.

'Anything new from the search site?' she asked Penn.

'Most of the volunteers were gone due to the rain, but nothing found by the time I left.'

Damn it, they were almost twenty-four hours into Archie's disappearance. The houses closest to the edge of the park had been visited, but as yet no one had seen a thing. By the end of the day they would all be visited again to double-check on family members not present during the first visit.

'Stace, I know you've been busy but anything yet on Ella Nock?'

'Nothing so far that would cause concern. She has no police record, not even a parking fine or speeding ticket. Like her brother, she works in sales, but she makes around double his salary selling luxury items like Jacuzzis and hot tubs. Andrew sells inkjet printers to trade clients. He does okay, works a lot more hours but makes nothing like his sister. Two speeding tickets for Andrew but no criminal record. From what I can see both went to university and excelled. At school, both were keen on sports and performed at national level. She at long jump and he at triathlon.'

'Parents?' Kim asked, feeling the disappointment land in the pit of her stomach.

'Both doctors and both dead. Mother was a gynaecologist who died seven years ago of an aneurysm, and the father a heart surgeon who, ironically, died of a massive heart attack four years later.'

Which explained the closeness, Kim thought. Their similarities so far may be a little strange, but there was certainly nothing there to indicate the capability or motivation for murder. And yet there was something gnawing in her gut. Something was missing.

'Keep looking, Stace.'

'Okay, boss, but…'

Stacey stopped speaking as a familiar figure appeared in the doorway.

'Damn it, I hate it when you get it right,' Bryant said under his breath.

She'd been sure enough to leave a temporary ID at the front desk, which was now hanging around Alison Lowe's neck.

'No, you don't,' Kim said as she waved their visitor through the door. 'In you come, Alison. You know where to sit.'

'You were so sure?' she asked, sliding into the seat at the spare desk, and tapping the lanyard around her neck.

'Yep,' Kim said, marvelling at the difference in the appearance of the woman now from when they'd first met during the kidnap case of two little girls. That day, she'd appeared in four-inch heels, stick thin and wearing a business suit that had sucked out any trace of personality, and the tightest ponytail Kim had ever seen. That day, she had looked almost ten years older than her thirty-one years.

Cut to the current picture of a woman wearing faded jeans, a college hoody with her blonde hair flowing down her back. The few pounds she'd gained suited her, and she looked exactly her own age.

'But thanks for helping us out.'

'Is that an admission that you finally trust us profiley, behaviourist folk?' Alison asked with a half-smile.

'Absolutely not,' Kim shot back. 'But let's just say I distrust you less than the rest.'

Alison laughed out loud, breaking the tension in the room, although Kim noted she hadn't looked at Stacey once.

'She didn't want to do it, Alison. She fought hard.'

Alison simply nodded.

Well, that was Kim's one and only attempt at salvaging their friendship. Having Alison's input on the letters was a higher priority than the BFF status of her colleagues.

Stacey printed off the two letters and placed them on Alison's desk.

She glanced at them.

'The killer is communicating with you directly?' she asked.

'Two murders, two letters,' Kim said as Alison began to read.

'So what do you think?' Kim asked when Alison appeared to have read them both.

'You want the quick answer?' Alison asked.

'Of course.'

'Bryant wrote them,' she said, nodding towards the sergeant.

Kim turned to her colleague. 'Bryant, did you write them?'

He shrugged and took a sip of his coffee.

Alison held up the printed sheets. 'You know I need more than this. Where are the incident reports, the witness statements, victim backgrounds? This is like giving me a plate with no meal on it.'

Kim wasn't surprised at her food analogy. During their last case together, they'd established Alison could out-eat a group of long-haul truckers.

'So how long until you can give us something?'

Alison smiled and shook her head. 'You never change, do you?'

Kim wasn't insulted. 'I try to be consistent.'

'The answer is that I don't know.'

'And you haven't changed either. Still refusing to—'

Kim's ringing phone cut her off.

Her heart leapt. No caller caused the same emotional response in her as Keats.

'Keats, you have to be joking,' Kim said as the whole room fell into silence around her.

'Come to Uffmoor Wood right now, and it's not so we can go for a walk.'

# CHAPTER FORTY-EIGHT

'You reckon we've got another one?' Penn asked, breaking the heavy silence in the squad room.

'Well, I don't think Keats has invited the boss out for afternoon tea,' Stacey answered distractedly. Alison had not met her gaze once yet. 'Hey, Penn, you wanna go get fresh coffee?' she continued.

'You don't drink coffee,' he said without looking up.

'Well, fetch me a Diet Coke then.'

'Bloody hell, Stace, since when did I turn into drinks-boy?'

'Penn, she wants you to leave the room so she can apologise to me,' Alison said.

Finally, Penn looked up and glanced from her to the profiler. 'Oh, okay,' he said, getting up. 'Toilet break.'

Stacey took a breath, 'Look, Alison, I'm really—'

'You really are a pain in my arse, but there's nothing to apologise for. I know how persuasive your boss is, and as long as you keep me well fed and away from tall buildings we're all good.'

'Like I'd try and keep food away from you,' Stacey said.

'But just so you know, Stace, I'm not gonna be your bridesmaid any more.'

Stacey laughed out loud. 'You never were. I'm not having any.'

'Well, that's settled then. We agree.'

Stacey tipped her head. 'Can you bake me a cake instead?'

'Hahahahahaha, oh you are so funny. That would be a big fat no.'

Stacey recalled something Alison had told her. 'Hang on, you said that when you arranged your ex-fiancé's birthday party, you baked him a three-tier red velvet cake, his favourite.'

'You must have misheard me, Stace. I told his mother that I baked it. I wanted her to like me. It didn't work: she still hated me, but the most I had to do with that cake was collect it from the bakery. Why, what's up?'

Stacey opened her mouth to explain that all the local bakeries and cake shops had laughed in her face at the short notice request, but then she closed it. Talking about it depressed her even more. At this rate, she'd be heading to the supermarket to pick up a kids' birthday party cake with Thomas the Tank Engine on the front.

'Never mind. But you're sure we're okay, yeah?'

Alison blew her a raspberry in response.

They were good.

She was sure of it.

# CHAPTER FORTY-NINE

Uffmoor Wood was a Woodland Trust site spanning over two hundred acres, just one mile south of Halesowen and sitting at the foot of the Clent Hills. Accessed from the A456 along Uffmoor Lane, a car park gave way through a squeeze post and two kissing gates to five miles of paths.

Kim had brought Barney on the occasional early morning walk during the summer months, when the Clent Hills got overcrowded as people amassed for the striking views.

Despite being an area of natural beauty, the site had no public rights of way and had been closed temporarily in 2017 due to ongoing issues with sheep worrying, dirt bike racing, drug dealing and dogging. Unsurprisingly, it had been named as Britain's Baddest Woodlands.

Kim followed Bryant past the vehicles she knew well and through the kissing gate.

'Follow the trail for about a quarter of a mile, Keats said,' Kim repeated as she hopped over one of the many streams that ran through the site.

'So who put Bella in the wych-elm?' Bryant asked.

'Bryant, have you finally lost your mind?'

He rolled his eyes. 'Do you even live around here?' He paused. 'Okay, seeing as you didn't ask I'll tell you anyway.'

She groaned as she pushed a brittle branch away from her face.

'In the forties I think it was, just over the way there in Hagley Wood, four boys were bird nesting and found a skull in the hollow trunk of a wych-elm. An almost complete skeleton with a shoe, gold wedding ring and some fragments of clothing were removed. The pathologist determined that she'd been placed in the tree while still warm, as it would have been impossible to get her in there with rigor mortis. He also discovered a remnant of taffeta in her mouth, suggesting she'd been suffocated. Graffiti messages have turned up since 1944, asking who put Bella in the wych-elm, but despite an extensive investigation, she's never been identified.'

'Bryant, do you go to special classes for this stuff?' she asked, taking a left when the trail forked.

'Nah, I just read local books.'

'I suppose you're gonna tell me the woods are haunted next.'

'Well, as it happens…'

'Enough,' she said, spotting activity about forty feet away from the main path. A young male she recognised was sitting on a bench beside a standing constable.

She headed there first.

'Hey, Plinky,' she said, using the force's nickname for a low-level drug dealer who got banged up a couple of times a year for drug offences and still went back to his same stomping ground every time. Brains were not his strong point.

'You out for your afternoon stroll?'

''S right, yeah,' he said, looking up at her with a glazed expression. She was unsure if he was still in shock or had been smoking too much of his own product.

'You weren't here doing a deal or anything like that?'

'Nah, nah, not me.'

'You see anyone?' she asked, unsure whether he was going to claim to have seen unicorns and fairies, looking at the state of him.

'Nah, just called you lot.'

A drug dealer and yet stays with the body. Suitably called Plinky, as he didn't have the brains to lie.

'Did you touch anything?'

'Fuck off, I ain't into bestiality.'

'Wrong sport, but I appreciate the sentiment and I didn't mean sexually. You didn't think about taking anything like money or phone?'

He shook his head, wearing an expression that said he'd never given it a thought but maybe had missed an opportunity.

'Plinky, you must be the most honest drug dealer we know.'

He smiled weakly at the compliment.

'Okay, we'll need to talk to you again. Now show this nice police officer what you've got in your pockets.'

He bristled. 'I ain't got nuffin. I ain't done nuffin wrong, so what you gotta treat me like—'

'Bloody hell, Plinky, I'm trying to get you off home, but I've got to make sure you've not got more on you than you arrived with.'

Jesus, you couldn't do a local weed dealer a favour without suspicion these days. 'But fine, you want to hang around for hours until—'

'Okay, okay,' he said.

He was doing as she asked as she began to walk away. Seeing as he could have discarded or at least hidden his stash before the police arrived told Kim the kid could do with some lessons in self-preservation.

She headed west to Keats and the rest of the team.

'What we got, Keats?' she asked as a couple of techies stepped aside.

'Female, late thirties, haven't opened her bag to identify her yet but—'

'Bloody hell,' Bryant said as his gaze rested on her face.

'You know who she is?' Kim asked.

'Oh yeah, I know exactly who she is.'

# CHAPTER FIFTY

Alison read both letters a few times. She wanted to get a feel for his mind-set before Stacey presented her with all the case details.

She also stared at the page to give her a few minutes to get her bearings on where she was and what she was doing.

It had been almost twelve months since she'd been seconded to assist the team in trying to catch a killer who had been recreating traumatic events in the DI's life, before trying to take the life of the DI herself.

She had been tasked to identify past associates of the detective to help find the person with enough hatred and motivation to carry out such horrific crimes. But she hadn't found the person. Instead, the murderer had found her and involved her in the sick, torturous game in which she had very nearly lost her life. Only the physical strength and determination of DI Stone had saved her.

She shivered, as she always did, and forced the memory from her mind.

Every day, it played over in her head, and even if she felt that she'd defeated it in her conscious mind, her subconscious mind was not yet prepared to give her a break and tortured her with nightmares, prompting her to wake drenched with sweat, fighting heart palpitations.

She knew that seasoned police officers often faced near-death experiences and got over them much quicker than she had. Trouble was, she wasn't a police officer and had never wanted to be one. She was a consultant, a pen pusher, a desk jockey who cheered from the sidelines. She studied people and patterns, behaviour and habits, traits and motivations. It was what fuelled her, what she was passionate about, and she had missed it even more than she realised.

Directly after the incident, she had been unable to face the thought of returning to her consultation role. The idea of writing a book had initially appealed to her, and she had thrown herself into the research with gusto. She'd taken a break from active – and what she now considered dangerous – duty but had still felt as though she'd been doing something productive. Something worthwhile.

Research done, she had reached the point months ago where she actually needed to write the words 'Chapter One', but she had been unable to do it. Reading about old profiling cases, the techniques, had been interesting enough, but it was stuff that she now knew. There was no new information being presented for her to dissect. There was no challenge in reciting facts and exploring theories.

She blinked away the tears as she realised that this was what she needed to do. Right now, this was where she needed to be. She coughed away the emotion as Stacey smacked three thick files of paper down on the desk before her.

'I can see them turning, you know.'

'What?' Alison asked.

'The cogs in that head of yours. They might need a bit of oil, but the pulleys are definitely moving.'

'Yeah, I've got one or two initial questions.'

'Shoot,' Penn said.

'Why Noah?'

Both police officers shrugged.

'We need to know, guys. He could have called himself anything. It's either his perception of himself or it's a clue to something, but we definitely need to know which one.'

# CHAPTER FIFTY-ONE

'Her name is Nicola Southall,' Bryant said to everyone who was suddenly looking his way.

'Friend of yours?' Kim asked.

He shook his head. 'Never met her, but she's pretty well known.'

She exchanged a glance with Keats who shrugged in response. For once the two of them were on the same page, and Bryant was out in the cold. For someone who was pretty well known, two-thirds of their collective had no idea who she was.

'She is… was an actress, appeared in one of the big soaps about ten years back, not sure which one now but the missus watched it. Loved the soap but hated her.'

'Why?' Kim asked. The blonde bob framed a pleasant, attractive face with clear, smooth skin.

'She played a kidnapper. Stole someone else's toddler cos she couldn't have kids of her own. I only remember it because I had to tell Jenny to calm down every time this woman came on the screen. Some folks get really involved.'

Kim knew that some people viewed soaps as though they were watching real-life events; that the incidents unfolding were actually happening in a street or square somewhere. She didn't think Bryant's wife was as susceptible to that level of disbelief.

'It was an incendiary storyline, guv,' Bryant said, as though reading her thoughts. 'It was aimed at every parent's worst nightmare. Imagine someone broke into your place and took Barney—'

'I get it, Bryant; I'm just not sure what relevance it has here.'

'Agreed,' Keats said, in harmony with her for the second time. She considered asking for his rectal probe to take his temperature. Clearly, the man was unwell. He continued, 'Same manner of death as both Katrina and Louise.'

Kim already knew. While Bryant had been talking, her gaze had sought any obvious wound or injury before checking out the angle of her neck.

The woman was dressed in dark jeans, trainers, a lilac T-shirt and a thick woollen cardigan; a satchel-type handbag had been dropped to her left.

'Strange,' Kim said, placing her foot near the satchel.

Bryant followed her gaze.

'These are normally worn across the body,' she said, picturing Stacey back at the office constantly lifting it over her head. That would also be the logical way to wear it if you were going off for a walk in the woods as her attire suggested. The murderer wouldn't have needed to remove it to break her neck, so what was it doing off her person?

'Has it been photographed?' Kim asked.

Keats nodded.

Bryant took out a pen and held it towards her. She used it to nudge the bag aside and touched the ground beneath it. The flattened patch was dry. The rain had started around eleven when they'd been at the Stevens Park search site, meaning Nicola Southall had been dead for at least three hours.

'I'd estimate between nine and eleven,' Keats confirmed.

Kim understood the havoc the elements could wreak on evidence collection. Since the killer had left the body, the breeze had increased, bringing heavy rain and evidence dispersion. Kim surveyed the ground around them: valuable evidence – a hair, DNA – could be somewhere right there. She could be standing on a link to their murderer, the person who was holding Archie, and she didn't even know it.

She used the pen as carefully as possible to dislodge the catch on the satchel. The bag opened easily.

Kim looked up at Bryant, who was watching from above.

'The bag is already open,' he said, echoing her thoughts.

'Ah, just the man,' Kim said as Mitch approached from the path.

'Oooh, got me feeling like a rock star with that greeting,' he joked, coming to stand beside her.

'Well, Bon Jovi, can you empty and bag this first?' she asked. 'I think our killer has touched it.' Which meant she didn't want to interfere with it any more than she needed to.

Mitch opened his bag and took out a white sheet of fabric. In seconds, his gloves were on and he was expertly moving the satchel onto the sheet, so that anything of interest could be collected.

He avoided the catch and opened the bag, laying out the contents: a small purse; a tiny manicure kit; three receipts and a pack of mints.

Kim turned to the pathologist.

'Keats, anything on her person?'

He shook his head.

'The killer took her phone,' she said to Bryant.

'He didn't take the others,' he replied.

'Exactly,' Kim said, standing up. 'Because this victim he already knew.'

# CHAPTER FIFTY-TWO

*The battery was out of the phone within five seconds of walking away from her limp and lifeless body. Choosing someone that I know is dangerous; but I like the thrill. Yes, I suppose I made this one more complicated for myself.*

*Not emotionally, I'm over that. But practically speaking, I've linked myself to my victim. Not that they will catch me. They'll never catch me. They will have to get up early in the morning to smell the skid marks I leave behind.*

*That game is a sideline, a frivolous distraction, like the breadstick you eat while waiting for your meal. It's entertaining and amuses me while I wait for the main course. But it's not the reason I'm in the restaurant.*

*She is good but not good enough. She will not win.*

*There was a marked difference in killing Nicola Southall. I missed the rush of choosing a life, of standing and watching and knowing that the person I chose was completely oblivious to my existence, that someone they had never seen or met was going to be responsible for their death.*

*But it was necessary to move it along. There had to be an escalation; there had to be something new. Nicola Southall had been a means to an end, a convenient acquaintance, a step up from the victim before. She should be proud that I chose her to play this part: the starring role she'd always dreamed of. But this one would not bring hate, rage and insults, but sympathy, love and flowers. Nicola would once again amass an adoring public, as in death she would be forgiven. If she could communicate from beyond, I know she would thank me.*

*The mechanics of the job are done, and my anticipation consumes me.*

*It's time for the purpose of the act to be fulfilled, and my favourite part bar none.*

*It is time to take out my phone and wait for whatever is to happen next.*

# CHAPTER FIFTY-THREE

'Alison, it's half past two, you've been here an hour and there are already three empty wrappers on your desk,' Stacey pointed out.

'Yeah, I'm cutting down.'

'I hate you,' Stacey said. Her own recent efforts to lose a few pounds before her wedding day had put her in the worst mood of her life. Luckily, she had accepted that both Devon and she preferred her the way she was.

'Okay,' Penn said, sitting back. 'Noah was chosen by God to undertake a mission of rescuing various animal species from a disastrous flood. Along with his family, he builds an ark to protect life on earth.'

'We all know that, Penn,' Stacey offered. She turned to Alison. 'You think he's saying he was chosen by God to do this?'

'Visionary serial killers,' Alison said.

'What's that now?' Stacey asked, raising an eyebrow.

'Okay, seeing as there are three victims, our guy qualifies as a serial killer. The motives of serial killers fall under four categories: visionary, mission-oriented, hedonistic and power or control.'

'Go on,' Stacey said. This was the reason they'd called her in.

'Okay, visionary serial killers suffer psychotic breaks with reality, sometimes believing they're another person or are compelled to murder by entities like the Devil or God. Remember Son of Sam, David Berkowitz, who was being given messages by his neighbour's dog?'

'Could be our guy.'

Alison shook her head. 'I don't think so. These letters don't indicate any kind of psychosis.'

'And the second type?'

'Mission-oriented killers typically justify their acts as ridding the world of certain types of people. They're generally not psychotic but could claim to be doing it in the name of a higher order. Normally, they seek to improve the world. They target specific groups of individuals. They are often perfectionists and highly compulsive. They're stable, gainfully employed and long-term residents of the geographical territory in which they kill. They're highly meticulous and they kill quickly and efficiently.

'Joseph P. Franklin, a former member of the Ku Klux Klan, was convicted in 1980 of four homicides, including a sniper shooting of two black men jogging with a white woman. He felt that race mixing was a sin against God and that God had instructed his work.'

Stacey looked hopeful. If they knew what kind of serial killer they were dealing with, maybe Alison could form a profile and give them somewhere to start.

'Is this our guy?'

Again, Alison shook her head. 'The victims don't fit. He's targeting straight, white, heterosexual women, two with children. Victims would normally be homeless, prostitutes, black, Asian. His perception would be that he is improving the planet.'

'Hedonistic?' Stacey asked, losing hope.

'Definitely not,' Alison said. 'Hedonistic serial killers are driven by lust, thrill or comfort. None of which are evidenced in any of the murders. There is no kind of ritual, no apparent pleasure in the act of killing itself, and the latest victim is even more unlikely, as power-driven serial killers almost always sexually abuse their victims, but not through lust, more through the need to dominate, like Ted Bundy who travelled around the United States seeking women to control.'

'So what kind of serial killer is he?' Stacey asked, confused.

'None that I've come across before,' Alison acknowledged, shaking her head.

'But if he's a serial killer, he has to fit one of those criteria,' Stacey protested.

'Hang on while I change decades of research to accommodate you.'

'Yeah, thanks,' Stacey said, feeling as though she'd learned a lot and yet it had given them nothing.

'How much further on Noah do you want me to go?' Penn asked, his voice showing the same level of despondency she was feeling.

'Leave it for now,' Alison said, moving around papers on her desk. 'I keep reading these letters and I can't help getting a picture of Norman Bates.'

'From the *Psycho* film?' Penn asked.

Alison nodded. 'This reference in the first letter to having no control, it's like he's absolving himself of all responsibility, as though he has no free will. What about if there's a voice in his head, a dead mother who speaks to him or something?'

'Like a whole other personality is doing the killing?' Stacey asked. Seemed a bit outlandish to her but stranger things had happened.

'Or more,' Alison answered.

'More than one personality?' Penn asked.

Alison nodded. 'There are many cases, but one that springs to mind is William Milligan. After committing several felonies, including armed robbery, he was arrested for three rapes on the campus of Ohio State University. He was diagnosed with multiple personality disorder. His lawyers pleaded insanity, claiming that two of his alternate personalities committed the crimes without Milligan being aware of it.'

'You are kidding me?' Stacey said.

'He was the first person diagnosed with multiple personality disorder to raise such a defence and the first to be acquitted of a major crime for this reason. He was never imprisoned and spent a decade in mental hospitals.'

'Bloody hell, Alison, I would hate to be knocking around in your mind with all these stand-up folks,' Stacey said.

'Been doing lots of research, haven't I?'

'Yeah, for a book I can't wait to read if it ever gets written.'

Alison blew her a kiss.

'So you really think our killer could have a split personality?' Penn asked.

'Maybe... or maybe not,' Alison said, thoughtfully picking up her pencil.

# CHAPTER FIFTY-FOUR

Russell Southall shook his head for the fourth time, denying the truth of the news they'd just delivered.

They had driven the short distance from the crime scene to Nicola's home, a comfortable four-bed detached property, to give devastating news for the third time in as many days to the partner of their latest victim. They had waited patiently while he tried to process the news, but he remained in a state of shock.

She guessed the man to be around five feet ten; he had dark hair beginning to grey around the temples. A tidy moustache and light beard gave his face a gentle, friendly appearance. His eyes were filled with pain.

'We understand how difficult this must be for you, Mr Southall, and obviously we want to catch the person responsible as quickly as possible,' she reassured as her eyes wandered the room and landed on a photo of three children in between two miniature model Vespa scooters. The children in the photo appeared to vary in age from early to late teens.

'Your children?' Kim asked.

'Mine from a previous marriage,' he said. 'Nicola and I don't have children together. We knew each other years ago but lost touch.' He smiled sadly. 'We met again in a friend's pub around eleven years ago. I had no idea she was now famous. She liked that, I think,' he said, wiping a tear from his eye. 'That first night we didn't even talk about it. We chatted about mutual friends and she wanted to know about my job as a sign maker. Despite the fame, she hadn't changed a bit. She still loved to read a good book, was passionate about cats, liked to go to the theatre and took a long walk every day.'

For a moment, it had seemed as though he had forgotten what he'd been told as he relived happier memories, but the mention of the walk brought him right back to Uffmoor and the fact that she was now dead.

He shook his head once again. 'Who?... I mean... I just don't understand...'

'Did your wife have any enemies?' Kim asked, seizing the opportunity to insert a question into his grief. 'Had she been threatened at all?'

The fact that her phone had been taken could mean that it contained a link to the killer. The first two phones had not been taken.

'Not any more,' he answered, shaking his head. 'All that was behind us.'

'All what?' Kim asked.

He sighed heavily. 'When Nicola got that part in the soap everything changed. At first, it was amazing to see her get the recognition she deserved. She was earning ridiculous money compared to the living on which she'd scraped by. For a while, we enjoyed a bit of high life until the writers came up with that storyline. Her character got pregnant and lost the baby, sending her into a spiral of grief. She was excited to play the storyline, welcomed the challenge. And she played it well, too well.'

Kim sat forward. 'Go on.'

'Her character was popular and had all the public sympathy and support until she kidnapped the newborn child of an even more popular character. Overnight, the public hated her. She was getting abused in the street. She couldn't leave the house alone. She tried to weather it for a while, but it was too much for her. She came off social media and begged the producers to write her out of the soap.'

Kim recalled examples of public perception when it came to soap characters, none more so than when Deirdre Barlow was imprisoned in *Coronation Street* and even the prime minister commented on it.

'What happened?'

'They agreed. Nicola kept a low profile, and once she was gone from the screen everything quietened down and went back to normal. But that was almost ten years ago. You don't think it's related to?—'

'We don't know at this point, but we can't rule it out. Were there any direct threats that you know of?' Kim asked.

He shook his head. 'Everything was dealt with by her agent. She took care of everything.'

'Nicola had an agent?' Kim asked, feeling her interest rise. It was a question she had never thought to ask.

'Yes, her name was Sewell. Kate Sewell.'

# CHAPTER FIFTY-FIVE

'I've met her,' Kim said once they were back in the car. 'I met Nicola's ex-agent, on Monday at the INEPT meeting. She's also the agent of the visiting celeb.'

'You're kidding?' Bryant asked and then thought for a minute. 'Although that probably shouldn't be a huge surprise. Not sure we have too many talent agencies around here, so probably not much of a coincidence.'

'Still like to have a chat with her, though,' Kim said, taking out her phone.

'You don't think this is our guy?' he queried.

'Could be someone copy-catting,' Kim answered, scrolling to Stacey's name. 'The manner of death has been in every news report. The agent should know if there was any direct threat years ago that might still be valid now. If it's not connected to the part she played, we need to rule it out.

'Stace,' she said when the constable answered her phone, 'I've sent you Nicola Southall's number. Get on to the network and see who she was in contact with. And get me an address for a talent agent named Kate Sewell. Thanks, gotta go.'

Kim ended the call as a beep and Woody's name appeared on the screen.

'Sir?'

'Where are you, Stone?'

Kim wondered if this was a trick question. She'd updated him about the third murder before entering Nicola Southall's home. He wasn't normally on her case this quickly. And clearly her answer didn't matter, as she was given no time to answer.

'I need you back here right now.'

Kim rarely felt irritation towards her boss. Usually he had a good reason for the things he did and the decisions he made, so she gave him the benefit of the doubt. Most of the time, even when he was sending her to pointless INEPT meetings.

'Sir, I just need—'

'The instruction wasn't debatable, Stone. I want you back here now. There's something we need you to do,' he said, ending the call.

Jesus, how was she supposed to solve this case if he kept pulling her off it to run errands. And more importantly, who the hell was 'we'?

# CHAPTER FIFTY-SIX

Within twenty minutes, Stacey had the call log from Nicola Southall's phone. The revelation of a missing child tended to light a fire under most people from whom she requested assistance.

The majority of calls were short ones to and from the same number that Stacey knew was Nicola's husband. She'd ruled out calls to friends and other family members and only one other number remained in the seventy-two hours prior to Nicola's murder. And that number had called the former actress at nine o'clock that morning.

'She really did get some shit over that part, you know,' Penn said, shaking his head.

He'd been tasked with finding out as much as he could on Nicola Southall.

'I remember it,' Alison piped up. Stacey had no knowledge, as her parents had never been into the soaps.

Alison continued, 'My mum used to shout "evil bitch" every time she came onto the screen.'

Penn agreed. 'Mine too. I know folks get into these programmes. My mum watched every one of them, but surely this level of hatred for a fictional character is unnatural. I mean, the intensity of it all drove Nicola out of the public eye, and it looks like she never returned to social media. She just disappeared.'

'Penn, why do you think people watch these shows?' Alison asked.

'Dramatic storylines that grow ever more outlandish especially for the Christmas specials?'

Alison laughed and shook her head. 'Nope, it's for the characters. Viewers are invested in their lives.'

Stacey stopped what she was doing to listen. She always valued Alison's insights when it came to the human psyche.

'Viewers spend a lot of hours each week with these people. They're not necessarily switching on to watch a programme. They're switching on to catch up with the lives of the characters. It becomes important to them. It matters. It's like ringing a parent or family member. People record their favourite soaps, unable to bear the thought of missing something. The more people watch the more engrossed they get. They are invested, so when something bad happens to one of their favourite characters they're hurt, angry. The characters are real people and the viewer feels as though they know them like friends and family, which is the purpose of the writers. They want the viewer to feel all these emotions.'

'But to what degree?' Stacey asked. 'How do the writers ensure that an element of realism keeps it from becoming obsessive?'

'They can't. They have no control over the intensity, and what that intensity can do to an individual. Most folks will feel the emotion, maybe take to social media to lament for a few minutes and then move on to the next show or put the kids to bed, read a book. Others will not. They'll take it personally, become enraged and take it further.' Alison paused. 'In 1989, a twenty-one-year-old actress named Rebecca Schaeffer was murdered by an obsessive fan who had been stalking her. He shot and killed her after being fixated on her for more than three years. Closer to home, we still have the case of Jill Dando, shot on her doorstep, case never solved.'

'Do you think that's what's happened here? A crazed soap fan finally caught up with Nicola and punished her?' Penn asked.

Alison shrugged. 'I think it's too early to rule it out.'

Stacey picked up the phone to call the network.

She needed to know who had been on the other end of that three-minute call.

# CHAPTER FIFTY-SEVEN

'Go check on the kids while I go and untwist Woody's nickers,' Kim said as they entered the station. It was after four and she couldn't remember the last time she'd had a drink. It felt like two days instead of the six hours that had passed since they'd been drinking coffee with the graphologist. 'Oh, and Bryant...'

'I'll get a pot on,' he said without looking her way.

She smiled. She guessed that soon she wouldn't even need to open her mouth at all.

Her hand was curled around the door handle before she remembered to knock. It was one of her boss's pet hates and a habit she struggled to break, much to his annoyance.

'Come in,' he called after two firm knocks.

She entered and took a moment to assess the two additional people sitting with Woody at the small, round conference table, which worryingly had one spare seat. She felt her inner groan trying to escape. Sit-down meetings indicated a lengthy stay.

'Take a seat, Stone,' Woody said in a tone she rarely argued with when they were alone never mind in front of other people.

'Obviously, you know Flora,' Woody said, nodding to his left as she sat.

Flora Bridges was with the press liaison team and was responsible for telling police officers what they could and could not say to reporters. She was in her mid-fifties and had a mousy brown perm that was as tight as the ill-fitting blouses she always wore.

Her glasses on a rope rested along with her identification on a chest that was testing the fabric and button construction of her shirt.

Almost all officers she knew dreaded getting Flora. Most of the press liaison team were happy to offer guidelines on content and delivery, but not Flora. Oh no, Flora wrote the whole thing word for word, with little notes like 'pause' and 'lower voice' like stage directions. Flora liked control.

Kim glanced to Woody's right.

'And this is Frederick Hammond, psychologist over at Ridgewood laboratory.'

'Okay,' Kim said, wondering what either of these people had to do with her. For clues, she looked to the paperwork on the table. Set before Frederick Hammond were copies of the letters the killer had sent. The sheets were covered in red notations.

Before Flora's folded arms was a single sheet of paper neatly typed without notations.

'We have a press briefing booked for five o'clock,' Woody stated.

That was little over half an hour away and still: what did that have to do with her?

'You'll be the one talking to the press,' Woody stated, answering her silent question.

If they'd been alone, she would have immediately offered an opposing argument. She hated talking to the press and Woody knew it.

She searched his expression for wiggle room on the matter. There was none.

Woody inclined his head to Frederick, who offered his hand across the table.

'Pleased to meet you, DI Stone.'

She ignored the hand and waited. Irritation flashed across her boss's face, but she didn't care. She didn't touch people unnecessarily for anyone.

He retracted his hand.

'These letters are addressed directly to you. There is something in you that he trusts. He's asking for your help. He wants you to help him stop.'

Kim waited. She'd worked that much out for herself.

'He looks up to you and has placed his faith in you. His anger at your failure to stop him is almost like a child waiting for boundaries to be set by a parent who—'

'Sir?' she said, looking at Woody. The words, *how long do I have to listen to this?* remained unspoken between them. She had little time for psychologists at the best of times, but this guy looked way too excited by his own observations.

Woody narrowed his eyes at her and turned to Frederick.

'He asked for your help in the first letter and showed his frustration with you after the second. I understand that no letter was found on the third victim today?'

'Not yet.'

'He still wishes to communicate with you but may feel his letters are useless. He might find another way to communicate his displeasure. He may feel you're ignoring him and choose to use the most valuable weapon he has.'

'Archie?' she asked, paying attention.

Frederick nodded. 'He may hurt the boy or worse, to get your attention, to make—'

'Yeah, I get it,' Kim said. She didn't need those pictures in her mind.

'The murder of the third victim needs to be communicated to the public, so this is an opportunity,' Woody said, bringing the attention back to himself.

'To do what?' Kim asked. She didn't like the way this was going.

'To speak to him, to answer him. To show he's got your attention,' Frederick interjected before Woody offered him a look.

Some juvenile part of her wanted to bob out her tongue at Frederick.

He got the message and closed his mouth.

'He'll be looking out for any sign that he's reached you. He wants a response from you. He needs you to connect, and we need to do everything we can to keep Archie safe.'

Kim said nothing, concerned that all this was on the recommendation of one psychologist that she'd never even met before today.

Woody nodded to Flora, who pushed the single sheet of paper towards her. 'This is what we want you to say.'

Kim started reading. It was pretty standard stuff at the beginning: 'body of a female…'; 'condolences…'; 'no stone unturned…'; 'the full force of the law…' and then she got to the third paragraph.

'You're kidding, right?'

Three heads shook in unison.

Frederick looked to Woody for permission to speak. Woody nodded.

'Given the nature of his letters to you, we feel this is the best way to address him.'

'You want me to berate him while he still has possession of an innocent little boy?'

'We strongly believe that this man sees you as a figure of authority, a person to be admired and respected. We feel he will respond to a level of sternness that this message conveys.'

'You don't think there's a chance it could have the opposite effect?' she asked, and then began to read from the paragraph that horrified her.

'"This is an unspeakable act carried out by someone with no conscience… evil individual… callous… unfeeling… deviant… punishment of the highest order… met with no mercy…"'

She paused. 'Hardly sending him to bed with no supper. Why not just tell him we're firing up the electric chair ready?'

Flora leaned forward. 'Because that's—'

'Yes, Flora, I know we don't do that any more, but even though I'd like to say all this and worse to him, I'm not sure it's going to have the desired effect.'

'And we are confident it will,' Frederick said, folding his arms.

'I think we have to do something, Stone,' Woody said. 'Three women dead in as many days and a child missing. Somehow, you have to reach him.'

Kim considered arguing further, but it was futile. Despite her own misgivings. These people were the experts and there were times she had to accept that someone else knew better than she did.

She just wasn't sure that now was one of those times.

# CHAPTER FIFTY-EIGHT

'So where are we, guys?' Kim asked, entering the squad room. 'What have you been up to?'

Stacey spoke first. 'Waiting for an email from the network provider for the burner phone that called Nicola at nine this morning. Tried calling it a few times, but it's going straight to voicemail. Really don't think he's going to answer, boss.'

*Well, that was one way of communicating with him that wasn't going to work*, Kim thought, still holding the piece of paper from the meeting in her hand.

From the window at the top of the office, Kim could see the press starting to assemble outside the building.

'Penn?' she asked, turning away.

'Looking for any crackpots who trolled Nicola and seeing if they're still unhinged now, but nothing so far.'

'I ferried you around all day and then made coffee,' Bryant offered.

'Valuable work,' Kim said, taking a sip from the mug he'd placed beside the printer.

She stared at the wipe boards. 'And I'm still trying to work out the reason for the differences in the crimes. First one – woman killed but child left. Second one – woman killed but child taken. Third one – woman killed but no child involved at all.' She paused and looked at Alison. 'Anything at all to offer?'

'We discussed split personalities earlier,' Alison said, although her response lacked the conviction she'd have liked if they were looking at a highly plausible theory.

'Is there any chance there's another personality inside him telling him what to do?' Kim pushed. 'Would that explain why there are differences, if both personalities are murdering but doing it slightly differently?'

Alison shook her head. 'I've not seen that before. Normally, with split personalities there's a dominant and a submissive; even with multiple personalities there is one clear voice that controls the rest, but we're learning new things about mental illness all the time.'

'And what do you think his personality or plural are gonna make of this?' she asked, dropping the sheet of paper on Alison's desk.

Kim watched her carefully as she read and saw the frown on her face as she neared the end.

'This is what you've been asked to read to the press?' she clarified.

Kim nodded. 'By my boss, a psychologist and a press officer, and yes that does sound like the first line of a joke.'

Alison read it again and this time there was no frown but a slight nod of the head as she reached the bottom.

She handed it back. 'Given his communication with you, it does make perfect sense to put you in the parental role and tell him off. I can definitely see the logic behind what they're trying to do. They're hoping your words will shock him into stopping what he's doing and to let Archie go.'

'But?…' Kim asked.

'There's no but. I think it's a sound plan. It could work.'

'Okay, thanks for that,' Kim said, glancing out of the window and then at her watch.

She stood and reached for her jacket.

'And I guess we're about to find out.'

Her colleague stood to follow.

'It's fine, Bryant, I can do this myself,' she said, appreciating the gesture. He knew she wasn't feeling confident about what she'd been asked to do.

'Yep, you go do it alone, guv, and I'll be right there with you.'

# CHAPTER FIFTY-NINE

Alison stared down at the papers on her desk and pretended to read, but the words began merging into each other and were making no sense. She felt as though she'd come full circle and didn't like where she had landed.

As a child, she'd never been great at fighting her own corner. She had shrunk from opposing opinions and deferred to what she always felt was a higher and more authoritative power. Afterwards, she would think of a hundred examples to substantiate her own viewpoint, but only once the moment had passed would she realise she did have an opinion after all.

Once she had trained in behavioural science and obtained two degrees, she had felt confident enough in her knowledge and her education to try life at the other end of the spectrum. The certificates on her wall had given her the confidence to offer her opinion with both gusto and conviction whether it was sought or not.

But a familiar sickness now started to rise up in her stomach. A feeling she could trace back to the day one of her nine-year-old classmates, Dorian, told her that kids on free school meals were stupid and had no parents. She knew that Molly, who lived next door, had free school meals and that was because her dad had been in an accident and couldn't work for a while. Molly wasn't stupid and had parents. Alison had disagreed, but as other kids had begun nodding in agreement with Dorian, Alison had felt herself fade away from the conversation. She had remained in disagreement, but she had also remained in silence.

As the sickness travelled upwards to her throat, she raised her head and faced the two people still left in the room.

'Guys, I think I just fucked up.'

# CHAPTER SIXTY

Kim felt her silent phone begin to vibrate as she stepped out of the building and into the glare of the press. Bryant sidled to the position he'd occupied a couple of days before.

The paper she'd been given was in her back pocket, and if Flora expected her to take it out and read it word for word she could think again. If she was being forced to talk to the press, then she'd talk to them properly. She knew by heart enough of what was on the paper to do what they'd asked.

Her phone stopped and started again as she approached the gaggle. She knew it wasn't any of her team. They all knew what she was coming out here to do. The only other person who mattered was Keats and God forbid he'd be calling her right now. Answering the phone to the pathologist right in front of this group of people with their powerful microphones and speakers would not be a good idea.

'Okay, folks, gather round.' She paused to give them chance to switch on whatever device they were using. Frost's choice was an iPhone pointed in her direction.

She forced her expression into neutral as she began to speak.

'I can confirm that the body of a forty-six-year-old female was found at Uffmoor Woods earlier today.'

Kim paused. Every word she spoke took her closer to the third paragraph, with which she didn't agree.

And yet, Woody had instructed it.

'The family have been informed and obviously our condolences go to her loved ones.'

Even Flora thought it was a good idea.

'It is too early to tell if the incident is linked to other cases under investigation. However, I can reveal that we have not yet ruled it out.'

Good old Freddie thought it was a great idea.

'The post-mortem will take place tomorrow, after which the identity of the victim will be revealed and witnesses to the incident will be sought.'

And even Alison agreed.

'I would like to reiterate that we will catch the person responsible for this crime and bring them to justice. I would like to take this opportunity to remind you that we still have not located a six-year-old boy named Archie. His family are desperate for news on their little boy who has now been missing for over twenty-four hours.'

First part done. Now on to the second paragraph about which every expert around her agreed. Every one of them.

'Thank you for your time, ladies and gentlemen, and there will be more for you tomorrow.'

She turned her back and walked into the building, taking out her phone. There was no live broadcast on the news, but the footage would hit the internet in about thirty seconds. Half a minute before Woody blew up her phone.

'What the hell was that?' Bryant asked, following her inside.

'In a minute,' she said, surprised that the missed calls were from Stacey. Well, she'd have to wait. She scrolled to the number she wanted and waited four seconds for it to be answered by a thin, incredulous voice.

'Stone, what the?…'

'Listen carefully, Frost, without making it obvious, meet me around the back of the building.'

'Stone, I only go round the back of buildings for a smoke or a snog, neither of which I wanna do with—'

'Just do it, Frost,' Kim snapped, before ending the call.

'Okay, now I'm even more confused,' Bryant said.

'Go see what Stacey wants and I'll explain all later.'

She put her phone back in her pocket, aware that the second Woody saw her abbreviated press conference he would be seeking answers, but regardless of the instructions she'd received, the public chastisement had not felt right to her. There was much she wanted to say to this man, preferably with a red-hot poker, but not while he still had possession of a little boy.

She agreed that the killer was awaiting some kind of response from her, and he was going to get one.

Kim heard the rhythmic clicking of the high heels three seconds before Frost came into view.

'Stone, I don't know what kind of game you're playing but those folks back there ain't happy.'

'Crying on the inside, Frost. Now I need you to do me a favour.'

Her face hardened immediately.

'Don't worry, there's something in it for you.'

'Go on,' she said, tipping her head.

'I want you to write your story, but I want you to add in some quotes from me.'

Frost frowned. 'I can name you?'

'You must name me,' Kim said.

Frost took out her notebook. 'Okay, Stone, what the hell are you up to?'

'Write this down. I want you to say that we fear for the safety of an innocent child, that there's no need for Archie to get hurt, that we understand how Archie has unwittingly become an innocent party. Add that we know his captor doesn't want to hurt him, we know to him there's a good reason why he's doing the things he is and that I would welcome the opportunity to talk to him about it.'

'Fuck me, Stone, I wish you were this empathetic to folks who weren't going round murdering folks,' Frost said with her pen poised.

There wasn't one ounce of empathy in her for someone who had killed three women in three days. It was a calculated move. If he wanted a parent, she didn't think harsh, cold disciplinarian was the way to go.

On cue, her phone started to buzz in her pocket.

'Can you do it, Frost?'

'Err… yeah, exclusive content from the senior investigating officer on a triple murder case, I'll do it, but why me?'

'I read yesterday's article online. There was no mention of any letters from the killer.'

Frost rolled her eyes. 'Yeah, sometimes I slip up and do the right fucking thing.'

Kim was grateful that she'd chosen not to divert the direction of the story and had kept the focus on the missing boy, but they still needed to know whose loose lips were going to be kissing their career goodbye. 'Look, your source…'

Frost looked up and to the left. 'You wanna tell that Mitch guy to be more careful when he's carrying plastic evidence bags around. I have zoom on my camera, you know.'

'Fuck, Frost, you said there was a leak in—'

'Yeah, I ain't all nice, you know. You guys pissed me off.'

'We all square now?' Kim asked, aware they used Frost when it suited them, and for once she'd done the right thing by them.

'For now,' she said, putting her notepad away.

'How long until it's live?' Kim asked.

'The article will be online within the hour and in the early print edition tomorrow afternoon.'

Kim prayed Noah was searching online. Every hour that passed where she didn't receive a call to attend the body of a young boy offered another sliver of hope that they could get Archie back unharmed.

Her phone rang again, reminding her that she had to go back and face the music.

But not before she'd played some music of her own.

# CHAPTER SIXTY-ONE

'Alison. Bowl. Now,' Kim said as she entered the squad room.

'Boss, she—'

'Not now, Stace,' Kim snapped. Her rage had been building as she'd mounted the stairs.

Alison closed the door behind her.

'What the fuck did you think you were doing?'

'I got it wrong. I'm sorry. I realised as soon as you'd left—'

'But you didn't get it wrong, did you, Alison? I could almost forgive you that because people make mistakes, but you read that statement and you knew it was the wrong way to go. You, who have been studying the crimes, the methodology as well as the letters, knew I was being steered wrong and you said nothing.'

The miserable expression on the woman's face did nothing to soften Kim's rage. 'What do you think could have happened to Archie if I'd read that bloody statement? I'm pretty damn certain he'd be coming back in a fucking body bag, and I also know that you knew that. You wanna come with me to tell his family, cos that's my job, Alison. That's my consequence when I get it wrong.'

'I'm sorry. I tried to—'

'Too fucking late, Alison. I need your opinion when I bloody well ask for it, not once the damage has been done. I didn't ask for your help here because you're shit at what you do. I asked for your help because you've always had the balls to tell me when I'm wrong. I rarely listen, but at least you've got the courage of your convictions. Or at least you did have.' Kim paused for breath as the face grew even more miserable.

'Look, I know you're not being paid to do this. You agreed to help and that makes this conversation all the harder, but free service or not, if I can't trust you to use and share your expertise then there's no point—'

'If anything happens to that little boy, I'll never—'

'I didn't use it,' Kim said, relieving her of some of her misery. 'You didn't?'

'I didn't agree with it, so I've taken another route. The onus is now on me, but seriously, Alison, dipping your toe in this thing is no good to us. Either get back on the horse or get out of the fucking stable. Your choice,' Kim said, opening the door back into the squad room.

She'd said all she needed to say and right now she had to go suffer an arse-chewing of her own.

# CHAPTER SIXTY-TWO

Kim had barely swallowed down her own anger by the time she walked into the full force of someone else's. Her own was rooted in a person's inability to make a decision, but the rage she faced was because she had.

'Do not let my calm exterior fool you that I am anything less than furious right now,' Woody said as she walked in the door.

'Sir, if you'll just let—'

'Let you what, Stone? Get away with bloody murder? Deliberately disobey a direct instruction from your superior? Decide your own course of action regardless of expert advice? Let you think you know better than everyone you meet despite their education, experience and credentials? What exactly do you think I should let you do?'

Oh, this was a tricky one. Should she try and insert her point of view and reasoning into the centre of his rage or let him shout it out and explain herself later?

She knew which was the safer option. Just let him get it all out, remain quiet and non-confrontational. That's what she should do.

'If you want the truth, I'm just as pissed off at you, sir,' she shot back. Waiting her turn had never been her strong point.

His head reared backwards, and his eyes burned even brighter. 'And what exactly do you have to be pissed off at?'

'Being given the wrong tools for the fight. I listened and I understood, and I disagreed. There were many things I shouldn't have done as a kid and I can tell you now that a hard, swift slap across the face wouldn't have prevented me from doing any one of them again. In fact, it would have just made me worse.'

'This is not about your childhood, Stone. It is about you taking accountability for your actions, which may well result in—'

'But we are talking about that, sir, because you three all assumed that this could only go one way. That he would be cowed by my anger and judgement. You never gave any thought to it having the opposite effect. Saying nothing would have been preferable to an outright bollocking.'

'Well, you got your own way then, didn't you? You ignored a direct instruction and missed a perfect opportunity to connect—'

'I didn't ignore your instructions recklessly without a plan of my own. I've tried to reach him another way, low-key, non-judgemental and through Frost.'

His face hardened more. 'Stone, are you trying to incite me to violence? Why on earth would you trust Frost with any part of this? She's already responsible for two internal investigations and won't divulge—'

'There is no leak,' she said. 'Frost saw the letter through the evidence bag that Mitch was carrying away from the scene and told me so. It was a shot at you for cutting her off.'

The fleeting relief was gone in seconds.

'Regardless, we always return to the same problem we have faced historically, Stone. You cannot follow orders from people who are paid to make difficult decisions.'

'So I'm supposed to do it anyway because your decisions absolve me of all responsibility? You think I'm going to follow instructions just so I can sleep at night if it all goes badly wrong because it wasn't my call? You really think I'm going to care less about a child's life because the call wasn't mine? Sir, you know me better than that, so…'

'I remind you, Stone, three people told you—'

'And those three people were wrong.'

Woody brought his fist down hard on the table. 'How dare you,' he raged. 'Who do you think you're speaking to? Your flouting of rules, regulations and procedures would have had you thrown out on your ear many times had I not supported your abilities. More than once I have been forced to fight for your job, and you fail to learn that there is an authority to which you must answer, and that authority is me.'

Kim stood firm, her gaze unwavering. 'All of that is true, but you were still wrong.'

The thick silence that filled the room was alien to her. Never before had she told her boss that he had made the wrong decision. She had disagreed, appealed, pleaded but never had she told him he was just plain wrong.

When he finally spoke his voice was low and measured.

'You'd better hope we were wrong, Stone. For the sake of a six-year-old boy.'

# CHAPTER SIXTY-THREE

'You're quiet,' Kim said as they got in the car.

'Guv, you've just ripped Alison a new one, took a lashing yourself from Woody and then told the whole team to pull their fingers out and get cracking. So it's safe to say I know when to keep my mouth shut.'

'But if you were a braver man?'

'I'd say that was the last thing the guys needed to hear when they've already been working twelve hours.'

'Bryant, I—'

'And I also think you already know that, which is why I'm not going to say it.'

'Fuck off, Bryant,' she said, turning towards the window.

'Absolutely, guv,' he said, guiding the car out of the car park. It was about six miles to the home of Kate Sewell in Belbroughton, but there was one stop to make first, which she'd already told Bryant, and now she'd just as soon spend the short journey-time in silence.

Her ass-chewing from Woody was in no way connected to the frustration she'd been feeling when she'd barked at her team. Yes, the air between her and her boss was as tense as she'd ever known it. Rarely, if ever, had they gone toe-to-toe in such a manner, but her annoyance with her team stemmed from the fact they were no closer to finding the killer than they had been after the first murder on Monday. Two more women were dead.

It wasn't a new situation, but Kim had the strangest feeling that the clues were there, all rolled together like a stick of dynamite just waiting for someone to light the fuse.

She just hoped that one of her team found a match before someone else lost their life.

'Okey dokey, we're here and I'd sure love to know why,' he said, pulling up at the entrance to Dobbie's scrap yard. It was exactly three minutes to seven.

'Your life might just be about to get a whole lot easier,' she said, getting out of the car. 'Or harder,' she added, remembering the circumstances. If she lost this frame, she was likely to buy them all crash helmets.

'Jesus, what now?' she said as her phone signalled a Google alert. 'Oooh, article from Frost is up,' she said, pressing the link.

She continued to walk slowly through the gates of the scrap yard as she read. She searched the piece for the phrases she'd quoted and found them all there.

*Good job, Frost*, she thought, putting her phone away. All she could do now was hope.

'So, you getting a new project?' Bryant asked hopefully.

'Oh, yeah,' she said as they headed towards the office at the centre of Dobbie's yard. The last time she and Bryant had been here together, it had been to view the mangled remains of a murder victim crushed to death in Dobbie's machine. A hand had been found protruding from a square chunk of moulded metal, earning their victim the nickname Rubik until they'd been able to make an identification.

In the distance, she could see two men, one in a suit, one in casuals, and Dobbie in his black T-shirt and jeans.

'Who are the guys?' Bryant asked.

'Potential thieving bastards,' she said. 'Now, do me a favour. Once the bidding gets over a thousand make it look like you're trying to stop me going any higher.'

'What the?…'

'Just do it,' Kim said as they met with the others.

The two men looked appreciatively in her direction as Dobbie looked at his watch.

'Thought you weren't going to make it, Inspector.'

The gaze of the two males dropped away.

'How could I possibly resist your offer?' she asked, glancing at the frame leaning against the wall of the office.

'Everyone come prepared?' he asked.

Kim tapped her back pocket where the notes were rolled.

'Okay,' Dobbie said, licking his lips, 'you all know what you're here for, so let's start this bidding at five hundred.'

Two hands shot up and she nodded.

'Six hundred?'

Two hands and a nod.

'Seven hundred?'

Two hands and a nod.

'Eight hundred and fifty?'

Two hands and a nod.

'One thousand?' Dobbie said. His eyes were glistening with excitement. Seven hundred pounds more than he'd agreed with her, and all three bidders still in.

'Twelve hundred?'

'Guv,' Bryant said once she'd nodded.

'Fourteen hundred?'

One hand and a nod. Suit man was shaking his head.

One down.

'Sixteen hundred?'

One hand and a nod as the suit man began to walk away.

'Eighteen hundred?'

'Jesus, guv, that's way too—'

'Shh,' she said, nodding.

'Two thousand?' Dobbie said, as though he could barely believe it himself.

One hand up and a nod, but the hand had hesitated.

'Two thousand, two hundred?'

Kim nodded. The hand itched but stayed where it was.

'You sure?' Dobbie pressed.

The owner of the hand agonised for a few seconds but shook his head. He looked longingly at the frame before accepting defeat and leaving the area.

'Looks like it's mine after all, Dobbie,' she said, motioning for Bryant to pick up the frame.

Dobbie licked his lips and smiled. 'I wanted you to have it to be honest.'

'Ah, bless you, Dobbie, you old sweetheart,' she said, reaching into her back pocket.

His meaty arm rose, and she slapped the money into his outstretched hand.

'What's this?' he asked as his considerable eyebrows drew together.

'It's the three hundred quid we agreed on a month ago, Dobbie. A deal is a deal and we shook on it. Only you would try and swindle a police officer,' she said as Bryant headed towards the car with her frame.

'But it sure was an entertaining night out so thanks for inviting me,' she said, walking away with her first genuine smile of the day.

Now it was time to go speak to Nicola's agent.

# CHAPTER SIXTY-FOUR

*I look towards the locked door and curse myself for my foolish actions.*

*What am I supposed to do now? What the hell was I thinking when I snatched the boy? It's not as though I wanted him or even had a purpose for him. He was there and in one stupid, impulsive moment I saw triumph. I saw victory. I had exceeded the murder of Katrina. I had not left the child. I had taken the child.*

*But now what to do with him? He has seen my face. He can identify me.*

*There is only one choice, I feel, as my palm wraps around the kitchen knife. I am horrified but I cannot let him live now.*

*With each step that takes me closer to the door, the weight upon my shoulders increases. The grip around my heart tightens, but I can't allow him to destroy everything.*

*My free hand closes around the door handle. I take deep breaths and try not to visualise what I have to do. I will count myself down.*

*Three.*

*Two.*

*My phone sounds the receipt of a Google notification. I have only two alerts: one for murder and one for DI Stone. Which one has raised the alarm?*

*I falter for a second. I must not put off what I have to do. The child cannot live. I take a final deep breath.*

*Three.*

*Two.*

*Murder or DI Stone. Which one?*

*Damn it. I have to see.*

*I swap the knife to my other hand and take out my phone. I refuse to put down the blade. That is defeat. I can do this. I must do this. Soon.*

*The alert is for DI Stone. She has been quoted in an article by a local reporter. Not a national but Tracy Frost from the Dudley Star.*

*I skim over the narrative. I'm not interested in those empty words and look only for what she has to say. That's all that matters to me.*

*'…fear for the safety of innocent child…'*

*'…no need for Archie to get hurt…'*

*'…Archie has unwittingly become an innocent party…'*

*'…Don't want to hurt him…'*

*'…good reason for what he's doing…'*

*'…welcome opportunity to talk…'*

*I am surprised at her empathy, her compassion. I know that I was right to trust her, to seek her help. She understands. She knows that I don't want to hurt the boy, but…*

*A second alert sounds. Murder.*

*I scroll to the article and the screaming headline tells me everything I need to know.*

LOCAL EX-SOAP STAR FOUND MURDERED IN THE WOODS

*I put down the knife and reach for the phone. My other phone. The message is there, but I already knew it would be.*

*Now I know what I have to do. It's the only thing that makes sense, I realise, as I head once more for the door.*

# CHAPTER SIXTY-FIVE

'You okay?' Stacey asked once Penn had left the room to call Jasper. It was after seven and it didn't look like they were leaving any time soon.

'I'm fine, Stace,' Alison replied, looking anything but fine. A Wagon Wheel had been sitting on her desk untouched for over an hour.

'You could always just leave,' Stacey offered, speaking as a friend instead of a colleague. 'None of this has to be your problem.'

The woman wasn't even getting paid for the privilege of being shouted at twice in one day. Once separately for not giving her honest opinion and again when the boss had scolded them collectively.

Right now, Stacey felt like walking out herself, but she wouldn't because deep down she knew the boss was right. There were things here they were missing, and they weren't trying hard enough to find them.

Problem was: twelve hours in and they were all bloody shattered.

'I still think we're missing something about Noah,' Penn said as he re-entered the room. 'I just think we can't see the wood for the trees,' he continued, pacing up and down the office.

'Maybe we're making it all too complicated and overthinking things,' Stacey added.

He paused for a second. 'Ladies, grab your phones and come with me.'

Stacey looked at Alison who frowned in response.

Stacey shrugged and grabbed her phone. She felt as though her behind had been glued to the chair for days. Alison did the same.

'Okay, ladies, we're going for a walk,' he said as they headed out the automatic doors.

'Clears the cobwebs from the head.'

'Err… where exactly are we going?' Stacey asked. It was a concrete building with a car park. Hardly the Clent Hills.

'We're gonna get some fresh air and do circuits of the building to get the blood pumping to our brains.'

Stacey couldn't help the smile that came to her lips. Her colleague really was crazy sometimes. She pulled her cardigan tighter around herself. The sun was setting on what had been a cold and miserable day.

'Clockwise or anti-clockwise?' she asked.

'Anti,' he answered. 'I'm feeling like a bit of a rebel.'

They all turned and began walking the other way with Penn in the middle. 'Let's break this down and go through it piece by piece.' He turned to his right. 'Alison, what strikes you the most from what you've learned so far?'

She thrust her hands into her pockets. 'I think it's the differences in the first two murders. Children involved in both, but he leaves the first and takes the second. Many killers escalate but the pattern remains the same. The escalation is normally in the type of crime, but he's either interested in kids or he's not. It's not something I've come across before.'

Alison paused to step back as an officer passed them on his way to a squad car. She waited until he was out of earshot to continue. 'No kids involved in the third murder but everything else is the same. Female, broken neck and she'd been in the public eye. Does that mean anything or not? So far we've found no link between the victims themselves, no common friends or places they visited. There's commonality but no commonality, if you know what I mean.'

'Okay, Stace, what about you?' Penn asked as they passed the bins halfway through their first circuit of the building.

'Why the rush?' she asked. 'What's happened to make him kill three women in three days? What prompted him to start now?'

Penn stopped walking, but she and Alison carried on. 'Unless these aren't his first crimes,' he said, drawing level with them again. 'What if he's done other things elsewhere?'

Stacey realised that showed just how tired she was because that was something she should have considered. She turned to her colleague as they passed the automatic doors and continued around again.

'What about you? What's bugging you?'

'The scratches,' he answered. 'Present on the first victim but not the second.'

Alison shook her head but waited to speak until an articulated lorry had thundered past the station car park on the dual carriageway. 'See, that's what makes no sense. If a killer leaves a calling card, either as a message or a taunt to the police, it's present in every crime. They don't pick and choose when to do it. It's part of the whole process, it's important—'

'Ooh, hang on,' Stacey said as her phone dinged an email. 'It's from the network provider for the burner phone that called Nicola earlier today.'

She sat on the wall to the car park before opening the attachment.

The document was shorter than she'd expected and tidy. Very tidy.

'That's strange,' Stacey said as Penn took a seat beside her. Alison sat on the other side.

'Other than calling Nicola's phone this morning, that phone has only been in contact with one other number.'

Penn looked at her screen.

'So eight calls to that same number in the last month?' he asked, trying to take a better look. 'And no incoming calls at all.'

Stacey checked the dates at the top of the page.

'It's not a monthly statement, Penn. This is the sole activity of that burner phone for the last twelve years.'

# CHAPTER SIXTY-SIX

It was almost eight when they reached the house of Kate Sewell, which stuck out sorely from the properties of her neighbours. The row of quaint, cottage-style homes appeared unchanged with their pretty, well-manicured gardens and low white walls, except for number nineteen, which had a dropped kerb and a black brick driveway.

Must have gone down well with the neighbours, Kim thought as Bryant blocked in the Toyota Corolla on the driveway.

The village of Belbroughton sat approximately four miles south of Stourbridge and was once at the centre of the north Worcestershire scythe-making district. It had a population of around two thousand three hundred and was famous for its scarecrow festival at the end of September. It was an area known for its affluence and peace.

The door to the cottage was answered on the second knock.

The face Kim recognised from Monday creased into a frown. 'Inspector…'

'Stone,' Kim said, helping her out.

The suit she'd been wearing when they'd last met had been replaced with a leotard and Lycra leggings. Kim spied a yoga mat on the floor behind.

'De-stresses me,' she said, following Kim's gaze before her head snapped back, her eyes shining with fear.

'Nothing's happened to Tyra, has it?'

Kim shook her head. 'No, we're here on a totally separate matter.'

Relief flooded her features as she stood aside for them to enter. The front door led directly into a small lounge that appeared to be a second living area.

'Where would you like to sit? Do you want coffee or?… I'm sorry, I don't know how it works when the police visit your home late at night.'

It wasn't quite eight, so it was hardly the middle of the night.

'I'm afraid the matter is urgent and couldn't wait until normal business hours, no coffee and right here will be fine,' Kim said, taking a seat on a white leather sofa.

Bryant took the single seat and Kate sat cross-legged on the yoga mat. She reached for her phone, checked the screen and put it back down again.

Kim hadn't really had a feeling one way or another when they'd met the other day. She hadn't needed to form an opinion, but one was beginning to form now.

'How may I help you?'

'We understand you once represented Nicola Southall?'

She appeared to think for a few seconds. 'Oh goodness, yes, I did but that was a few years ago now,' she said, reaching for a bottle of water. 'Why would you ask about Nicola?'

'I'm afraid to say that Nicola was murdered earlier today,' Kim said, feeling no need to soften the blow. This had been a business relationship and even that had been over for some time.

The woman paused mid-drink.

'Not the body in the woods. That's quite close to—'

'Yes, that was Nicola, I'm afraid.'

Kate resumed her drink of water before screwing the top back on to the bottle.

'Bloody hell, poor thing,' she said as one would of someone they had met once in passing and then had never thought of again. Kim could see that in her mind there had been a profit and loss calculation; she was no threat to profit and so was no huge loss. She was not warming to the woman.

'You represented her for some time?' she asked.

'Yes, I signed her when she was doing adverts. She looked good on the telly and was a reasonable actress, so I thought someone would snap her up, but I never guessed it'd be a national soap.' She smiled as her eyes lit remembering the excitement. 'They were good days. Magazine interviews, radio spots, photoshoots and an interview on BBC Breakfast. But...' she opened her hands expressively.

'It all went wrong when they changed her part?' Kim asked.

'Oh yeah, the story was fictional, but the hate was real. She was getting abuse online, spat at in the street and it got too much for her. I told her it would pass and that she could keep making the money, but she was too frightened by it all.'

*More like she could have carried on and you could have carried on making the money*, Kim thought.

'So she retired?'

'Slunk away is how I think of it. She just didn't have the mettle to see it through. Wouldn't go out alone, got her own protection and wouldn't go for auditions; obviously, we had to part ways eventually.'

*When the cash cow dried up*, Kim thought.

'But was there any direct threat to Nicola's life?'

Kate frowned as she took another sip of water. 'You think someone hated her enough to wait all this time?'

'It's something we have to consider. Death threats were made.'

'Yeah, but they weren't really serious. Keyboard warriors, most of them.'

'Most?' Kim pushed.

'We had the odd couple that were worse than the rest, were a bit more specific but that was ten years ago.'

'And what did you do with those letters?'

'Burned them and gave them the respect they deserved.'

'And did you tell Nicola about them all?'

'Most of them, but there was no point making her even more paranoid.'

'And you're sure—' Kim's words were cut off by a ringing phone, but not the one next to the water bottle.

Kate sprang to her feet and glanced towards the kitchen.

'Sorry, got to get that: client phone.'

Kim stood and suddenly remembered Kate's reaction when they first arrived.

'Your first thought on seeing us was that something had happened to Tyra Brooks. Do you have reason to suspect that something might?'

There was no hesitation as she opened the door to let them out as the phone in the kitchen continued to ring.

'No, Officer, no reason at all.'

Kim opened her mouth to question that point, but two things happened: the door closed in her face and her phone began to ring.

'Charming,' Bryant noted as they headed for the car.

'Stone,' she answered.

'Marm, it's Craig Harris, FLO at the Webb-Harvey home.'

He was an officer she'd worked with years before and was a good match for this home.

'Go on,' she said, unable to stifle the ridiculous hope that Archie had turned up safe and sound.

'It's Robyn, Marm, she's absolutely raging and is demanding you come here right now.'

'Fuck,' Kim said, ending the call.

Not normally one to respond to other people's demands, in this case she'd make the exception. She instructed Bryant to head to the Webb-Harvey home.

She now had some explaining to do.

# CHAPTER SIXTY-SEVEN

Kate tried to push down her rage as she stared at the phone that had stopped ringing and now started again. She knew the number well; he really should know better than to call her. That wasn't how they did things. She considered returning to her yoga session, but there was no way the downward dog on a chair position was going to relieve the tension that had now built in her shoulders.

The visit from the police had unnerved her, as had the conversation about Nicola Southall. Not least because it had reminded her of what could have been if only the woman had been made of sterner stuff.

Kate had brokered an initial deal on Nicola's behalf of £1,400 per episode with a guaranteed 100 episodes a year and a repeat fee. It was a nice deal and they had celebrated together with a glass or two of the bubbly stuff. Kate had celebrated even harder alone once she saw the direction they were taking Nicola's character. Good characters make decent money, but hated characters make a lot more.

Every daytime show wants an interview, every newspaper wants a story and every magazine wants a photoshoot with the most heinous characters being portrayed on the small screen.

And Kate had been poised to start making big money from interviews and personal appearances. She'd been ready for them both to milk the exposure for every penny it was worth.

She'd learned the hard way not to overshare with her clients. She'd made the mistake of talking to Nicola about her ideas. The minute she'd unveiled her plans, the woman had folded under the pressure of the abuse.

No, she'd learned by now that the less the client knew the better. They could thank her later when they, and she, were laughing all the way to the bank.

Best if she didn't involve them at all, she thought, picking up the phone once it stopped ringing. She wasn't going to speak to the caller. Conversations could be recorded.

She pressed the text message icon.

She typed:

*I've told you not to ring me. What's up?*

The reply came quickly:

*All ok 4 tomoz?*

Kate swallowed her irritation at the abbreviation in text messages. Just how much time did people save by using non-words?

She typed:

*If there was any change I'd have let you know!!!*

The reply:

*Just chkg c u tomoz*

She typed:

*No, you won't and stick to the plan. Don't contact me again.*

She threw the phone to the side in disgust and took a deep breath.

There was a feeling in the pit of her stomach, and she couldn't ignore the sensation that something was going to go horribly wrong.

# CHAPTER SIXTY-EIGHT

'She's in Archie's bedroom,' Craig said, opening the door. He nodded towards the stairs. 'Second on the left.'

Bryant offered her a questioning glance. She shook her head. She'd deal with Robyn alone.

'We'll make tea,' Bryant said, following Craig to the kitchen.

The door was already open, and Robyn sat on the edge of the racing-car bed with her head in her hands.

Kim coughed to signal her arrival.

'You,' she accused, reaching to the right for her phone. 'You said all this to the man that murdered my wife and abducted my son?'

She thrust the phone forward as though she wanted Kim to read it.

'Robyn, let me explain,' she said, stepping into the room. The walls had been painted white then decorated with hand-painted colourful cartoon characters. Kim had the sudden vision of Robyn and Louise clad in overalls, paintbrushes in hand, preparing for the birth of their child. The thought brought a deep sadness to her heart.

'Explain what? That you understand why he took my child? Why he murdered my wife and left me with nothing?'

Kim pulled out a stool nestled beneath a small table holding colouring books and crayons. Two grown adults sitting on child-sized furniture.

'I mean, are you trying to make new friends or something? You want to pat him on the back for ruining my fucking—'

'Robyn, I'm trying to keep your son alive,' Kim offered gently. In hindsight, she wished she'd taken a moment to explain to Robyn what she was trying to achieve. To read the article without warning or explanation must have been like a knife to the heart.

'I should have spoken to you. I'm sorry, but there is a method in our madness. Believe me when I say we are every bit as angry as you are, but we believe in this particular instance a gentle approach will yield the best results. We all want to bring Archie home safely. And we will,' she said with conviction.

The anger seemed to drain out of her at the mention of her son's name.

Kim waited.

'Monday night,' she said, shaking her head as her thoughts relocated and attached themselves somewhere else. 'Just two days ago, we were talking about a brother or sister for Archie. Something that's impossible now. Archie is biologically Louise's child but he's still—'

'Of course he's your son,' Kim said. She guessed that though Louise had given birth to Archie, Robyn had never regarded the child as anything other than her son too.

'Not everyone feels that way. Many people feel that I have no claim to him at all: my own brother being one of them.'

'You have a brother?' Kim asked, surprised. Why wasn't he here now supporting her? In fact, where were any family members?

'He's a dick,' she said honestly. 'He's travelling back from a conference in Geneva, but quite honestly, I'd prefer him to have stayed where he was. If you get the misfortune of meeting him, you'll see what I mean.'

'You're not close?' Kim asked, remembering her own brother, Mikey, who had died in her arms when he was exactly Archie's age. She would have given her own life to save his. She knew that if he'd lived beyond their mother's neglect and torture, they would have been as close now as they had been back then.

'Pah,' she said disgustedly. 'It's not possible to get close to Robert. He places himself in competition with everyone he meets, and if he can't beat them he dismisses them. We see each other rarely, but no meeting goes by without some kind of snarky comment or judgement on my chosen lifestyle,' she said, making speech marks around the word chosen.

'Aah, he's one of those,' Kim said, raising an eyebrow.

Robyn smiled weakly. 'Oh yes, he's definitely one of those. I could have a perfectly normal heterosexual life if I wanted to. Says he just wants me to be happy.'

'So he means well?' Kim asked charitably.

'Absolutely not. He wants a sister with a normal, conventional family. He doesn't like how my sexuality reflects on him, as though I'm defective, and that people will think he's tainted with some kind of imperfection brush. Appearances are everything to Robert. He buys likes for his business in textiles which he markets on all social media platforms.'

'Buys likes?' Kim asked, not really interested, but the longer Robyn talked the calmer she became.

'Yeah, you can buy likes for your social media pages that make you look much more popular than you are, and Robert does this all the time. It validates him and then he ends up believing it himself. It's hilarious. Louise and I laugh about it all…' her words trailed away as she realised that just for a few moments her mind had allowed her to forget the reality of her current situation.

'Did they get on?' Kim asked.

Robyn shook her head. 'I've grown accustomed to his ways, and I've learned not to react because it just fires him up. Louise couldn't let any snarky comment go and would challenge him on everything.'

Kim got the feeling she would have liked Louise. She felt a sudden wave of sadness wash over her. She remembered walking into this home just yesterday, an interloper in a family that had been primed for normality. The food had been cooking, the wine had been poured and she had walked in and destroyed it for ever.

'It's him I hate,' Robyn said, as though reading her thoughts. 'Every fibre of my being wants to meet him face to face and make him suffer the way I'm suffering now. I want to take the most important things in his life and smash them to pieces.'

'Absolutely normal,' Kim said.

'But I can't do it,' she said as a tear slid over her cheek. 'I can't hold on to it. There are so many emotions running round inside me that I don't know which ones to try and hang on to.'

Kim understood. How did one grieve while trying to maintain hope? How could she fall apart when she still needed to stay strong? How did she even begin to find a new normal when her son was still missing?

Kim stood to leave. There was nothing more she could give Robyn right now.

'Why?' Robyn asked suddenly as her eyebrows drew together.

Kim turned and waited.

'Why would you believe this is the best way to handle him when it's clearly not normal practice? What makes you think he'll respond to this tactic?' she asked, demonstrating that her quick mind was still in attendance.

However much Kim wanted to, she couldn't divulge the contact that had been made. She trusted Robyn with the information; she just didn't trust whomever Robyn chose to trust with the information.

'I can't answer that, Robyn. Not yet.'

'Bring him back to me, Inspector,' she whispered as fatigue set in and her eyes began to droop.

'I plan to,' Kim said as she quietly left the room.

# CHAPTER SIXTY-NINE

Stacey was sure the wave of tiredness was being passed around the room like a Mexican wave. All three of them were covering their mouths to stifle yawns.

The ten-minute walk around the building had temporarily revitalised both her and Penn, but had had the opposite effect on Alison, whose eyes were drooping and growing heavier by the second.

'Alison, get off home. You don't even have to be here.'

As an unpaid consultant, Alison didn't have to wait to be dismissed by the boss. She could leave whenever she wanted.

'Hey, the team that walks together stays together… or something,' she protested, stifling a yawn.

Stacey turned back to her computer as the clock hit nine and a loud thunk sounded from the spare desk.

'Was that her head?' Stacey asked, looking over.

'Yep,' Penn said, wheeling his chair over to Alison.

He touched her lightly on the arm and a loud snore sounded, startling him.

Stacey felt the giggles rising in her stomach. The more she looked at Penn's efforts to gently wake Sleeping Beauty, the funnier it became.

'Bloody hell, she's out colder than a knocked-down prize fighter,' Penn said.

Another loud snore reduced Stacey to fits of laughter. Whether or not it was the effects of fatigue kicking in, she couldn't stop the tears from rolling over her cheeks.

'Stop it, Penn, you're hurting my stomach,' she said, wiping her eyes.

'Stace, stop laughing and help me wake her. I don't want to startle her.'

Stacey managed to get hold of herself and fought the laughter away. Just for a moment it had felt so good.

'Okay, Penn. Step aside, I've got this,' she said.

Penn rolled his chair back to his own desk.

'Hiya, boss,' Stacey shouted.

'What?… Where?…' Alison spluttered as her head shot up.

Both Stacey and Penn couldn't contain their laughter at her panicked expression.

'Alison, seriously, go home,' Stacey said.

The woman conceded defeat and reached for her handbag.

'I swear to God, you pair…'

'Hang on, that's it,' Penn shouted, standing up and looking at Alison. 'Noah, the name. We've exhausted every other theory except one. The animals came in pairs.'

# CHAPTER SEVENTY

'Thanks for dropping me home, Bryant,' Kim said as he pulled up outside her house. That last meeting with Robyn had drained her last reserves of energy. She'd left a house that a couple of days ago had been filled with normality, a family, and now it held only strangers. Right now all she wanted was a hot shower, strong coffee and a late-night dog walk.

Bryant killed the engine. 'I'd love to come in for a coffee, thanks for asking.'

'You okay?' she asked, getting out of the car. She was running on fumes, but if Bryant needed to talk she'd summon the energy from somewhere.

'I'm tickety boo,' he replied, following her to the front door.

She unlocked and pushed it open to see her favourite sight.

'Barney, my boy,' she said, leaning down to pet him as Bryant walked around her.

'I'll put the kettle on.'

'So what's up?' she asked, rubbing Barney's head as he walked beside her.

She opened the back door for Barney to go out. Their night walk would come after Bryant had left.

'You have a fight with the missus?' she asked, concerned.

It would be unusual for the two of them, but every marriage, even the best ones, hit rough patches. And Bryant's was the best example of a good marriage she'd ever seen.

'We're in your home, so I'm still Bryant but you're now Kim, right?' he asked.

'Yeah,' she said. That was her rule.

'And we're officially off duty after a fourteen-hour day?'

'Bryant...' she warned. It was too late in the day for these kind of games. 'Out with it.'

'You were dead wrong to speak to the team the way you did earlier today.'

'Is this because of Woody's call?' she asked, reaching for a carrot when Barney came in from outside.

Her boss had called her once she'd left Kate Sewell's address to ask why her team was outside walking around the building.

The news had both made her smile and prompted her to instruct Bryant to send them home.

'Alison had just left, the other two sounded delirious and I'm not sure I mean that in a good way,' he said, reaching for the mugs. He looked at the one she reserved for him and put it back.

'I don't really want a coffee; I just wanted to get in the door to give you a reality check.'

'Go on then, let me have it,' she said, sitting on the bar stool where he normally sat. He took her position, standing against the work surface with his arms folded.

He was a bit late with his bollocking. She'd realised her error two hours ago, but it was important to let him have his say.

'That team will do anything for you. They'll follow you anywhere. They don't expect a pat on the back, a gold star or for you to bake them cookies. They don't expect you to big them up for doing a good job. They also don't expect to be shouted at for working long hours and trying their best.'

'Absolutely.'

'They also don't expect to take the brunt of your frustration that this guy is getting ahead of us at every turn.'

'Agreed.'

'Penn has just lost his mother. Stacey is getting married in ten days' time and Alison… well, Alison actually deserved the bollocking, but still, you could have gone easier.'

'Is there any language in which I can say I agree with you that you'll understand?'

There was nothing he'd said that hadn't already gone through her mind since she'd left the office.

He uncrossed his arms. 'I mean, to be fair, it does look like the bollocking had a positive effect. Penn was telling me some interesting stuff they came up with on their little walk.'

'So make your mind up: was I right or was I wrong?'

Now she was just playing with him.

'You were right in content but oh so very wrong in delivery.'

'Message received and talking of delivery, go take your wife an average husband home until she can find a decent one. I'm sick of the sight of you today.'

He smiled. 'Yeah, the feeling is mutual,' he said, heading for the door.

'She's all yours,' he said, patting Barney on the head.

'Oh, and Bryant,' she called as he reached the front door.

'No, it's okay, no thanks are necessary for my honesty and bravery in pointing out to you that—'

'I was gonna say don't forget to take my bike frame out of your boot,' she said, cutting him off.

He was laughing out loud as he closed her front door behind him.

Kim moved to the other side of the breakfast bar to finish making the coffee that Bryant had started.

'Jesus, what now?' she asked Barney as her phone tinged receipt of a message.

It was from Frost.

*Check out my article.*

Kim keyed in a response.

*Already done. Thanks!*

Kim had checked the news piece the minute it went up. It was perfect, and Frost had quoted her word for word. She hadn't realised the woman would want a pat on the back for it.

A response tinged back.

*Rolling eyes emoji. Check it again!!!*

Three exclamation marks.

Kim searched for the article, which sprang onto her screen. She reread the piece Frost had written. Nothing had changed and it hadn't been updated. Only one thing was different. The comments. A Google alert had told her when the article had been uploaded. She'd read it when it was clean. There were now 133 comments.

She scrolled down. The majority of what her eyes passed over were exactly what she expected.

*'Evil Bastard'*
*'Probably a Paedo.'*
*'Catch the bastard and string him up.'*
*'Wot yo on dumb pig?'*
*'Stone's a fucking pussy.'*
*'Kid's probably already dead.'*
*'This ay gonna help catch the wanker, is it?'*
*'Give me ten minutes with him. I'll sort him out.'*
*'Does this bint copper wanna shag him or summat?'*
*'Pandering to a fucking murderer.'*

The comments and the insults went on, and there were no names she hadn't been called before, but three comments from the bottom was a post that almost stopped her heart.

> *'Sorry to disagree, folks, but the officer concerned seems to be showing compassion and understanding. Who is to say that these crimes are about hate, and why should she meet violence with aggression? How do you know that her measured and objective response didn't just save that little boy's life?'*

Her heart skipped another beat as she read that the post was from someone called Noah.

# CHAPTER SEVENTY-ONE

Penn parked outside his house just a minute before ten and paused. The lights were on, but some small part of him didn't want to go in. Never had he thought that such a distance would open up between the two of them following their mother's death.

The time she spent in the hospice should have prepared them, but it hadn't. They were both in unchartered territory, and he had no road map. All he knew was that he had to stay strong for his brother: try and keep the routine and the continuity, no matter how much he wanted to break down. Especially after a day like today. He had no choice but to keep it together.

As he opened the front door, the first thing he heard was laughter. A woman's laughter.

'Lynne?' he questioned, reaching the kitchen.

His brother and his old colleague were comparing two trays of chocolate muffins.

'Jasper called me. He wanted to cook,' she said, shifting uncomfortably. Reading the surprise on his face, she reddened. 'I'm sorry, maybe I shouldn't have...'

'No, no, it's fine,' Penn said, getting over the shock. Jasper knew he wasn't allowed to cook in the house alone. The two of them had struck up a friendship over the course of police social events where Jasper had been his plus one.

'Hey, bud,' Penn said, reaching over to ruffle his hair. Jasper ducked out of the way as his face hardened.

Lynne caught his look and planted a big smile on her face.

'Hey, matey, you wanna finish up your computer game while these cool?'

'Okey dokey,' he said, leaving the kitchen in his apron.

'He's angry cos I'm late again,' Penn observed, sighing deeply.

'That's not why he's angry,' Lynne said, removing her own apron. 'He's pissed at you for being strong.'

'What?' he asked, dropping down into a seat at the dining table. The exhaustion of the day suddenly caught up with him.

Lynne joined him. 'Bloody hell, Penn, you're an intelligent man but you often don't see stuff that's right in front of you.'

'Like what?' he asked.

'Never mind,' she said, shaking her head.

'Lynne, I don't…'

'What qualities does Jasper possess?' she asked, using the tone he knew she reserved for young children and difficult witnesses. 'Describe him to me.'

'He's kind, sweet, thoughtful.'

'Indeed, he is, and where did he learn those qualities?'

He shrugged.

Her head rolled back, and she groaned.

'From you, you bloody idiot. He's been watching and copying you his whole life.'

'But I…'

'Do you remember that pile-up we went to years back?'

Penn nodded. He didn't need to ask which one. Two families including three children had been wiped out that day.

'I still think about it now,' she said. 'I remember everything about that day: the weather, the victims, the placement of the mangled metal, the smell of charred flesh and something else.'

'What?'

'That you sent every other officer away for a breather before you went yourself.'

He could still see the stricken faces of the officers dealing with the incident. Some had kids of their own.

'It's not that you don't feel, but it's like you've got this extra reserve of strength, another gear that is only to be used when it truly matters.'

Lynne paused and waited for the penny to drop in his mind.

He shook his head as the fatigue continued to wash over his body.

'Blimey, Penn, it must have been a long day. He's trying to stay strong for you.'

'But he's so angry with me.'

'Because he wants to break down. He wants you to break down. He needs you to, so that he can do it too.'

'Aww… shit,' he said, rubbing his hand through his curls.

'He needs you to talk about her, not pretend she didn't exist. He needs to remember her and mourn her.' Lynne's hand moved towards his but stopped an inch away. 'You both do.'

He met her gaze fully for the first time. 'I fucked up, didn't I?'

She smiled. It was a smile he liked. He really did miss working with her.

'Yeah, you did, but you can put it right,' she said, nodding towards the lounge.

He was suddenly overcome with gratitude that she had been there for Jasper, that she had dropped whatever she was doing to help his brother.

'Listen, Lynne, thank—'

'Forget it, Penn. It's what friends do. Now get in there and talk to your brother. I'll let myself out.'

He nodded his thanks and headed into the lounge.

Jasper was holding the game controls, but nothing was moving on the screen.

'Hey, bud, what are you playing?' he asked cheerily and immediately understood that was exactly what his brother didn't need him to do.

He sat on the sofa, resting his forearms on his knees and realised that neither of them had yet sat in the armchair that had been their mother's favourite place to sit.

He heard the soft click of the front door closing behind his old colleague. For a second, he wished her reassuring presence was still in the kitchen. But right now, he had to focus on making things right with his brother.

'Hey, bud, the house doesn't feel the same without Mum, does it?' He felt the emotion thicken his voice and for the first time he didn't try and swallow it down. He didn't try and hide it.

'See, when she was in the hospice she wasn't really gone, was she?'

A slight shake of the head from Jasper.

'We could still go and see her, touch her, speak to her and maybe a part of us could hope that she'd still come back.'

Penn made no effort to stop the tears from falling over his cheeks.

'We're gonna miss her, buddy. It's gonna hurt like hell and I don't know how we're gonna get through it,' he said, dropping his head into his hands. The tears flowed and with them the acknowledgment of his loss, his grief.

He felt Jasper's trembling body come to rest beside him on the sofa and the heart-breaking sound of his own grief. Penn pulled him close and held him tight.

'But we will get through it, buddy. I promise. We have each other and that will never change. We'll help each other, and we'll talk and remember all the great things about our mum. She knew we'd be okay, mate,' he said, reaching into his pocket for a tissue.

Jasper's arm snaked around his back as he rested his wet cheek on Penn's shoulder.

'We'll be okay, Ozzy, we'll be okay.'

# CHAPTER SEVENTY-TWO

The coffee pot was on and Kim stood waiting for her team to arrive and start the day.

Bryant was first.

'What the bloody hell are those?' he asked, glancing at the edge of his desk.

'They're cookies,' Kim said defensively. 'I baked.'

'Oh Jesus, I knew I should have kept my mouth shut,' he said, removing his jacket and taking a closer look.

He picked one up and banged it against the plate.

'You know when I played hockey we used to hit something…'

'Bryant, if you've got nothing nice to say, I suggest you shut your damn mouth,' she snapped as the rest of the team entered the office together.

Safety in numbers.

'Oooh,' Stacey said, appraising the plate. 'Oh,' she said once she got a better look.

'Feel free to take one,' Kim said.

'I'm good, boss,' Stacey said.

'Just eaten, boss,' Penn offered.

'Not hungry,' Alison said.

'Well, I know that last one's a lie, Alison,' Kim said as they all eyed the plate with caution, as though it was about to attack.

'We being punished again, boss?' Stacey asked.

'Oh come on, guys, you always like to start the day with—'

'Penn, save us, for God's sake,' Stacey pleaded.

He reached into his man bag and produced a Tupperware box. Every pair of eyes landed on him expectantly.

'Muffins,' he said, opening the lid. The aroma filled the office immediately.

'Jasper's?' Stacey asked.

Penn nodded with a smile. Stacey stared longingly at the box.

'Well, I've got no chance of competing with Jasper, have I?' Kim asked, folding her arms.

No answer.

'Is no one gonna try the cookies I baked at one o'clock this morning?'

'Go on, Alison, you'll normally eat anything,' Bryant said.

'You're not wrong, providing it's actually edible,' she shot back.

Kim marvelled at the woman's metabolism.

'Go on then,' Bryant said, reaching forward. 'I'll take one for the team.'

He bit into it and placed the remainder at a point on his desk that was directly above his bin.

'Okay, okay,' Kim said, moving the plate of cookies out of the way.

Seeing this as permission, they all descended on Penn's offering like flies to a fresh pile of dung. She wasn't upset. They were Jasper's muffins and even she'd be grabbing one for herself later.

'Okay, guys, sounds like your stroll around the building last night yielded results. Want to tell me about it?'

'We're wondering if there's anything to do with pairs, boss?' Penn said. 'It's the only thing we can link with the name Noah.'

'So we're wondering if there are any other crimes that come in twos,' Alison added.

'But we've had three murders?' Kim queried.

'But the first two were similar: women with children,' Penn answered.

'And yet different,' she said, turning to Alison for an answer.

'Still working on it.'

'And the phone records of the phone that called Nicola yesterday?' Kim asked.

'Only been used eight times in ten years other than the call to Nicola.'

'No incoming calls or messages?'

'Not one. Not even from the only other number it's making contact with.'

'Stace, stay on that. I want everything you can find. Penn, I want you looking at any crimes that have come in pairs.'

Both officers nodded their understanding.

'Alison, I want you to take a look at the scratches on the wrist of our first victim. What do they mean and what is their purpose?'

'Got it.'

'But not before you've taken a look at this.'

Kim reached behind to the printer for the copies of the comment she'd screen-shotted and printed from her phone.

She handed the first copy to Alison and then circulated the rest.

'Our guy?' Kim asked impatiently.

Alison read the comment and then spread the other two communications around it.

The room waited in silence until Kim could bear it no longer. 'Well?'

'I can't be sure.'

'I'm not asking you to bet your house on it. Your opinion?'

'My opinion is that yes, I think this could be our guy.'

'Why?' Kim asked.

'His sentence structure is similar – both handwritten and typed – which will show likenesses because it's the pattern of thought, the style of writing, if you like. Many of the words are used in the same way. I'm pretty confident it's him, and if it is…'

'Thanks, Alison,' Kim said, taking the piece of paper and heading out the door, but not before she heard Alison finish her sentence.

'I think she might just have saved that little boy's life.'

# CHAPTER SEVENTY-THREE

'If this means what you think it means, you were lucky and it changes nothing that I said to you yesterday,' Woody said after he'd read the comment from Noah three times.

If that was how he wanted to refer to her judgement call, then so be it. Either way, she hoped she'd given the kid a fighting chance until they were able to find the bastard who had him.

She had to admit that she'd wondered how warm the temperature would be in this office following their heated exchange the previous day, and normally she would have kept a low profile for a few days, but that wasn't an option. She needed something from him, and she had an idea what his answer was going to be.

'Any chance of tracing the comment?' he asked.

Kim shook her head. 'It's gone now, sir. Removed half an hour after it was posted. He gave me enough time to see it before taking it down.'

'So?'

'He wants to engage with me. He posted that answer so that I'd see it. He wants me to know he's listening, otherwise he wouldn't have bothered.'

'Go on,' he said, sitting back in his chair.

'I want to do it again. I want to use Frost to try and reach him before anyone else gets hurt.'

'You know my answer is no,' Woody said. 'Your first interaction was accidental. He made contact with you without invitation. The process of actively trying to engage a killer one-on-one without the full support of police resources is not something that can be decided in this room and you know it.'

Yeah, and the full resources of the police force had done them no good at all the day before, but damn it, that's what she thought he'd say. Protocols demanded that a roomful of experts would be needed to examine every shred of evidence before sanctioning an order for her to interact on her own. That could take days, and the answer would most likely be no. But she didn't have days to wait any way. With one murder every day she had to get his attention.

'Sir...'

'The answer is no, Stone. In fact, I'll be doing the press conference later today. I don't think talking to the nationals is right for you right now.'

Kim hid the smile that was forming on her lips. Some days, Woody exceeded even her expectations. Just one word was all she needed, and he'd given it to her. Nationals.

As usual the man had been fair and objective and had weighed the benefits of what she was trying to do. As ever, he had not let her down.

'Sir, about yesterday. I'd—'

'I think that's best left where it is, don't you, Stone?'

'I disagree.'

The hint of a smile pulled at his lips. 'Why am I not surprised?'

'I shouldn't have spoken to you the way I did,' she said, and meant it. There were few people she respected as much as this man, and it was important to her that he knew that. 'It won't happen again.'

His fingers knitted together in front of him. 'I trust it won't, and your passion and conviction are to be admired, most of the time.'

She turned to leave, content the air was now clear between them. Woody didn't hold a grudge and neither did she.

After their previous exchange, he could be forgiven for barely giving her the time of day, never mind listening and agreeing to her proposal.

And if there was any doubt in her mind on that score, he clarified it when her feet reached his office door.

'And do give my regards to Frost if you just happen to bump into her later today.'

# CHAPTER SEVENTY-FOUR

'So Jasper baked?' Stacey asked once the boss and Bryant had left the office.

Penn felt the smile lift his lips as he remembered the night before.

'Yeah, he was cooking up a storm last night with Lynne while I was still here.'

Penn felt brighter today. The heavy weight that sat upon his grief was a few pounds lighter this morning.

After Lynne had left, the two of them had cried and talked and cried some more. They had a long way to go, but he now knew they'd make it.

'Lynne?' Stacey asked. 'Isn't she one of your old colleagues from West Mercia?'

'Yeah, Jasper and Lynne hit it off the first time they met.'

'That's cos your brother is awesome,' Stacey said. 'But tell me more about Lynne.'

'Nothing to tell, sticky beak. Now get back to work,' he said, reaching for the headphones in his drawer.

Stacey got the message and picked up her phone.

Putting on his headphones gave him the privacy to be alone with his own thoughts. He had to admit, it had been quite a surprise to see Lynne in his kitchen cooking with his brother when he'd got home the night before. He'd been pleased to see her smiling face and had felt thankful to her for spending time with his brother.

It was only later when an exhausted Jasper had finally climbed the stairs to bed that Penn had returned to the kitchen and had found it feeling emptier than normal. He could still see her there behind the counter, dressed in his naked-man apron, comparing muffins with his brother.

It was no secret to him that he missed working with her. They'd shared the same humour and had often found things funny that other people had not. He had always been able to talk to her about anything, and she had become a really good friend.

Only, last night he'd also noticed just how brown her eyes were and the way she tipped her head slightly when speaking.

He shook the thoughts away. Lynne was engaged. She was happy. Her whole life was ahead of her: a glowing career and probably a family. He knew his own situation hardly made him the catch of the year, and Jasper would always come first.

Anything further with Lynne was not an option for more reasons than one. He pushed the thoughts firmly away and focused his attention on work.

# CHAPTER SEVENTY-FIVE

'Hey, Frost, how are you doing?' Kim asked when the reporter answered her phone.

'What the fuck you want, Stone?' she asked groggily.

Bryant smiled at her response as her terse voice filled the car on loudspeaker.

'Oh, Frost, who hasn't yet got out of bed the wrong side this morning?'

'You do know you're not funny, don't you?'

'Bryant thinks I am, don't you, Bryant?' she asked, moving the phone closer to his mouth.

'Bloody hilarious,' he answered.

'Stone, what the hell do you want at this ungodly hour of the morning?'

Kim could hear from the background noise that the reporter was now up and moving around.

A sudden, unwelcome thought occurred to her. 'Err… Frost, you don't sleep naked, do you?'

'No, but my breath smells like a son of a bitch.'

'Okay, TMI, Frost, way too much information and, just so you know, it's almost eight o'clock.'

'Which is way too early to listen to you quoting and then explaining acronyms to me. Now just get to the point. Clearly, you want something from me, so hurry up unless you want to accompany me into the shower.'

'Ugh… no thanks. Bryant here would like to buy you a coffee this morning if you've got a minute.'

'Why?'

'Cos you're his favourite reporter and—'

'Stone, it's too early for this shit. For fuck's sake, spit it out.'

Kim did the calculations between their first visit of the day and Nicola Southall's post-mortem at ten.

'Meet us at Sam's Bostin Bites, Old Hill, at nine fifteen. Now go get clean: you stink.'

Bryant chuckled as she ended the call.

'You think she'll go for it?' he asked of her plan. She'd already told him what she wanted to do.

'I think so if we make it worth her while.'

She'd cross that bridge later, but right now she was on her way to see what was left of a family and offer them the smallest ray of hope.

# CHAPTER SEVENTY-SIX

'Bloody hell,' Stacey said, slamming down the phone.

'Wassup?' Alison asked, raising her head.

'Damn network provider for the other phone, the second burner, are being a lot less helpful. It's not registered, but they're playing hardball with the data because its link to any crime is tenuous at best,' she said, quoting the assistant who'd said she'd look into it, which was code for I'm going to forget about your call the second I put this phone down.

'I mean, who uses their phone like this?' Stacey asked, waving the single sheet around.

'Have you asked the provider of the first burner for content?'

'No, Alison, I never made sure to do that before I went home last night,' Stacey said, softening her words with a smile.

She'd done it the second she'd realised the phone had been used for texting only, except for the call to Nicola. But now she was desperate to know who the hell it was texting, and the network weren't too keen to help her find out.

'Stace, you got a minute?' Penn asked, removing his head-phones.

'Unfortunately, yes,' she answered, seeing as her leads appeared to be going nowhere.

'Can you look up the murder of Rhona Stubbs and see if you can find any mention of scratches? She was stabbed eight months ago in Walsall, and the same on the scratches for Bryan

Thompson, who was assaulted six years ago outside a chip shop in Kingswinford.'

'Bloody hell, Penn, what are you up to? You want me to look at a case from six years ago?'

He nodded distractedly as he looked at the screen and then scribbled something down.

'I can find no way to link the scratches to anything,' Alison said. 'They're not present in every crime, which fits no pattern, and they don't actually say anything.'

Alison had been tasked to investigate the scratches further, and that was her way of telling Penn he was wasting his time.

'So what are you thinking, Penn?' Stacey asked, even though she agreed with the profiler.

'I've got more stuff to look at, but I think there might be something in the pairs theory, and I think it's been going on for years.'

# CHAPTER SEVENTY-SEVEN

'She's outside,' the family liaison officer said as he opened the door.

'How's she doing, Craig?'

'As you'd expect. She fell asleep on Archie's bed once you'd left last night but was awake before six. She's alternating between crying and wanting to get out there and search for Archie.'

*Completely natural reactions*, Kim thought.

'Just one thing, though,' he said, closing the door and dropping his voice to a whisper. 'Her brother's been here since sevenish and he's err—'

'Who is it, Craig?' said a strong voice from the kitchen.

Kim said nothing and waited for the owner to come into view.

'DI Stone, this is Robert Harvey,' Craig said. 'Robyn's brother.'

Kim could see a vague resemblance, but the features of this man were harsher, sharper. He matched Bryant's six-foot height but with an additional couple of inches' width.

He stepped towards Bryant with his hand outstretched. 'Inspector Stone, my sister—'

'That's DI Stone, but I'm still pleased to meet you,' Bryant said, pointing her way before returning the handshake.

He glanced at her without offering an apology for his error. And already she didn't expect one.

'Do you have news?' he asked, standing in a way that prevented her moving further into the house.

'Mr Harvey, I'm here to speak with your sister,' she said, stepping forward.

He didn't move, meaning she was now very close to him and could smell the cause of the tidemarks at the armpit of his powder pink shirt.

'And I would prefer you to share any news you have with me first.'

'As you are not directly related either by marriage or blood to our victim, that is not going to happen, so please, stand aside.'

'The vic… oh, you mean Louise. I assumed you were here with news of Archie, seeing as you can do nothing for Louise now. Any news would be better for my sister if it was delivered by me,' he said, standing aside now that he felt he'd made himself clear and had had the last word.

Kim was surprised at the dismissive nature of his manner towards Louise, his sister's wife.

'Any information will be shared with your sister first,' she said, edging past him and taking the last word for herself. 'But she'll be safe with us if you'd like to take the opportunity to freshen up.'

She continued walking to the rear of the house, choosing to ignore the fact he was following Bryant. The man did not take a hint.

Robyn sat outside on one half of a wooden companion set, with a single mug on the triangle piece that linked the two seats. The oversize cardigan appeared to swamp her slight frame, which was clad in the same clothes as the night before. Her long brown hair had been tied into a haphazard ponytail.

Kim was suddenly struck by the lonely figure who might be thinking that she would never share that seat with her wife again. Her gaze was fixed on the small playhouse at the end of the garden.

'We knew he was too big for it,' Robyn said softly as Kim approached. 'But we didn't have the heart to throw it away. We can't throw anything away. You see, there's a memory in everything. I have every piece of Archie's clothing. Sounds crazy I know, but I remember something different for every single item. Just one small thing that stops me from being able to part with it.'

Kim lowered herself onto the seat beside the woman, who finally turned. Kim's breath caught in her chest. Never had she seen a woman more haunted and bereft of emotion. It was as though every feeling had been sucked out of her.

'I don't want to be here, you know,' she said, turning away again.

'Robyn, I need—'

'Please, let me gather myself for a moment, Inspector. I'm speaking because I'm terrified of what's going to come out of your mouth if I stop, and I'm trying to prepare myself.'

'I understand that…'

'No, you don't,' she said with authority but without anger. 'Everything I love in this world has been taken away from me; my wife is dead, my son is…'

'Well, strictly speaking, he's not your son, is he?' Robert asked from the kitchen doorway. 'Well, not biologically anyway.'

'Piss off, Rob,' she snapped.

'I'm just trying to help.'

'How does that help?' Robyn asked. 'You think I love him any less because I didn't give birth to him?'

'Well, technically…'

'How about technically you fuck off,' she spat, rising from the chair and turning.

Bryant, who was standing closer to the brother, looked to her for guidance. Should he step in or not? Kim shook her head. She would have liked to have responded to his insensitive and cruel comments herself, but by her own admission, Robyn had rarely stuck up for herself, allowing Louise to be the reactive one in the marriage. Robyn needed to do this for her own piece of mind.

'You never liked her, and you hated our life together. You've never taken our marriage seriously or treated Archie like your nephew. Look at your face; you're not even sorry she's dead.'

The tension that burned between the two was palpable, causing Kim to wonder why he was here at all. They obviously weren't close.

Kim wondered if Robyn could hear her thoughts as she continued.

'Why did you come? Just to talk about your perfect wife and your two perfect daughters? Did you come to gloat because I'm miserable and hurting?'

The rage burned in Robyn's eyes, but Kim was surprised to see amusement in the expression of her brother.

'You always wanted to be better than me. All our lives you've competed for attention. You always wanted to win at something. Well, here you go. I have nothing, but just so you know, your wife is a bitch and your daughters are brats.'

'You evil cow,' he said as his face reddened. 'You couldn't get a man, so you settled for a woman, and now you're pissed off with me because my life is great and yours is—'

'Mr Harvey, I think it's time for you to leave,' Bryant said, taking a step forward.

The man hesitated for a few seconds before storming back into the house.

'I'm sorry you had to witness that,' Robyn said, collapsing back into her seat. 'As I explained last night, we've never got along. We used to pretend for our parents, but there's no need for that any more. Both gone,' she explained.

The woman expelled a deep breath and braced herself.

'Go on, Inspector, I'm ready for whatever you've got to tell me.'

'Robyn, I'm here to tell you not to give up hope. We firmly believe Archie is still alive.'

# CHAPTER SEVENTY-EIGHT

Kate applied a second coating of lipstick before popping the cosmetic into her handbag. She wanted to look her best later.

She was due to collect Tyra in half an hour to commence what would be their last day of the book tour. Two more signings and the deed would be done. The two-week tour had gone without incident, except for a few mean shout-outs from people passing by the bookstores. All moved on quietly by security.

Only last night, Tyra had messaged her for an update on book sales. Kate had promised she'd have an accurate figure later today, but that had been a lie. She had an accurate figure almost by the hour.

Sales of the book were not what she or the publisher had expected or hoped for. The initial buy-in had been promising but reported till sales were less than twenty per cent of the initial orders after two weeks. Kate hadn't expected the book to make the *Sunday Times* bestseller list, but it was barely making any list at all. The e-book wasn't faring much better, but priced at almost ten pounds, it seemed the publishers failed to understand that most readers wouldn't pay that for something they couldn't physically hold.

She'd hoped the book tour and associated interest would bring potential foreign deals and translations. Just a week ago, publishers in Germany, Hungary and Spain had been showing interest in making a deal, but the conversations had ended, and the emails had dried up and Kate was no longer receiving responses to her messages. What appeared to have been a passing interest had died completely, and this was what happened if you didn't seize every single opportunity.

The public and press were losing interest. The requests for interviews were dying off and even social media appeared to have softened towards Tyra. Fascination in the ex-glamour model and her story was waning.

But there was a spring in her step as she locked the door of the cottage behind her because she was sure that would have changed by the end of the day.

# CHAPTER SEVENTY-NINE

'Not sure the brother was as supportive as he could have been,' Bryant said once they were sitting in Sam's Bostin Bites in Old Hill. The café was double fronted with seating and a takeout counter for homemade products. Bryant had bagged a couple of Scotch eggs and two red onion sausage rolls to take home later.

Kim thought Bryant's assessment was a little on the charitable side.

He continued. 'Seemed a bit of an…'

'Arrogant prick are the words you're looking for,' she offered, just to help him out.

'Yeah, but there was more to it than that. He was superior, judgemental, dismissive, almost like he was gloating.'

Kim nodded her agreement as she sipped her drink.

'You think it was wise to tell Robyn about Archie, that we think he's still alive?'

'Absolutely, the woman needs something to hope for.'

'You really think we can bring him back safely?' Bryant asked, and she swore she heard an element of doubt in the question.

'We're about to find out,' Kim said as Frost entered the café and tottered towards them in her four-inch heels.

Once upon a time, Kim had been amused by the woman's insistence on wearing the tallest shoes she could find despite appearing clumsy and awkward. Until she had found out that the woman had one leg shorter than the other and had been teased about the limp all her life.

Bringing even more attention to the way she walked was Frost's unique way of hiding her own insecurities.

'Hey, Frost,' Kim said as she took a seat and placed her studded Michael Kors bag on the spare chair.

'Knock it off, Stone. You're giving me anxiety. This courteousness unnerves me, and I prefer you being a bitch. It's a persona I know and expect.'

'Frost, we agree on something,' Bryant said. 'Because her being nice freaks me out too.'

Kim offered her colleague a look.

'I want to do it again,' Kim said.

'You think that was definitely him?' Frost asked, not needing any further explanation.

Kim knew that she was treading a fine line with what she should or shouldn't reveal to the reporter, but she was asking for a favour. She had suspected he would respond better to a message sent through a small local paper rather than a national. It wasn't fame and notoriety he was after. It was contact, and this was more intimate and personal. Like it or not, Frost's articles were now the medium through which she and the killer spoke.

She also knew that engaging with a man who had killed three women was not without risk. Just saying one thing wrong could destroy the rapport he thought he had with her. Her fear in doing that was for the safety of Archie.

'So you want another online article?'

Kim nodded.

'Anything new to add?' Frost asked hopefully.

'Nice try, but no.' She wasn't offering the woman an exclusive. 'Can you not do some kind of round-up of events so far?'

Frost raised one eyebrow. 'Yeah, cos my editor just loves me to write stuff that goes over the same ground we've already covered.'

Kim appreciated Frost's subtle reminder that she had a boss too.

'Sorry, Stone, can't—'

'For an intelligent woman, you're not thinking very clearly,' Kim said, having anticipated Frost's resistance. 'I can give you nothing, except the fact I'm asking you for a favour. Do you want to think about that for a minute?'

A slow smile spread across her face. 'So you'll owe me one?'

Kim nodded.

'Which I can call in any time I want?'

'Not a fucking chance,' Kim said. 'But I will pay you back and you know it.'

Frost hesitated for only a second before reaching for her notebook.

'Okay, what do you want in there? I'll work the article around that.'

'Okay, I want you to say that not every murderer is evil, that if they want to stop they can. That no one else has to die and that help is available and—'

'Bloody hell, Stone, do you want to tuck him in and read him a bedtime story too? This monster has killed three women and—'

'I'm trying to make sure he doesn't kill a fourth. Unless he chooses you and then I'm not all that—'

'Okay, carry on,' she said, shaking her head.

'You must mention my name, and you must emphasise that no one else needs to die. Got it?'

'Yeah, yeah, but working it into a bloody news story is another matter.'

'I have every faith in you, Frost,' Kim said, pushing back her chair.

'Whatever,' she said, taking out her laptop and making herself comfortable at the corner table in the café.

As they stepped outside, Kim glanced back at Frost's fingers flying across the keyboard.

Whatever words she'd chosen to use, it was a plea for him to stop what he was doing, and with it being almost twenty-four hours since the last murder, Kim only hoped that she wasn't too late.

# CHAPTER EIGHTY

'Penn, what the hell are you doing?' Stacey asked as he wrote furiously on the wipe board.

'Give me a minute, Stace,' he said without turning.

'You're just writing random incidents on the board that have nothing to do with—'

'Okay, I'm done,' he said, standing back.

Stacey looked at the completed board and tried to take it all in.

*May 2010 – Burglary – Scratches in sideboard*
*May 2010 – Burglary – No scratches*
*August 2012 – Peeping Tom – Scratches on window sill*
*August 2012 – Peeping Tom – No scratches*
*January 2014 – Assault – Scratches on hand*
*January 2014 – Assault – No scratches*
*February 2019 – Murder – Homeless Woman – Scratches on arm*
*February 2019 – Murder – Homeless Woman – No scratches*
*Current – Murder 1 – Katrina Nock – Scratches*
*Current – Murder 2 – Louise Webb-Harvey – No Scratches*
*Current – Murder 3 – Nicola Southall – ???*

She reached the bottom of the list and looked to Penn for explanation.

Alison looked just as puzzled as she felt.

'I've been searching for unsolved crimes involving scratches. I've also searched for unsolved crimes with similarities to another crime and for crimes that happened closely together. After a lot of cross-referencing, this is what I've got. Every one of these crimes happened within days of each other, and every single one of them is unsolved.'

He paused, looked at the board and then pointed to the first listing. 'In May 2010, there was a burglary at a house in West Hagley. The scratches had been carved into the sideboard that held the jewellery that was taken. You couldn't miss it. Second burglary was a similar MO but just round the corner, in Pedmore. No scratches.'

Stacey listened as his pointing finger moved down to the second pairing. 'In August 2012, a twenty-seven-year-old woman in Bilston reported seeing a shadowy figure staring at her through the bedroom window at around 11 p.m. She lived alone and was terrified. When shown where she'd seen the figure, officers noted fresh scratches in the paintwork of the outside window sill. A photo was taken and held on the file. The next day, the same thing happened to a twenty-five-year-old woman in Coseley. Exactly the same, even the same time of night. The victim saw someone peering through the window, but no scratches were found. Still with me?' he asked.

Both she and Alison nodded.

'In January 2014, a thirty-nine-year-old male was knocked unconscious as he walked home from his job at a tool-making factory in Wall Heath. The scratches were cut into his hand, and no other injuries were found. The following night, a forty-two-year-old male, Barry Thompson, was hit from behind as he left a pub in Kingswinford. No scratches and no injury other than the head wound. Both made full recoveries but could offer no information about their attackers.'

'Bloody hell,' Stacey said. Hearing the explanations behind the one-line notations on the board was causing her to wonder if Penn really was on to something.

'In February 2019, a fifty-four-year-old homeless woman was found murdered by one single stab wound, on the outskirts of Walsall, at the back of a twenty-four-hour service station. They got a partial print but no match. Scratches were found on her lower arm. The following night, Rhona Stubbs, a sixty-three-year-old homeless woman, was found murdered in exactly the same way just outside a new housing development in Great Bridge. No partial print and no scratches. The local team originally had a suspect for Rhona's murder, as the building site was having a lot of problems with looters and vandals, but there was no physical evidence to link him.'

'So you think Noah is responsible for all these crimes and he's escalated over the years?' Stacey asked.

'I think it's possible,' Penn answered.

'But why always a pair?' Alison asked. 'Why does he do everything twice?'

'I have no idea.'

'And why are there only scratches noted on the first incident of each pair?' Stacey asked.

'I have no idea.'

'Penn, right now you're posing more questions than you're answering.'

'I know,' he said, taking a seat and staring up at the board.

'You know, Penn, there's something not right about that list,' Alison said, breaking a Kit Kat in half. 'Look at the stages of escalation. There's a proportional elevation from one crime to the next, except for assault to murder. The leap is too big.'

'So what are you telling me?' Penn asked, frowning.

'I'm telling you that you're missing some incidents. There has to be something in between.'

# CHAPTER EIGHTY-ONE

'Nothing yet,' Kim said, checking her phone as Bryant pulled onto Russells Hall Hospital car park.

'Guv, it's been twenty minutes. Give her a bloody chance. She's gotta write the article first, and it's not like you've given her a lot to work with.'

'Doesn't normally stop her from making something out of nothing,' Kim shot back.

'I swear, sometimes…'

He left the thought hanging as they got out the car.

'You know, Frost does puzzle me,' he said as they headed across the road. 'I can never work out if she's a decent human being or a ruthless journalist with no morals.'

'Assume the latter and hope for the former,' Kim said as they headed towards the morgue. But she agreed with Bryant and often felt the same confusion.

Over the years, Frost had been a consistent pain in the backside: needling, goading, prying and pushing for information. And yet, at times she'd also done the right thing and held back from publishing information she'd unearthed or been given access to. Not least when she'd been presented with the entire social services file of Kim's childhood, gifted to her by someone who hated Kim enough to murder people in recreations of the most traumatic events in her life. It was that same case that had almost cost Alison her life.

Kim shook away the memories. Frost had handed her back the file, unread. No matter what the woman did, Kim would always remember that.

'Hey, Keats, did you miss me?' Kim asked, entering the morgue. The hours since they'd seen each other were barely into double figures.

'Only if my aim was off,' he said without turning. 'And where's Penn?'

'Bloody hell, Keats, anyone would think you didn't like me after all the years we've accrued of mutual understanding and respect, whereby we value each other's opinion and expertise.'

He turned to Bryant. 'Is she drunk?'

'Keats, I am cut to the quick,' she said, clutching her chest. There were few reasons to look forward to coming to the morgue, but baiting Keats was definitely one of them.

'Inspector, I have no idea what a "quick" is nor where it is found on the human body, but I very much doubt that you possess one.'

Ah, a point she wasn't sure she could argue with.

'I see you started without us,' she said, observing the state of the body on the table. The Y incision had been closed neatly.

'The dates and times published by the management of this establishment are offered in an advisory capacity only and are subject to change whenever I say so.'

Kim opened her mouth to retort something along the lines of his estimated times of death having that same level of fluidity but noticed the pinched expression on his face just in time.

'Something else come in, Keats?'

'Two children in a house fire.'

The room fell silent. Bad enough imagining two young souls lost in such a horrific manner, but to have to pick through their remains for answers took a stronger stomach than she had.

The retort died in her mouth.

'Okay, Keats, we'll take the edited version and let you get on.'

'Thank you. As usual, all weights and measurements will be on my official report which will be with you later today. The victim appeared to be in reasonable health and, although we're pretty sure our killer doesn't share a meal with his victims prior to death, so it's unlikely to help, her last meal was scrambled eggs and bacon.'

Normally, Bryant would have asked what kind and Keats would have shot back a response, but now was not the time. The vision of two dead children awaiting his attention was still firmly in the mind of all of them.

'Not really that helpful, Keats, to be—'

'Inspector, cases have been solved through the examination of stomach contents.' He shook his head as he launched into full lecture mode. She had five minutes spare to indulge him.

'Two men held up a coffee shop in Eugene, Oregon. The barista shot the first man, but the second got away. CCTV wasn't working, so the second masked gunman couldn't be identified. The post-mortem of the first gunman revealed food that had barely been digested, and investigators could make out a certain type of fry served by a local fast-food restaurant. CCTV checks showed both men eating a meal at that restaurant and also trying the masks on prior to the event. Gotcha.'

'Gotcha?' Kim asked, raising an eyebrow.

'Just using a vernacular you might understand.'

'Thanks for that, Keats, now—'

'No signs of a struggle with this one,' he noted, returning to the job at hand.

'We think this victim knew the killer,' Bryant said.

'But not the other two?' he queried.

Kim shook her head.

'Okay, well, as I'm pressed for time I have only one thing of interest to reveal and there'll be no dramatics.'

That was a first for the pathologist.

'Photos or actual?'

'Both,' he said, standing to the left of the trolley.

Kim followed suit and moved towards the body.

He took the right arm and turned it so the wrist was facing up.

'Scratches,' Kim noted.

'There was no watch or jewellery on this wrist, so could not have come from that and definitely inflicted after death.'

'Just like Katrina,' Bryant noted. 'But why on the wrist?'

'Easy place to get to,' Kim answered. 'It's October, it's cold, and all our victims have been heavily clothed. It's almost like he doesn't want to violate the body, but that's not what's puzzling me.'

'I've already checked and there's nothing,' Keats said, reading her thoughts.

What the hell were the scratches and why were they only present on two of the three victims?

# CHAPTER EIGHTY-TWO

Penn ended the call from the boss and wrote the word 'scratches' against the name of Nicola Southall.

'Okay, why every other one?' Stacey asked, staring at the board, hoping for some kind of inspiration.

No one answered, and she could feel a sense of frustration growing in the room.

'Anybody else feel like we have all the puzzle pieces on the table but just can't find the corners to get it started?'

Both Alison and Penn nodded at her miserably.

'We've got post-mortem reports, incident reports, letters from the killer. We've got dates of incidents we think are connected and we've got…' her words trailed away as those last words kicked at something in her brain.

'Hang on one sec,' she said, rifling for one single piece of paper.

She looked at the phone records of the phone that had called Nicola Southall the morning before.

'Penn, have you got the exact dates for all those incidents?' she asked. Just the month of the incidents he'd listed was not detailed enough for what she wanted to check.

'Somewhere,' he said. 'Why, is it important?'

'Might be,' she said, looking at the list on the board and the paper in her hands.

'Okay, what do you?…'

'Call out the date and stand by the board with your marker pen.'

'You know it's a good job I don't mind being bossed around,' he said, pushing a roll of curls out of his eyes.

'Okay, first burglary, twenty-second of May.'

'Put a tick by that one,' Stacey said.

'Second burglary, twenty-third of May.'

'Put a cross by that one,' Stacey said as he added the symbols beside the crime.

'First Peeping Tom, eleventh of August.'

'Tick.'

'Second Peeping Tom, twelfth of August.'

'Cross.'

'First assault, fifth of January.'

'Tick.'

'Second assault, sixth of January.'

'Cross.'

'First homeless murder, ninth of February.'

'Tick.'

'Second homeless murder, tenth of February.'

'Cross.'

'Our first murder, nineteenth of October.'

'Tick.'

'Our second murder, twentieth of October.'

'Cross.'

'Our third murder, yesterday.'

'Tick.'

Penn stood back.

'The second incident is always one day later than the first,' Alison noted, which was true but not what she'd been trying to establish.

She held up the piece of paper.

'The phone that contacted Nicola yesterday morning sent a text message to the unknown number on the day of every first incident in the paired crimes.' She paused for a minute, allowing that to sink in. 'But no text back, except there's one date missing,' Stacey said, following the cross-referenced tick marks. 'A text was sent from the burner phone on the third of May 2018, but we don't have an incident for that.'

'That date falls between the assault and the first murders,' Alison said, staring at the board. 'I said that was too much of a leap. We're missing another pair of incidents.'

Stacey looked again at the date on her list without a check mark.

Her heart began to race.

It was a date she already knew.

# CHAPTER EIGHTY-THREE

'It's up,' Kim said once she'd finished the update call to Penn.

'Yeah, I see it,' Bryant said, scrolling through the article.

'What the fuck?' Kim asked as she began reading. They both read Frost's online article in silence. Kim could feel her rage growing with every sentence.

'Even the bloody headline,' she spat. '"Are the police going soft?" I swear to God, I should never have trusted that woman. She's…'

'Very clever,' Bryant finished.

Those were not the words she'd been about to use.

He continued, pointing to his phone. 'She phrases it as a question and uses every word you asked her to as one side of the argument and poses cases of police brutality as the opposing side.'

'Yeah, but this is a judgement piece.'

Bryant shook his head. 'It really isn't, guv. It's a reporter trying to find an angle to write a piece you've requested, using the quotes you instructed. You didn't give her any new facts around the case to weave the quotes around. In my humble opinion, for one hour's notice she's done an amazing job.'

'Bloody hell, Bryant, start a fan club.'

'And are we really bothered that much about the content of the article? Isn't it the comments we're after?'

'Yeah and there are none of those yet,' she snapped.

'Be patient,' he said, starting the car.

Yes, that was Bryant. Always asking the impossible of her. And she had demonstrated patience. It was twenty-four hours since she'd given Reginald the two letters she'd received from Noah, yet she hadn't banged on his door at 6 a.m. this morning. Surely, for her, that was progress.

'You know, Bryant, sometimes your sensible, level-headed approach is…'

'Refreshing, reassuring and a solid, steadying influence on you.'

'Well, I was going to say annoying but if—'

Kim stopped speaking as her phone signalled an alert.

She scrolled to the comments on Frost's article.

'It's from him,' she said, seeing the name 'Noah' at the top of the post.

'Read it out,' Bryant said.

'"I for one find it refreshing to see that the police force is willing to empathise with people who are committing crimes and who may have varying reasons for the acts they are carrying out. Yes, there are criminals committing heinous acts through deviance or to seek some form of gratification, and then there are others that commit despicable acts through no fault of their own; they are compelled – one might even say forced. Some may wish to be stopped, to be understood; but even though there are two types of killer, there does remain one single commonality. They will carry on until they are stopped."'

'Jesus, guv, that's an awful lot of words in response to the article,' Bryant said.

Kim read it again as other comments began to appear.

'Yes, Bryant, it's an awful lot of words to give us one simple message.'

'Which is?'

'That he fully intends to kill again.'

# CHAPTER EIGHTY-FOUR

'The sexual assault of Gemma Hornley happened on that date,' Stacey clarified as Penn began to make changes to the wipe board, to accommodate the two new crimes.

'Now that makes more sense,' Alison said, nodding her head. 'The escalation from assault to sexual assault to murder is more logical than the leap we had before.'

'Except, we currently have a man called Sean Fellows serving a seven-year sentence for the rape of Gemma Hornley, and two days ago I was trying to get him to confess to the rape of Lesley Skipton.'

'If we're right, he's gonna be your new best friend soon,' Alison noted.

Stacey ached to pick up the phone and call Brierley Hill station or the CPS or anyone. But she couldn't. The thought of Sean Fellows spending even a moment longer in prison than necessary was abhorrent to her, but they had to be absolutely sure before they put any wheels in motion.

Stacey hit herself on the forehead.

'Bloody scratches. Gemma was the first rape victim, and after he'd finished he used some kind of knife to scratch her. Damn it, I should have…'

'You got any photos?' Penn asked, printing something off behind her.

She reached for the file that had been pushed to one side.

'Here,' she said, pushing the open file across the desk at the page he was after.

He took the file to the copier and then handed it back.

'You know something,' Stacey said as a sudden thought occurred to her, 'if we're right, I've actually spoken to two of his victims.'

Both Penn and Alison looked her way as she continued, 'And there was a great disparity in their accounts. Gemma's attack was vicious, brutal and included a knife. Lesley somehow got a sense that when he attacked her he didn't really want to do it, that there was emotion, tenderness.'

'You're kidding?' Alison asked, and even Penn was frowning hard.

'Tenderness and rape do not go in the same sentence.'

'Exactly, but where does that leave us now?'

'More confused than ever,' Alison said, turning back to her notes.

# CHAPTER EIGHTY-FIVE

Having learned from their first visit to the graphologist's house the previous day, Kim accepted Reg's wife's offer of coffee, aware that she was going to get it anyway.

'Okay, let's get started,' Reg said, taking a notepad from beside the well-watered plant.

'So we're going to start with the letter T, which shows more personality traits than any other letter of the alphabet.

'Our subject is ambitious and self-confident. The T bars are high but not right at the top. That would be overly ambitious with distant goals. The heaviness of the subject's T bars in relation to the rest of the writing indicates lower than average levels of willpower.'

'Our subject—'

'He,' Kim interrupted.

'I cannot state that,' Reg said, peering over the top of his glasses.

'You can't tell the gender?' Bryant asked.

He shook his head. 'As all people possess both masculine and feminine components, it would be at best a guess. Not unlike a painting in a gallery or a novel with an androgynously named author. You may guess at the gender, but you couldn't be sure. Similarly, we are unable to detect the age of the subject. Some people are mature for their age and others are immature.'

'Okay, please continue but refer to the subject as male.'

'As a reference, I will, but not as a judgement. The sub… sorry… he does not exhibit any traits of domination, as the T bars don't slant down. There is enthusiasm in the long sweeping T bars, but it does not demonstrate procrastination. His T's do show a measure of initiative, but the upsweep of the T bar shows self-castigation. Blame for things not his fault.'

'Really?' Kim said, sitting forward.

'He doesn't show a tendency to temper, as the T bar is not to the right of the stem. When the T and D stems are very high, there is vanity and ego has taken over; but see these loops on the T and D stems, they indicate he is sensitive to criticism.'

Kim glanced at Bryant. Thank goodness she hadn't publicly berated him as she'd been instructed.

'And this wide gap between the upstroke and the downstroke at the base of the letters T and D: he is stubborn.'

'But you said he lacked determination,' Kim said, frowning.

He thought for a moment, taking time to find an example as Henrietta brought in a tray laden with coffee, mugs and delicately cut pieces of Battenburg cake.

All three of them thanked her, and Bryant moved forward to pour from the cafetière.

Reg held up his hand to signal no coffee for him. 'Okay, look at it this way, determination is the ability to climb to the top of the tree for the best apple even though you're tired. Stubbornness is the refusal to move out of the way so someone else can't get past you and take the apple.'

'Okay,' Kim said, understanding the difference.

'Do you see here where the T and D stems are carefully retraced all the way down?'

Kim nodded.

'That tells me he possesses a high level of dignity.'

For a reason that Kim couldn't fathom, this did not surprise her despite the fact he'd murdered three women and abducted a child.

'His writing is without loops, which often shows a loner. But see here where the lines of writing run into each other. This demonstrates confusion. The absence of figure-eight formations shows there is little fluidity of thought.

'As I've said before, handwriting will show a trait but doesn't show if you use it.'

Kim nodded.

'And now, if you look at the lower case m and n, we can determine his thinking style. There are four: logical, investigative, keen comprehension and analytical. Our subject has rounded tops, which would indicate a logical thinking style, with a couple of worry loops on the m and n.'

Kim was captivated by everything he had to say, and a picture was starting to build in her mind.

'With the time given, that's all I was able to deduce on stroke formations and individual personality traits.'

Kim hid her disappointment, even though she had a feeling she was getting to know their killer well.

'The rest of the time was spent gauging his emotional response, which is critical in knowing what kind of person you're dealing with.'

He produced another sheaf of papers.

'And this is where it starts to get interesting.'

# CHAPTER EIGHTY-SIX

Penn pressed refresh on his email and, just as though he'd wished it, Keats's name appeared at the top. At 11 a.m. he'd asked for the official post-mortem report to be sent through urgently and it had been the longest fifteen minutes of the day.

He scrolled through to the attachments and stopped at the one marked 'scratches'.

He enlarged the photo and turned it around, looking at it from all four sides. There were curves and straight lines but nothing obviously legible.

'There has to be,' he said out loud. The scratches mattered. He knew it, but how was he to make sense of them?

'Has to be what?' Alison asked.

'Never mind,' he said, laying all the printed sheets in front of him on the desk.

He moved from one to the other, turning the sheets around. He could feel his frustration growing. He couldn't do it like this.

Suddenly he had an idea. All the images of the scratches had been saved in the same folder.

He clicked on each image individually, enlarged its size to where it could just fit on an A4 sheet of paper and then stood by the printer, tapping it impatiently as it printed them all one by one.

'Stace, I'm borrowing the boss's office for a minute…'

'Yeah, whatever,' she said, waving him away dismissively.

'You okay?' he asked.

'Yeah, just got the content report in from the network provider for the burner phone.'

'And?'

'The text messages are short and all eight say the exact same thing.'

'Which is?' Alison asked.

'Every single message says: "Tick".'

# CHAPTER EIGHTY-SEVEN

Reg handed both her and Bryant two sheets of paper as Henrietta entered with more coffee. Kim wasn't going to complain. Full faculties or not the woman made great coffee.

'So what are these?' Kim asked. The sheets were the letters sent by Noah, but they were now covered in straight lines rising from the base of the word, drawn so that they brushed every letter like a thousand spikes pointing in all directions.

'Emotional response. Do you see the letters at the end of each stick?'

Kim nodded as he reached to the table and produced a plastic semi-circle with a gauge running around the edge.

'Most people have a mixture of slants, so it's a matter of working out an approximate percentage.'

Kim took a look at the sequences of letters, wondering what they all meant.

'There are seven measures on the gauge; however, we're looking at five key emotional responses. The F's and the FA's show someone with little or no emotional response. They're loners and have trouble relating to others. Your typical sociopath would score highly here.'

'You can really see how someone responds emotionally from a plastic gauge?' Kim asked doubtfully. Surely the science had to be more technical than a piece of flimsy plastic.

Reg looked at Bryant. 'And here was me thinking he was the doubting Thomas.'

He reached to the side and passed a piece of paper to her colleague. 'Once I've explained it, you tell me if it's accurate, and then you can explain it to your boss.'

Bryant smiled as he looked at the paper. She looked over, but he hid it from view like a child not wanting their answers copied.

'So do you get many people who register up there in the F's?' Kim asked.

'Not many, but I do remember being asked some twenty years ago to analyse the handwriting of the staff of a medium-sized investment company. It had become clear to the owners that one member of staff was embezzling ever-increasing amounts of money and managing to hide their tracks electronically. One subject threw up flags immediately. The person concerned demonstrated predominant traits of greed, ego, ambition, ruthlessness. Their emotional responsiveness was the highest I've ever seen in the F range and signalled total emotional detachment.'

'So this person could easily be deceitful without feeling any level of guilt?' Kim asked.

Reg nodded. 'And wouldn't show a shred of emotion while discussing the issue at director-level meetings.'

'That takes a lot of neck,' Bryant observed.

'What happened?' Kim asked, wanting to hear the rest of the story.

'With the information they had, they were able to start isolating the activities of individuals. Given the ego, it was only a matter of time until she struck again.'

'She?'

'Yes, a forty-six-year-old woman who had been with the company for fifteen years. She'd been at it for pretty much the whole time. The amounts had started small but had grown with her ego and confidence.'

'And?' Kim asked.

Reg laughed. 'Yes, as a police officer I'm sure you want the rest. She was convicted of seventy-six charges and served eight years in prison. But, luckily, people like her don't come along all the time.

'The middle three sections of the gauge show the most common area into which people generally fall. AB dominant markers are cool, calm, collected, not sociopathic but very measured and reliable. You'd want an air-traffic controller to register here. BC offers more emotion: they're quick to sympathise but still logical. Total middle ground and equally balanced. Great counsellors, as they can empathise but also remain objective. The CD slant shows someone who openly displays their feelings. They get overly emotional and don't always make logical decisions. The final category is DE and E: these are people driven purely by emotion. They are warm, empathetic but they get too involved; they are prone to emotional outbursts and offer little logic in their emotional response. They could cry from a single look. They could also attack from a single look.'

He nodded towards Bryant. 'So how am I doing so far, knowing what you know?'

Bryant took a look at the piece of paper he was holding and smiled. 'Yeah, you got me. I'm sold.'

'What the?…' Kim said, grabbing the piece of paper.

She wasn't surprised to see her own handwriting sample from the day before. She was even less surprised to see she was AB dominant.

'A few more run-ins with Woody and you could always retrain as an air-traffic controller, guv,' Bryant said, taking back the page and putting it in his pocket.

Kim ignored him and looked at the two letters from Noah side by side with the knowledge of what she'd just learned. She'd make sure Bryant destroyed that page later.

'These are both showing a majority of BC's and CD's,' she noted.

He nodded. 'Absolutely, he shows emotion, he is logical, can tend to be overly emotional at times but has enough analytical ability to rein his emotions in when it matters.'

'So given everything you've observed with your T bars, loops and this, can you draw me an overall picture?' she asked, waving the two sheets around.

'To perform a full character analysis, I'd want a week, but an outline sketch of your killer indicates that he, your determination not mine, is highly intelligent with reasonable ambitions. He is confident but not conceited. He is not dominant and does not procrastinate. He is not prone to quick temper but may be sensitive to criticism. He does not have a huge ego and is dignified. He is a bit of a loner; there is confusion and there is guilt. He is in touch with his emotions, considers them, but doesn't allow them to shape his decisions.'

He paused. 'Basically, if you were to meet him in the street you'd probably call him a nice guy.'

Yes, that was the picture Kim was starting to get, which made the one question on her mind all the more puzzling.

Why was he murdering innocent women?

# CHAPTER EIGHTY-EIGHT

Penn placed every printed sheet on the floor in the boss's office. He knew she wouldn't mind her desk and chair being pushed to the wall; he needed the space to get a clearer picture.

He'd laid the pages out in date order with the oldest set of scratches first.

He stood at the foot of the seven pieces of paper, one for each set of crimes.

Immediately, he could see that they were not identical. Some had more curves and others had more straight lines. He moved around them and found commonalities in some but not all.

He took a bandana from his pocket and tied back the curls that were already breaking free from the holding gel and falling over his eyes as he looked down.

The more he observed, the more his brain became overwhelmed with data and possibilities. He moved position and looked again. Sometimes just glancing away from a situation for a few seconds was enough to offer a fresh perspective. Still nothing jumped out at him.

He stroked his chin as he realised he was trying to solve seven different puzzles at the same time.

He'd already scanned the images and googled them, trying to match them with any kind of ancient symbols or hieroglyphs, but nothing had shown as a match.

It was too much, he realised, as his eyes darted from one sheet to another. It was overload, distracting.

He gathered up the sheets and placed them on the desk, holding back the first from the burglary over ten years earlier.

His cluttered brain breathed a sigh of relief as he stared at the single sheet, but something still wasn't right. The scratches were separate but contained on one sheet of paper. There was no fluidity, no movement.

He had an idea.

'You got any scissors, Stace?' he said, stepping out of the Bowl.

'Life ain't that bad,' she said, reaching into her drawer. 'And there are easier ways.'

He took the scissors and stepped back into the Bowl.

He sat on the floor and cut out the individual scratches and discarded the surplus white paper.

His legs were formed into a v shape with the cut outs set before him.

Now he had the fluidity to move them around. Place them against each other, upside down and back to front.

He changed their position time and time again like a magician performing a hidden-object-under-a-cup trick.

'Damn it, it's still…' his words ran out of steam as he put the first and last pieces together. The arcs of the two symbols together appeared to form a perfect zero.

'Hang on one second,' he said as the other pieces slid together in his mind's eye.

He looked at what the scratches had formed.

'No bloody way,' he said, shaking his head at the simplicity.

He stood and reached for the rest of the sheets and began cutting as quickly as he could.

# CHAPTER EIGHTY-NINE

'How long's he been in there?' Kim asked, peering through the glass into her office.

Penn, sitting cross-legged on the floor, had acknowledged her presence with a wave before returning to his project.

'About an hour,' Stacey said. 'Only came out for scissors and glue.'

'What the bloody?…'

'Boss, you know what he's like trying to solve a puzzle.'

Yes, she did. And that was the only thing stopping her from storming in and kicking both him and his art project out the window.

Kim leaned against the printer cupboard at the top of the room.

'Well, I hope once he collects his Blue Peter badge he can tell us how we find our guy Noah, who by all accounts, is a jolly nice chap.'

'Who has no intention of stopping,' Alison said, having read the response Kim had screen-shotted over to her.

'But, boss,' Stacey said, 'there's been a few developments here, and Alison and I think we might be dealing with—'

'It's a score card,' Penn said, storming out of her office. 'He's keeping score with someone,' he added, crossing the office with a sheaf of papers and sitting at his desk.

'Penn, what the hell are?…'

Alison nodded her agreement. 'That would make perfect sense with the conclusion Stacey and I reached about five minutes ago.'

'Which is?' Kim asked, getting whiplash looking from one to the other.

'That we're dealing with two killers, not one.'

# CHAPTER NINETY

Kim could feel the frown forming on her face.

'You're telling me I've been gone a few hours and we've gained a killer?'

'Makes sense,' Penn said, holding the sheaf of papers while he wrote something on the board.

'Noah told us everything happens in pairs,' Stacey offered, taking the lead on giving her an explanation.

'Of those pairs on the board, the phone that contacted Nicola Southall yesterday sent a text message to another phone saying "tick".'

'Like a clock?' Bryant asked.

'Nope, I think it's tick like the game?' Stacey said. 'Which basically means you're on or it's your turn. I played it with my cousins as a kid. That message is followed by a similar crime within a day. It's like goading, a nudge. There's never any return text or communication from the other phone.'

'Okay, got that,' Kim said. 'But what about the scratches?'

'They only happen on the first of the crimes as well, just like the text message. Never the second.'

'And this is what the scratches mean,' Penn said, handing around pages of his project.

Kim looked at her page which said '2-1'.

'The numbers follow,' he said, pointing to the board. 'The burglary said 1-0; the Peeping Tom says 2-1; the assault says 3-2, and on and on. The first killer is keeping score.'

'But why isn't the second doing the same?' Kim asked.

'I think Noah is our second killer,' Alison said. 'Remember his letter came after the first murder. He didn't kill Katrina Nock at the Shop N Save, but he knew his partner in crime had done it because he got the text message. When he posted the letter, he hadn't killed yet and he was hoping you'd stop him before he killed too. He's an unwilling killer. But there was no way we could find him in time; he responded with the murder of Louise Webb-Harvey at Stevens Park, taking little Archie with him.'

'Boss,' Stacey said, reclaiming her attention, 'I spoke to both women who were allegedly raped by Sean Fellows, and though the crime was similar, the first rape was more brutal, more vicious, whereas Lesley said it felt like her attacker was going through the motions, that he didn't really want to do it.'

Kim was trying to get her head around everything she was being told. She had to admit that it was making a lot of sense. A lot but not all.

'But what I don't understand is why he doesn't stop if he doesn't want to kill people. Why does he allow himself to be goaded? That part makes no sense.'

'But it does,' Alison said. 'Noah feels compelled, as though he has no choice. Somehow his will to fight back has been broken. There is no domestic abuse sufferer who wakes up praying for a beating or a put-down. They go to work, look after kids while hiding bruises. There is a door that they can use. There is no physical barrier to prevent them from leaving. They have been conditioned to stay, to accept the abuse. It doesn't happen overnight. It's gradual.'

'You think it's a domestic abuse situation, like husband and wife?'

Alison shook her head. 'It's a rivalry situation. The similarity in victims, in crimes, the escalation. Each one is trying to do better than the other.'

'So the game—'

'It's not a game,' Alison interrupted. 'It's survival. It's matching your opponent, showing strength, besting your rival. There's no game here. It will only end when one of them dies.'

'But what kind of rivalry is as sick and enduring as this?' Kim asked, pointing towards the board.

'One that's been going on for a very long time.'

# CHAPTER NINETY-ONE

'You're saying they're related?' Kim asked, crossing her arms.

Alison took a breath. 'I can see the doubt in your body posture but hear me out. The sibling relationship is the longest we have. It's often seen as the training ground for life. How to share, take turns, love and nurture, reason, solve problems; how to cope with disappointment; how to get back up after being defeated. Constructive sibling conflict is learning how to be assertive without being aggressive.'

Kim tried not to show her reservations and waited to be persuaded. Finally, Alison had an opinion and she was going to consider it.

'Siblings have significant impact on key developmental milestones. The acquisition of interpersonal skills, cognitive development, emotional development and social understanding.'

'But there are millions of siblings out there not in competition,' Kim said.

'Look closer and you will often find some level of competitiveness, but it's usually pretty harmless and indicative of how it was originally handled by the parents.'

'Explain,' Kim said. Everyone in the room was listening.

'Okay, so siblings spend more time together during childhood than with their parents. The bond is complicated and is influenced by birth order, personality, parental treatment and experiences outside the family. It's particularly intense when children are very close in age. From the age of one, children are sensitive to differences in parental treatment, and by the age of three they have a sophisticated grasp of social rules, can evaluate themselves in relation to their siblings and know how to adapt to circumstances within the family.'

'But surely this ends as they grow up?' Bryant asked.

Alison shook her head. 'In many cases it gets worse. Fighting with siblings as a way to get parental attention may increase in adolescence. One study found the age group ten to fifteen reported the highest level of competition between siblings. It often continues into adulthood, though it can change dramatically over the years due to parents' illness or death, or marriage. Approximately one-third of adults describe the sibling relationship as rivalrous or distant.

'Each child competes to define who they are as an individual and wants to show that they are separate from their siblings. It can all be made worse by children receiving unequal amounts of attention, discipline, responsiveness.'

Kim was struggling to suspend disbelief. 'Alison, I don't—'

'I asked you to hear me out and then make your mind up. Siblings are striving for significance. Birth order is an important part of personality development, as well as age and gender. For an older sibling to respond aggressively to a new baby is a common feature of family life.'

Penn leaned forward. 'A female black eagle lays two eggs. The first hatched chick pecks the younger one to death within the first few days.'

Alison nodded. 'Among spotted hyenas, sibling competition begins as soon as the second pup is born.'

'And if we were filming an episode of *Springwatch* this would be riveting, but…'

'How about Cain and Abel, Esau and Jacob, Leah and Rachel.'

Kim frowned. 'Stace, I'm not sure the Bible is—'

'It's not just the Bible,' Alison added. 'Sisters and actresses Olivia de Havilland and Joan Fontaine were rumoured to hate each other.'

'The Gallagher brothers,' Penn added.

'Rudolf and Adolf,' Alison said.

'Who?' Bryant asked.

'Dassler. German brothers. Couldn't get along; one established Puma and one established Adidas.'

'Same businesses?' Kim asked.

Alison nodded. 'Competitive siblings will often follow each other into similar careers. Siblings tend to fight because one has displaced the other. In many Asian countries the roles are determined by cultural norms. The eldest son is expected to assume greater responsibility for the family's welfare and receives a greater share of the inheritance.

'Younger children are expected to show respect and obedience to elder brothers and sisters, and in return they expect care and guidance. In other cultures, parents include the older child in caring for the new child. Sibling rivalry is considered the most common form of bullying.'

'How does it all begin, though?' Bryant asked. 'I have siblings but we're not competitive.'

'Obviously, it starts with the parents. If there's a lack of structure, tension from above, no family hierarchy, negative attention or no attention and lack of problem-solving solutions, childhood becomes an adventure sport.'

Alison turned to Bryant. 'If one of you had a toy and the other wanted it, what was your parents' response?'

'My mum would ask us who had it first.'

'Exactly. A simple statement with guidance. The first child who had the toy gets to keep it. What if your mum had said to sort it out yourselves?'

Bryant considered. 'We'd probably have fought.'

'Exactly, rivalry has to be kept within healthy and constructive bounds. There are guidelines like ignoring tattling, don't compare, allow expression of feelings without blame, encourage sharing but don't force it, individually value and spend time with each child, decrease—'

'Enough,' Kim said, holding up her hands. 'I'm sure that checklist is on the minds of every mother struggling to make ends meet after finishing an eight-hour shift somewhere. She's probably just relieved the kids didn't kill each other.'

Kim had little time for perfect parenting checklists. For the most part, they were unrealistic, unachievable and managed only to make most parents feel inadequate.

'I'm more interested in warning signs. Is there any kind of obvious escalation?'

'Sibling rivalry is marked by elevated levels of hostility, resulting in delinquent behaviour, issues in adolescence, depression, anxiety, self-harm.'

'That's a big list,' Kim acknowledged. And one they didn't have time to work through. 'But there's one thing that still bothers me about this theory, which is that I get the sibling rivalry, I get the competitiveness of the examples you've used – but how often do these rivalries lead to murder?'

'Chaw Cheng Hong, aged twenty-six, was stabbed to death by his twenty-three-year-old brother,' Alison stated. 'A seventeen-year-old boy in Karnataka recently stabbed his ten-year-old brother to death because he was jealous of—'

'But that's violence towards each other, not towards other people. Bring me some examples of—'

'Boss, it's probably nothing, but just thinking about what Alison said about career paths and all that.'

'Go on,' Kim said, turning to face Stacey.

'Just looking at the details I dug up on Ella and Andrew Nock.'

'The husband and sister-in-law of the first victim?' Bryant asked.

'Yeah, the boss asked me to get background on Ella after she turned up at the search for Archie. There are so many similarities that it's a bit weird; they both joined the athletics club at school, went to the same college, both joined the chess club, both worked part-time in fast-food restaurants, went to the same university and both ended up in sales.'

Kim looked to Alison.

'Even for competing siblings that seems a bit much,' the behaviourist answered.

'But is it a competitiveness that could have evolved and spiralled out of control?'

Alison considered carefully before speaking.

'I think it's a definite poss—'

'Boss, I've just had another thought,' Stacey said, looking into space, appearing to do sums in her head.

'Go on, Stace, you're on a roll.'

'The first letter was sent on Monday, to you specifically?'

'Yeah, Stace, but…'

'So it had to have been posted by five thirty to reach you the following day.'

Kim frowned. Was there a point coming any time soon?

'You spoke to the press briefly on Monday but it wasn't until late in the evening.'

Kim got Stacey's point. Noah hadn't seen her on the television or in the press as being the SIO because that hadn't happened when the letter was posted, which could only mean one thing.

The letter had been sent by someone she'd already met.

Someone like Ella Nock.

# CHAPTER NINETY-TWO

'You really think one of them took Archie?' Bryant asked as they banged on Ella Nock's door for the second time.

If Ella was home, she wasn't answering her door; but with no car on the drive, she was guessing no one was there.

After the updates from her team, she and Bryant had sprinted to the car to track down the woman who had shown a little too much interest in the abduction of Archie and was definitely a controlling older sibling.

'Do you want to go in?' Bryant asked.

Kim thought for a second, shook her head and took out her phone.

Stacey answered immediately.

'Stace, I need you and Penn over at Ella Nock's address right now. Get a team to meet you here and force entry on my authority.'

'On the way, boss,' Stacey said and ended the call.

'Guv, we're right here,' Bryant said, looking back at the house.

'But Ella isn't and she's the person we need. If half of what we suspect is true, then another person is due to lose their life soon. Come on, we have to find her,' Kim said, heading back to the car. 'And the search begins with her brother.'

As they pulled away, she glanced back at the house. Her instinct told her that Archie wasn't in there; Penn and Stacey were now on their way and had her full authority to break in and search for him.

For once, she had to believe in the integrity of Noah who had assured her that Archie would not be harmed.

# CHAPTER NINETY-THREE

'Bloody hell, Penn, is this even legal?' Stacey asked as they pulled off the station car park. The car was a wreck.

She'd already spoken to Inspector Plant, who had dispatched a team to meet them at Ella Nock's address with the big red key, or enforcer as some called it, which could apply more than three tonnes of impact force from its 16kg weight.

'Oh yeah, fit and well, passed her check-up with flying colours.'

'Is the mechanic a good mate of yours?'

'You're safe, Stace, I swear,' he said, taking a sharp left. 'We'll be there in no time, and if Archie's there—'

'Do you think he is?' Stacey asked, pushing back further into the seat. She knew Penn was rushing to get them there, but she wouldn't even stake tomorrow's lunch on this car's airbags activating. 'You think Ella Nock could have taken Archie?'

'I saw her briefly at the search for Archie, and she was pretty cool and calm, but how do you tell if someone is capable of abducting a child? If emotional distance was a precursor, our boss could have a houseful.'

'Can't imagine that, can you?' she said as he crossed a green light at the very last second.

'The thing I'm not sure about is this: we know Noah has Archie, so of the pairs Noah must be doing the second kill. Noah must be the one being prodded and poked, but Ella is the older sibling, which means she would have committed the first murder of her own sister-in-law and—'

'Do we really think that Andrew Nock would have continued this bloody competition if his own wife was lying in the morgue?' Stacey asked.

'Yeah, but our theory means that if Ella didn't kill her sister-in-law, then Andrew killed his own wife. One or the other.'

'So how much faith do we have in our own theory?' she asked as he turned sharply into the street where Ella Nock lived.

He left her question unanswered as he parked the car.

As they approached the house, Stacey couldn't help wondering if somehow, despite all the evidence, they had taken the wrong direction entirely. But then again, too much of what they'd uncovered made sense.

No, they were right. They had to be.

She pushed her doubts aside as Penn gave the nod for the officers to use the big red key.

# CHAPTER NINETY-FOUR

'Have you caught him?' Andrew Nock said as he opened the door.

'I'm sorry to say we don't have a result,' Kim said, stepping into the house. 'But we are making progress.'

If Andrew wasn't involved, then she needed to manage his expectations about her visit, and if he was, she'd sent a shot across his bows that they were on to something.

'We just wanted to drop in and check on you all. Is Ella not here?' Kim asked as Andrew showed them through to the lounge, although she already knew the answer given the single car on the driveway. She only wanted to mention the woman's name. Right now, she could be sitting in front of Noah: she had to choose every word wisely.

'She was here earlier but she said something about going shopping. I'm relieved, if you want the truth,' he said, softening his words with a smile.

'The two of you are close, though?' Kim asked, seizing the opportunity.

'Sorry,' Bryant said, before sitting, 'may I use your bathroom?'

No hesitation. 'It's upstairs, first left but please be quiet. Mia's taking a nap.'

Bryant nodded his understanding. Seemed a bit late in the afternoon for a nap, Kim thought. Especially if he wanted the child to sleep at night.

'What routine?' he said, as though reading her thoughts. 'Been all over the place since… Monday,' he said, still unable to say the words. 'Late nights, early mornings. Right now, if she's tired she sleeps.'

She understood. Grief didn't wear a watch.

'How is she?' Kim asked.

'Eating now, so that's one less worry.'

'Ella must be such a help to you, but we could still arrange for a family—'

'It's fine. I don't want strangers around Mia at the minute. Ella is indeed a great help, but there are times when I really wish she'd just leave.'

'Older sisters mean well, but—'

'They always know best, Inspector. They can do everything better,' he said with an edge of bitterness in his voice.

'Like with Mia?'

He rolled his eyes. 'With Mia, with everything. She knows everything; she's always right, always does better. If I buy something, she buys the same but better. She's a competitive person.'

'Even as kids?' Kim asked.

It might appear to Andrew Nock that they were making idle conversation, but Kim was getting to ask exactly what she wanted to, given everything that Alison had told her.

'Hell, yes, Mum was a single parent and pretty much left us all to get on with it. We never found alternative ways to find resolutions and just fought for what we wanted. Bless her, our mum compared us all the time. I don't think we ever did a lot together as a family.' He smiled. 'Mum always said Ella didn't get enough time in the cot.'

'Sorry?'

Kim hoped that the conversation and memories were distracting him from the amount of time Bryant was out the room.

'As she had us, Mum would keep us in a cot in the bedroom with her. As another came along, the last one would be moved to the second room.'

Kim wondered if something that happened so young could affect a child for life. Was it perceived as rejection, causing a wedge of resentment between the eldest and the next in line?

'And what kind of things did Ella do to you when you were children?' Kim asked, trying to keep her tone light.

She was trying to prolong the time until Andrew realised the conversation had nothing to do with the case.

At that second, Bryant entered the room and offered a brief shake of the head to say he'd found nothing untoward in the time available. Her gut wasn't telling her that Archie was here either.

'Oh, she was bossy and controlling. Wanted all the good toys, wanted to be in control. Anything anyone else did had to be done better by her.'

He rolled his eyes fondly, and Kim's stomach began to turn. This man did not hate his sister. She annoyed him and frustrated him, but she was sensing there was a deep layer of love beneath his irritation. This man was not taking lives in a sick, twisted rivalry with his sister. Their whole theory had been blown to smithereens.

'Okay, Mr Nock, thanks…' her words trailed away as something occurred to her. 'You said something about "all of you"?' *As opposed to just the two of them*, she thought. They had made a foolish assumption. 'How many siblings are there?'

'Four altogether. Ella's the eldest and I'm the youngest, so I wasn't really on her radar. If you really want to know how bad she can be, you should talk to my older brother. He hates her guts, and the two of them haven't spoken for years.'

# CHAPTER NINETY-FIVE

'Nothing upstairs,' Penn said, meeting Stacey in the hallway, 'except a master bedroom, a comfortable guest room and a small boxroom for anything that doesn't fit in the other two rooms. Guest room shows no evidence of being used recently.'

Penn had trailed his finger through a very light layer of dust on the bedside cabinets.

'Nothing in any of the rooms downstairs either that I can see,' Stacey said. 'No sign of a child having been here, no wrappers or anything in the bins and they've not been emptied for a couple of days.'

Penn tried hard to quell the unease in his stomach. He remembered one time he'd been driving his mum and Jasper to a hospital appointment when his brother had an ingrown toenail. His mum had directed them by memory to the hospital, and despite her insistence he'd felt they were going the wrong way. Every metre he'd driven, he'd known he was going in the wrong direction and moving away from the destination.

That knowledge had stoked a fire of aggravation in his stomach, knowing they had an appointment to keep, that they were running out of time. And that's how he felt now.

Somehow, somewhere they had taken a wrong turn; despite all the clues and pointers, this dog was barking up the wrong tree.

'We have to be right, Penn,' Stacey said, reading his expression, 'Nothing else makes any sense.'

He knew Stacey was speaking with her brain and not with her instinct, but he couldn't quieten his own.

Maybe his gut was guiding him wrong this time. He remembered what Lynne had said to him recently. He sometimes didn't see the things that were right in front of him.

'Okay, Stace, let's swap. You take upstairs and I'll do down here. Second sweep with fresh eyes.'

Stacey nodded her agreement.

With another murder imminent and a six-year-old boy still missing, they had to try and find something.

# CHAPTER NINETY-SIX

'I'm not kidding, boss,' Bryant said as they got in the car, 'there was not one thing—'

'I know. I believe you. I don't think Andrew has hurt anyone. He's the wrong sibling. If Ella is in some kind of twisted competition, it wouldn't be with Andrew. He didn't usurp her position; it would be with Steven, the next sibling born.'

'Who also happens to be a sales manager for expensive holiday homes,' Bryant noted as Kim took out her phone. Andrew had been kind enough to offer them his older brother's phone number.

'Straight to voicemail,' she said as a low, deep voice kicked in. She ended the call.

'Want me to head towards his?—'

'No,' Kim said, tapping the phone on her knee. Andrew had told them Steven lived on the outskirts of Bridgnorth. 'Driving round trying to find siblings isn't going to help us right now.'

'But, guv, we might be on to something. We have to—'

'I know, Bryant,' she snapped. She too could feel the sand slipping through her fingers. They were running out of time. The response to the murder of Nicola Southall was imminent.

'Maybe we have to stop focusing on the players and concentrate on the game,' Kim said, picturing the wipe board back in the squad room.

'Go on,' Bryant said, switching off the engine and turning her way.

'The crimes themselves come in pairs. The assault, the rape, the murder, they're all pairs. Nicola Southall was the first of the pairing. How is our second killer going to respond? How are they going to match the challenge and in their own way surpass it?'

'Another ex-soap star?' Bryant asked.

'Perhaps, but tracking one down and…' Her words trailed away as the thoughts came thick and fast. 'Not even a soap star, Bryant, but someone in the public eye. Maybe some other kind of celebrity?'

Their eyes met as he appeared to catch up with her.

'Tyra Brooks, the footballer's mistress.'

Kim checked her watch. 'Who is due to arrive at the shopping centre in ten minutes' time.'

Bryant wasted not one minute in starting the engine and pulling away from the kerb.

# CHAPTER NINETY-SEVEN

*I can only take so much.*

*There are so many parts of my body that hurt so bad, but no one listens.*

*I'm telling tales. I'm exaggerating. I'm clumsy. I'm hurting myself. I'm a baby, but I'm not any of these things. Really, I'm not. Honest.*

*I watch as the latest red welts turn to purple bruises and the lines of scratches gurgle with little bubbles of blood that harden and rise up from the skin.*

*Every time it happens I hope it will be the last time. I pray that boredom will set in or another interest, fascination will come along. Sometimes I pray for death even though I don't know what it is. Death happened to Nanna Helen and I was told that I would never see her again, that it was final, so maybe death needs to happen to make it stop.*

*I wait for a long time but nothing changes.*

*I am scared, but I make a plan.*

*And so one night I stop myself from sleeping. I blink away my drooping eyelids and try to stop my body trembling in the dark. I have to make it better myself. I have to make it stop.*

*I know the door will open when everyone has gone to sleep.*

*It does and I am ready.*

*I know it is time to fight back.*

# CHAPTER NINETY-EIGHT

'There are supposed to be two people here,' Kim said as they approached the barrier to the service yard. The security officer was manning it alone.

'Where's the police officer?' she asked, opening her window. It was her understanding that the constable who accompanied Lena Wiley would remain at the barrier to support the security officer.

He shrugged. 'Got called away. Ran down into the building.'

'Shit, let us through,' Kim demanded.

Already, something was kicking off.

'I'm under instruction—'

'Mate, for your own safety, press that fucking button,' she snarled.

He did so and the barrier started to rise.

'Listen, I ain't taking the blame for—'

Bryant cut off the security officer's words as he drove underneath the barrier before it reached the upright position.

'You trying to write off this car already?' Kim asked, getting a closer look at the red and white striped pole than she would have liked.

He ignored her and pulled up behind the West Mercia squad car that was parked right behind the car of Kate Sewell, Tyra Brooks's agent. Damn, she'd been hoping that Tyra and her agent were running a few minutes late, but she guessed that Lena Wiley was pretty adept at keeping everyone on track.

'You're alone too?' she asked the officer at the entrance to the service corridor. Both of these points were supposed to have been double manned. Leaving people alone to manage potentially dangerous situations went against every operational order she'd ever seen, both by the police and private security companies and was not what had been discussed and agreed at the INEPT meetings.

Unless there was some kind of dire emergency.

'Yeah, Darren got called away by the boss. Something to do with an abandoned kid found wandering the service corridors.'

'Boy or girl?' she asked, holding her breath.

'Err… little boy, I think.'

Kim glanced at Bryant who looked as confused as she felt.

'Did you get a name?'

He shook his head. 'Just heard that a cleaner had found a little boy wandering around the corridors and everyone went running.'

'Some kind of diversion, guv?' Bryant asked as they entered the building and headed for the stairs.

'Fucked if I know what's going on,' she answered. The thoughts were flying around her mind as they headed up the stairs. Had their killer held Archie to use as some kind of distraction? Was that why he'd been kept alive?

Her heart was thumping as she knocked hard on the back door of the bookshop.

The door was opened by a frazzled-looking shop assistant, anxiously clutching the lanyard around her neck.

'Where's the boy?' Kim asked, showing her ID. She had many things to think about, but her overriding priority right now was identifying Archie and ensuring he was unharmed and safe.

'He's in the kid's section. The police have been—'

'Okay, thank you,' Kim said, walking through the staff area and into the rear of the store.

The shop had been closed ready for the book signing; only people purchasing the book would be allowed in to present it to the celebrity.

As she walked through the centre of the store, Kim spied the boy sitting on a beanbag in the kiddie's corner beside a staff member and a police officer on the other side.

Her heart settled as a sense of relief washed over her. It was Archie, and other than his tear-stained cheeks, he appeared to be doing fine.

'Go check on him while I track down our celeb,' she instructed her colleague. 'Get one of the security officers with him and put in a call to Robyn. She needs to know he's safe. Once you've done that, get centre security to start checking CCTV to see how he got into the service corridor.'

Bryant nodded and headed over to the child.

Although her heart had slowed down, her mind still raced ahead. It was obvious that whoever murdered Louise Webb-Harvey at Stevens Park had hung on to Archie. She had to believe that person was Noah – the person who had asked for her help – because the boy was still alive. He had listened.

If that was true, then some part of him did not want to kill again. She had to make sure no one else lost their life.

She spotted Kate Sewell at the front of the store amongst a few more staff members, but she couldn't see Tyra Brooks anywhere.

Kim was ten feet away from the crowd when her phone rang.

It was Stacey, calling from the home of their prime suspect, Ella Nock.

'Stace?'

'Yeah, boss, we got a problem here.'

Her heart thumped harder until she remembered that Archie was safe and well. Perhaps they'd found evidence that Archie had been there at some stage. 'Go on.'

'Ella Nock's just got back from Asda, and she is not very happy at all with the hole where her door used to be.'

*What the hell was going on?* Kim wondered as her thoughts went into overdrive. Their prime suspect was at home with her weekly groceries.

'Stace, tell her to put a cardigan on and get yourself and Penn over to The Book Store in Halesowen. There's all kinds of shit kicking off.'

'Kid's fine,' Bryant said, appearing beside her. 'One of Chris's guys is with him, and centre security are already looking at footage.'

Kim ended the call from her colleague as the spinning in her head grew worse.

'Noah's not Ella,' Kim said, continuing her journey to the crowd of staff at the door.

Her mouth dried as she got closer and realised the celebrity was missing.

Her eyes fixed on Kate, the woman's agent. How had the woman lost her client?

'Kate, what the hell is going on here?'

The woman's face coloured and was quickly accompanied by a guilty expression.

'What are you?—'

'You haven't realised you're missing someone?' Kim snapped. 'Where the hell is Tyra Brooks?'

Kate looked at her as though Kim had truly lost her mind.

'Tyra's out there walking the crowd. She insisted despite my—'

'Let me see,' Kim said, stepping to the front of the group.

And there she was: about forty metres away, walking the long line of customers, shaking hands and smiling.

Suddenly, the girl disappeared into the line and the line lost form. It coiled like a snake around the spot where Tyra had last been standing.

'Shit, guv, she's been pulled into the crowd,' Bryant shouted, running out of the store.

She didn't bother to answer as a few things fell into place. She looked around and assessed the situation before she turned and ran in the opposite direction.

# CHAPTER NINETY-NINE

Kim headed away from the commotion taking place at the front of the store because her gut was telling her that the real problem was going on elsewhere.

She did a quick visual check on Archie as she headed back out the way she had come in. She was pleased to see him sucking on a lollipop and reading a book with the shop assistant, with a security officer just three feet away.

She considered stopping to ask him questions, but her mind was telling her to forge ahead. None of the other murders had been lingered over and drawn out and she had no reason to think this would be any different. If she didn't find Noah soon, another person was going to die.

The second she'd seen Tyra amongst the crowds, she'd felt their entire theory crash down around her ears.

And then she'd looked around to see who was missing, and she'd thought about the escalation.

Their killer wasn't interested in a kiss-and-tell celebrity. Yes, she was current, unlike the ex-soap star, but she wasn't the most attractive target. Who better than someone who had been in the public eye and also held a senior, responsible position in the police force?

Kim raced through the back door of the store and down the stairs to the officer at the entrance to the building.

This was the last point where they'd been seen, and she'd noted the presence already of the West Mercia squad car.

She had to find them as quickly as possible, as her gut told her their killer now had in his possession a police superintendent.

# CHAPTER ONE HUNDRED

Bryant was surprised to see the guv wasn't chasing behind him as he neared the baying group that had Tyra Brooks surrounded. Not that he needed her help to break up a scuffle. Security guards watching the crowd were heading towards her as well. Damn it, where had she gone now? He briefly considered turning back to find her, but both his instincts and his training told him to deal with what was right in front of him.

'Let me through,' Bryant called out, moving people aside to get to the centre of the biggest rugby scrum he'd ever seen.

He turned to the officers who had come running.

'You two, get back to your posts and you grab a paramedic from that corridor and then get on to your boss and get him up here.'

He could do without anything else breaking out at another spot in the line.

The remaining officer turned away to use his radio as Bryant began picking up the bodies. At the bottom was the crumpled, dishevelled figure of Tyra Brooks. Bryant reached down and pulled her to a standing position.

'Are you okay?'

She nodded and smiled as Kate appeared beside them. She glanced around the crowd, her gaze lingering on one male with short, blond hair and a stud earring.

'Oh my god, Tyra, what happened?' Kate asked, horrified.

Bryant heard the concern in her voice, but he'd interviewed enough criminals in his career to be picking up something else there too.

'I d-don't know. I was just walking along the line, shaking hands when someone grabbed me and pulled me in.'

Bryant saw a thin trail of blood travelling down her neck.

'Let me take a look at that,' he said, lifting her hair. A deep scratch an inch long was reddening behind her ear lobe. A paramedic arrived and instantly moved Tyra a few feet away to check her over.

'Did anyone see who did this?' Bryant said, addressing the crowd. 'We have an injury.'

He watched as the blond-haired boy tried to slink away.

'Not so fast, fella. You seemed pretty close to the action. Did you see who did it?'

He shook his head and reddened.

'It's nothing, officer.' Kate said, pulling Tyra back towards them. 'It's just a scratch. You're fine, aren't you, Tyra?'

'I th-think so,' she said, smoothing her clothes down for the second time.

'It's just a scratch,' the paramedic said. 'I think she's fine.'

Kate nodded her agreement eagerly. 'Of course she's fine and I'm sure she wouldn't want to press charges anyway. She needs to do what we came here to do.'

Bryant was sensing a dynamic here that he didn't like.

He turned to Tyra. 'You want the paramedic to check you?…'

'I'm fine, honestly. But thank you.'

Bryant was pleased to see the colour was returning to her face.

'Okay, back into the store,' he said to the two women before placing his hand on the young man's shoulder.

'And you can come along as well.'

# CHAPTER ONE HUNDRED ONE

Kim retraced her steps back to the entrance to the building. The single security officer stood in the middle of the open double-doors.

'Everything okay?' he asked, covering his radio. She could hear a colleague of his calling for assistance. 'I daren't leave my post,' he said by way of explanation to her.

'Do not budge from this spot,' she said, frantically looking around. 'Who was here fifteen minutes ago?'

The superintendent must have been snatched right here during all the confusion.

He shrugged. 'Dunno. I was up at the barrier and there was all kinds of noise over the radio. I came down to see what was going on, by which time the area was deserted, so I stayed. Boss said this had to remain manned at all times, so I ain't shifting even if Beyoncé herself comes walking through.'

She turned a full circle and looked around again. *Where the hell could she?…*

Her thoughts trailed away as her gaze rested on the door to the old staircase.

Staircase 9.

The lock was broken.

'Shit,' she said, pushing the door wide open.

She took the stairs two at a time. The stairwell was bathed only in the emergency lighting that illuminated every twenty feet.

There were doors on either side of the disused corridor, which was around seventy feet long and grew darker and more ominous as it came to the end.

Kim moved along the corridor, slowly moving left and right to check that the padlocks to the doors were still intact.

As well as checking the locks, she paused at each one, listening keenly for any sound from within. She closed her eyes for a second, concentrating her hearing above the low hum of distant voices as people shopped in the mall. Ambient music sounded from speakers located on the other side of the wall.

As she neared the end of the corridor, she stepped into a dark corner not quite covered by the emergency lighting.

'Damn,' she cursed quietly when her foot met with a black rubbish bag that had clearly been dumped by someone. Plastic food containers spilled out into the corridor.

Only two doors remained – neither had a lock – a cleaner's room and an old plant room.

She stood between the two doors and listened, blocking out every other sound around her.

A noise to the left caught her attention. She took a step towards the old plant room. It was a sound she recognised.

She moved closer and listened again.

# CHAPTER ONE HUNDRED TWO

'Sit, and don't move,' Bryant said, closing the door to the bookshop behind him. The youth took a seat at the signing table. 'And keep your hands where I can see them.'

He placed his hands in front of him on the table beside a pile of books waiting to be signed.

'What's going on?' the store manager asked, stepping forward.

'We have a situation,' he said as Tyra rubbed the area behind her ear.

'But we need to get this—'

'It's cancelled,' Bryant said flatly.

'You can't do that,' Kate said, flicking her hair and frowning. 'You're not high enough to make that—'

'As the senior officer in attendance, I absolutely can. Dynamic risk assessments are performed on the spot. As there's been a public order offence and an injury before the event has even begun, it would be foolhardy to allow it to continue.'

'I'm really fine,' Tyra offered, glancing at the pile of books.

He understood that Tyra might want to go ahead, and he was pretty sure Kate Sewell did too, but it was no longer their call. If he allowed it to go ahead and a further incident occurred it would be his neck on the line.

'Send 'em away,' Bryant said, nodding towards the crowd outside.

Yeah, the boss might receive a couple of complaints, but she'd support his decision. The visiting celebrity had been attacked and allowing the event to continue was reckless.

Everyone stared at him as though he was going to change his mind any minute. He wasn't. And if the collateral damage of that decision was some people losing a few quid from the loss of sales of a book about an extra-marital affair, he'd sleep easily enough when he went to bed.

He stared at the door to make his point.

'I'd like your superior's name,' Kate said as her face filled with rage.

'DI Kim Stone; you've met her a few times already, and if that's not high enough, go for DCI Woodward at Halesowen police station; but before any of that I'd like you to take out your phone.'

'Excuse me?' she said as the store staff left and began talking to the waiting crowds.

Bryant held out his hand as Kate frowned.

'Just for a minute.'

She reached into her bag and handed him the iPhone that had sat beside her on the yoga mat when they'd visited her house.

'The other one,' he said, referring to the one that had sounded from the other room.

'I don't have another one,' she lied.

He considered continuing this conversation down at the station, but he needed to resolve this right now and find the boss.

He turned to the kid sitting at the table.

'Give me your phone, buddy.'

He hesitated.

'Right now, you're in a lot less trouble than she is.'

The kid took out his phone and opened it with his thumbprint.

Bryant scrolled through the messages and shook his head, returning to the call register. He pressed on the third one down.

Kate's bag began to ring.

'That's the phone I was asking for.'

'I don't get it,' Tyra said. 'You two know each other?'

'Not only do they know each other, but this lady, who has been taking such good care of you, instructed this fella exactly what to do.'

Tyra shook her head. 'No, you've got it wrong. She would never—'

'Arrange someone to physically assault you? I'm afraid that's exactly what she did, Ms Brooks. More hype, more publicity, more bookings, more money.'

Genuine tears filled Tyra's eyes as she turned to her agent. 'How could you?'

Bryant watched as the ruthless woman considered finding some kind of lame explanation. She realised she couldn't and just shrugged in response.

'Tyra, if you lay down with dogs, you are going to get fleas,' Bryant said, putting both phones on the signing table. 'This will be continued down at the station.'

Now, he just needed to find someone to stay with the three of them.

'Hey, Bryant, need some help?' said a familiar voice from behind.

'Penn, thank goodness,' he said, looking around at his colleague.

'Stace has gone straight to the control room to check on CCTV.'

Of course she had.

'Right, don't let these folks out of your sight until I get back.'

Penn looked around. 'Where's the boss?'

'That's exactly what I want to know,' he answered as he turned and left at speed.

# CHAPTER ONE HUNDRED THREE

In the few seconds it had taken for her to clarify the source of the noise, the week had flashed before her eyes and information gleaned from people around her started to fall into place.

She heard the crackle of the radio and pushed the door open.

'You don't want to do this, Chris,' she said to the security manager, who was sitting beside the bound and gagged superintendent. A knife glinted in his hand.

A flutter of the police officer's eyelids confirmed the woman was still alive.

Chris stared at her as she continued to edge into the room, but not too far. She didn't want to spook the man into doing something rash, and if she could keep the door open, anyone in the corridor would see the shaft of light coming from the room.

'You don't understand.'

Kim was surprised at the lack of emotion in his tone. She heard nothing but resignation. As though he'd already committed the crime and was holding out his wrists for the handcuffs. She had to steer him away from that mode of thought, or the act of using that knife wouldn't matter because in his mind he'd already done it.

'It doesn't have to end like this, Chris. She's still alive,' Kim said. 'Just like Archie; you kept him alive. No one else has to die.'

Lena's eyes flicked between the two of them, and Kim couldn't help wondering if the woman wished she'd have been a bit nicer to him earlier in the week. Maybe then she wouldn't have made herself into such a target.

'You don't get it,' he said, losing patience.

She lowered herself to the ground. She had to create an intimacy with him, get him to focus his attention on her and not his hostage. The blade was moving perilously close to the tender skin of her wrist.

'I do, Chris, I get it,' she said, sitting on the floor. In doing so, she'd had to let the door close behind her, aware that there were no breadcrumbs to her current location. No one knew where she was in staircase 9. Previous experience told her there was no signal beyond corridor 8.

'I understand that you didn't want to hurt anyone; that you wrote to me after we met at the EPT briefing. You begged me to stop you from killing. You didn't want to kill the woman in the park, but you'd been challenged, goaded into doing it.'

He nodded. 'It's there, you see, the voice. It's in my head, always there, telling me what to do. I thought that once I fought back it would get better, but it got worse.'

The way he closed his eyes as though blocking out the sounds caused her to wonder if they'd been right in the first place: the voices were in his head. It wasn't the first time she'd dealt with a split personality, but that time only one of the personalities had been doing the killing. The other had been unaware.

'The messages,' he said. 'I kept getting messages. I'd think it was all over and then I'd get another message.'

Could he have been sending the messages to himself?

'The crimes escalated, didn't they, Chris?' she asked. 'It started with crimes that didn't hurt anyone and then it turned violent. The sexual assault of Lesley Skipton was you, wasn't it? She was leaving the music festival: an event that you managed,' Kim said, remembering the details of the crimes. 'Rhona Stubbs, the homeless lady you killed, was close to a housing development that was being looted. The site was being guarded by your team.'

These were the facts that had run through her mind outside the door, along with the fact that Noah had to have been someone she'd met before the press conference on Monday. The letters had indicated to Reginald that the person would appear to be a decent, upstanding guy: almost the exact words Bryant had used to describe this man. They had focused all their attention on Ella, and they'd been looking the wrong way the whole time.

'I'd had the text and I wanted you to help me. I trusted you to help me. I knew you were the only one to stop—'

Chris stopped speaking as Lena made a choking sound.

Shit, this was taking too long. The woman was struggling to breathe.

Kim had to convince him to take the gag off her. Right now, she didn't care that she was a police superintendent, and an unpleasant one at that. She was a victim in very real danger of losing her life.

'Shut up,' Chris spat at the officer. Rage burned in his eyes.

'Chris, it's not too late. No more innocent people have to die,' she pleaded.

His expression changed to disappointment mixed with regret, and she could tell she was losing the bond she'd been trying to establish.

'I thought you understood.'

Damn, what had she said wrong?

The knife in his hand nicked at the skin on Lena's wrist. Blood appeared instantly.

'Please, be careful, Chris, you could cause some damage there,' she warned. The tip of the blade was perilously close to the artery.

His eyebrows drew together.

'Why would I be careful when it's what she's been doing to me all my life?'

# CHAPTER ONE HUNDRED FOUR

'Tell her, go on, Lena, tell her,' Chris screamed, loosening the gag.

Lena gasped before shaking her head, confused.

'I have no clue what you're talking about, Mr Manley. I arrived here with Tyra Brooks, there was some kind of commotion and you dragged me up here.'

Kim looked from one to the other. What the fuck was going on?

Lena turned her way. 'Officer, I suggest you disarm this—'

Kim ignored her. 'Hang on. Chris, are you saying Lena Wiley is your sister?'

He pointed the knife at her and nodded. 'It has to end, and it will only end in death.'

'Don't be so ridiculous,' Lena cried, having found her voice. 'You're out of your mind. You've fixated on me. Don't believe a word he—'

'I believe him,' Kim said quietly as the final pieces fell into place.

The first murder and the third murder had taken place on Monday and Wednesday. Both days that Lena had been in the area for the INEPT meetings. Her derision of Chris at the meetings had nothing to do with viewing him as inferior. She simply hated him.

Lena had been in close protection about ten years ago before joining the police, Chris had told her. She must have helped protect Nicola Southall during the death threats. That's how she had her phone number.

'You called Nicola and arranged to meet. You knew she'd see you because you'd protected her from abuse and threats in the past.'

Kim remembered what Alison had said about competitive siblings ending up in the same line of work. Lena was a police officer and Chris had tried. He had been set to join the force until that one incident of public order had ended that career path; instead, he had made a career in private security.

'Nicola who?' Lena asked, keeping up the pretence, but Kim could see the wavering in her eyes.

'You've been goading him the whole time. Using your scratches to keep score, to flaunt in his face that you were ahead and then sending him a message to goad him into following suit.' She turned to Chris, the knife forgotten for the moment. 'What the hell happened to you as kids?'

She glanced between the two. Lena's gaze was no longer filled with confidence. She had put more together than she'd imagined.

'I happened,' Chris said. 'I was born, and Lena didn't like that very much. She's abused me since I can remember. She was almost three when I was born, pinching and scratching me when I was small. As I got older, she'd creep into my room at night to hurt me. She'd put a pillow over my face to try to kill me.'

He glanced at her as though waiting for some kind of rebuttal. She simply stared at him with cold hatred in her eyes.

'Our parents were not the loving or demonstrative kind, but they did like babies. When I came along, Lena got no attention at all. I tried to tell them what she was doing, but they wouldn't listen. They called me careless and clumsy and almost convinced me I was hurting myself. They didn't want to believe they had a child capable of violence and hate at such a young age, and if they did believe me they hoped it would just sort itself out.'

'So what did you do?' Kim asked, wondering what he could have done as a small child being physically abused by his sister, with parents who turned a blind eye.

'One night I waited for her to come and I punched her in the face. I thought it would stop. I thought that if I stood up to her she would leave me alone, but she didn't. The torture just changed, and as we grew up we competed for attention, stupid stuff at first but Lena would always raise the stakes. She'd do something and then tick me for my turn.'

'But couldn't you just walk away?'

He shook his head. 'No, because I want to win too. I have to beat her. I have to show her she's not in control, that she's not better than me. All my life she's been there, in my ear, haunting me. It'll never end as long as she's—'

'Oh, you pathetic piece of shit,' Lena said in a tone filled with boredom.

Kim wondered if she'd forgotten who was holding the knife.

'You are ridiculous. You've always been a follower. You're weak and have no will of your own. I define you, you ineffectual prick. Everything you have is because of me. I made you. I moulded you. It's beyond ridiculous that you would ever consider hurting me. You think you want this to stop? I'm the only person in your life that has meaning. No wife, no girlfriend and no real friends, because you're invisible, you're nothing. No one ever remembers you. You're like a glass of water: colourless, tasteless, devoid of personality and totally forgettable.'

Kim watched silently as every barb hit its mark. Still he didn't use the knife. She could see the control that Lena had over him. Right now, this was between the two of them and Kim had no clue how to stop him using the weapon in his hand.

Lena continued, 'I validate you, you pointless wanker. Everything you've achieved was because of me. You've followed and tried to compete on every level. You think you're better than me when all you do is equal what I've done. You never get ahead.'

'I took a little boy,' he said in a childlike voice.

'And brought him back unharmed, so what was the fucking point in that?'

As the exchange continued, Kim saw two things: the way their lives had always been and something else – Chris was also seeking approval from his older sister. And then she got it: if Lena was the only person who had paid him attention as a child, it was her attention he craved now, as well as her approval.

And if Lena had the sense to understand that, there was a chance they could all leave this room unharmed.

She now understood that Chris had reached out to her specifically because she'd stood up to his sister in that first meeting. It was what a small part of him wished he'd done years ago.

Kim was silently praying that Lena would use her influence to ensure everyone's safety, because right now no one knew where any of them were.

'You've never surprised me, Chris,' Lena said with a heavy sigh. 'You've never exceeded my low expectation of you. Not once have you taken the initiative and proven yourself worthy of any affection or respect.'

Yes, she got it, Kim realised. Lena knew what he wanted from her. She could use that influence to ensure everyone's safety. *Tell him to drop the knife*, Kim thought. *He'll listen.*

'You've never liked me,' Chris whined.

'You've never given me a reason to. You're vanilla, Chris. You're boring and predictable. You don't take risks. You allow yourself to be led, to be manipulated. You're pointless. Right now, you have the chance to do something spectacular and you don't even realise it.'

This did not sound like she was trying to get him to put the knife down. This sounded more like a goad, a call to action and somehow that action was going to include her.

Some people used their power for good and others did not.

Kim knew she had to somehow break this bond.

'Don't listen to her, Chris,' she said.

He glanced her way, as though he'd forgotten she was there.

'It's your one chance, brother, to show me what you're made of. You wanted a police officer in the public eye. Well, there's one right there. She's alone. Kill her and we get to leave and no one—'

'Ignore her, Chris. She's doing what she's always done. She's trying to—'

'You could give us back our freedom, Chris. Let her live and we both spend the rest of our lives in prison. I'll be protected, but a pretty boy like you will be gang—'

'Chris, wake up,' Kim snapped, trying to remove that picture from his mind. 'She's using you to get out of facing justice for all that she's—'

'How could I not respect the man who set us free?' Lena asked, shouting over her.

Damn. Lena was offering him everything he'd ever wanted from her. Attention, respect, even affection.

All Kim could offer him was a lifetime in prison. She was losing the battle, but she had one last shot, she realised, as he moved to the centre of the room at equal distance from them both, demonstrating that Lena had turned his attention her way.

She was sitting against the double doors, and she knew there was no way out. Her only choice was to play the same game as his sister.

'Chris, you came to me,' Kim said gently. Empathy and understanding had saved Archie's life. If she tried to shout above Lena, there would only be one winner.

'There's a part of you that wants this to end. Inside—'

'Don't listen, Chris. She knows she's in danger. She knows she's not going to—'

'Inside, there's a part of you that wants to sever that control. You see, I know things about you that your sister doesn't.'

He turned his attention towards her.

'I know that you didn't want to hurt any of these people,' she said, remembering the graphologist's report. 'You are a decent—'

'Oh, shut the fuck up,' Lena cried. 'Just do it, Chris. For once you have the power—'

Kim tried to tune her out as she fought to hold his attention.

'You are decent and have integrity. You mourn for your victims; you empathise with—'

'Do it, Chris,' Lena shouted. 'Just take the knife and do it. How could I ever beat you? Finally, you will have won.'

Chris moved towards her.

'Don't do it,' Kim said, trying to remain calm. 'If you do, you'll never be free of her and—'

Suddenly, he lunged towards her holding the knife forward. She saw the blade heading towards her chest and the determined look in his eyes.

Lena had said the magic words. She had told him he could win.

Kim threw up her arms to shield herself from the knife.

Lena chanted in the background as Kim slunk down to the ground and writhed around to avoid his hand.

He used his free hand to grab her hair and pull her head down to the cold concrete floor. She kicked out, but he had moved around her body so her feet were meeting with thin air. She tried to sit up, but his hand grabbed her around the throat and kept her still.

She fought for breath while trying to push him away and keep her chest covered.

He raised the knife and looked into her eyes.

'I'm sorry but I have to win.'

She watched in horror as the knife travelled down towards her heart.

She opened her mouth, but any words were cut off as a searing pain thundered into her head and the world went dark.

# CHAPTER ONE HUNDRED FIVE

'What the fuck just?…' Kim asked, opening her eyes to a flurry of activity. Instant panic engulfed her at the figure leaning over her. Chris and his knife heading towards her chest.

The man was dressed in green.

She swatted away the paramedic. 'Get off me,' she said, trying to sit up.

'Just need to check—'

'She's fine,' Bryant said from behind.

'Jesus,' she said, rubbing the top of her head.

'You were pretty close to the door, guv,' Bryant offered.

'You did this to me?'

'Better than a knife in the heart, but that's okay, you can thank me later.'

Her second attempt at sitting up was more successful.

'What the hell happened?' she asked as two police officers hauled Christopher Manley to his feet.

Bryant turned away as he helped Lena Wiley to her feet. 'Are you okay, Superintendent? Let me—'

'Bryant, cuff the bitch,' she said as everything came rushing back to her.

Her colleague turned with a horrified expression. 'Guv, that bang to the head—'

'Trust me, Bryant. She's Chris's sister. Cuff her.'

He hesitated for just a second before motioning another two officers in from the doorway. 'You heard the DI. Put the cuffs on her.'

As they moved into the room, he came to stand beside her.

'How'd you find me?' she asked, rubbing her head.

'Asked the officer downstairs if he'd seen you, and we both started searching. Knew you couldn't be far,' he said, holding up his phone. I tried to call, and it went straight to voicemail. You were in a black spot. Saw the spill of the rubbish bag in the corridor. I shoved open the door as I heard the superintendent shouting something, which I'm sure you'll explain to me later once you're feeling better.'

Kim nodded and swallowed down the nausea as the cuffs cracked around Lena's wrists. Kim hauled herself to her feet. After what she'd witnessed, she wanted to face this woman head-on.

Their eyes met as Lena drew level with her.

'I won, you know,' Lena said. 'He was going to kill you.'

Kim marvelled at the triumph in her eyes. Even now, when she was being led away to police custody, her focus was still on the game.

'What exactly did you win, Lena?' Kim asked. 'You can't beat someone who isn't even in the game. You've thrown away your whole life to triumph over someone who didn't ask to be born, just because you were jealous. I once respected you as a strong woman who had succeeded in this difficult environment, but now I see that Chris would have been a much better addition to the police force than you. Somehow, he managed to keep some shred of decency even while committing horrific crimes. He is human but you are not.'

Her face reddened. 'You can't speak to—'

'Oh shut up, I'm not finished yet and you'd better get used to not having the last word. I saw with my own eyes how you've manipulated and shaped him. Innocent people have died, and a young boy terrified and taken away from his family in your efforts to be the best, but there is something so incredibly twisted and warped that you don't even realise yourself.'

'Like what?' Lena said, sticking out her chin in defiance of any insight Kim had to give. There was nothing this woman didn't already know.

'Everything you said about your brother is equally if not more true of you. You're pathetic and desperate because you always kept it going. Chris would have stopped but you were always the first. You couldn't let it go. It was you who wanted the attention, the love, the approval from your brother, so fill your boots with triumph: it's a victory you can savour and enjoy for the next twenty to thirty years.'

'Oh, we'll see about—'

'Fuck off, Lena. You're not in control now, and I don't want to look at you any more.' She nodded to the officers. 'Get her out of my sight.'

'Okay, I think I'm starting to catch up now,' Bryant said as Lena was led from the room.

'Not before time,' she said, leaning against the wall. The room that had emptied around them was now spinning every ten seconds or so.

'Go on, guv, it's just us now,' Bryant said. 'You can admit it. I saved your life, didn't I?'

'By knocking me out cold?'

'Yeah, but you're alive, so go on, just between us, you can say it.'

Oh, how he wanted to hear those words. Such a simple gift for a simple man.

'Bryant, you…' she paused, '…could have got here a bit sooner.'

He laughed out loud and looked to the back of her head.

'Yeah, definitely no permanent damage.'

She let go of the wall and took a few tentative steps as her aching head caught up with her movement.

Bryant walked beside her, knowing better than to offer her help. The dizziness had passed, but the rage had not.

She now had to tell three families they'd lost loved ones all because of a fucking game.

# CHAPTER ONE HUNDRED SIX

'You okay?' Kim asked Alison as they got back into the car.

'Allergies,' the behaviourist said, wiping a tear from her eye.

'Nothing to do with seeing Archie surrounded by a ton of Lego while his mum beamed with love and relief from the couch.'

'Nope, nothing to do with that at all.'

'You helped make that scene,' Kim said.

Kim had been prepared to visit all three families alone but had decided to bring Alison along for two reasons.

'I know why you asked me to come,' Alison said, cutting into her thoughts. 'You think I'll return to active service.'

Kim shook her head. 'That's your decision. I asked you to come so you could explain the dynamics of sibling rivalry, to offer the families some understanding of what happened.'

Kim knew that nothing either of them said was going to ease their grief, but she and Alison had at least been able to offer peace of mind that the people responsible had been caught.

'And that's the only reason?' Alison asked, putting her handkerchief away.

'Okay, I also wanted you to see first-hand the fruits of your labour. I know I've been hard on you this week and you didn't have to take even a minute of it, but it yielded results.'

She'd also wanted Alison to witness the comfort and closure her findings would bring to the families of the victims, that her input had value and that she could make a difference. She sincerely hoped the woman would reconsider her role in active duty and once again consult for teams that would benefit from her expertise.

'My head wasn't in the game as much as it should have—'

'I'm not accepting that, Alison. It was you who understood the intense, consuming kind of rivalry we were looking at, and I don't think any one of us would have made that connection. If you want to stay away from consulting, do it because it's not right for you or because you want to focus on something else, but not because you're going to convince yourself you're shit at it. You're not.'

Alison shook her head in wonder. 'Who'd have thought after all these years I'd hear those words coming from you?'

'Yeah, well, enjoy them cos you won't hear them again. You're not so bad for a profiler.'

'Behaviourist,' Alison snapped as she had during their first meeting.

They both laughed.

'So do you think she's going to crack?' Alison asked, and Kim didn't need to ask who she meant. It was the second day of questioning and already Chris had spoken freely, against the instruction of his brief, unlike Lena Wiley, who had not yet uttered a single word. And despite Bryant and Penn's best efforts, Kim suspected this was not going to change.

Kim shook her head in response. 'What would she even say in defence of her actions? Would she deny the picture Chris has painted of systematic verbal, physical and psychological abuse carried out in the absence of parental control?' she asked.

Would she deny the cuts and bruises, the pinches and the slaps? Would she refute his claims that she'd tried to smother him with a pillow or hold his head under the bath water?

'The physical injuries don't even come close to the psychological damage she's done to him over the years,' Alison said as Kim started the car.

The methods of which Kim had caught a glimpse. That level of degradation – the insults and put-downs over the years, with nothing positive on the other side to even attempt to offer balance – was far more damaging than any violence.

'Chris has barely even mentioned his parents,' Kim said. 'It's almost as though they didn't exist.'

'If they were remote and distant, then really Lena and Chris's existence became all about each other,' Alison explained. 'If rivalry was brewing from an early age and went unchecked by the parents, where are the boundaries?' she asked, speaking rhetorically. 'Our boundaries come from our parents and without them we flounder and make up our own.'

'Chris has explained how Lena had always been competitive, always goaded him to prove his worth but that it grew worse when their parents died together in a hotel fire in the Philippines.'

Alison nodded. 'That's often a catalyst for sibling rivalry to escalate. In Lena's mind, her chance of gaining approval and attention from them was lost for ever and for that she blamed Chris.'

Throughout his interviews, Chris had told his own story and, in doing so, had revealed Lena's. Inadvertently, he had painted a picture of a three-year-old child who had been simply cast aside when her brother had been born; she had resented him from the moment she'd set eyes on him. In her own simplistic way she had just wanted him to go away. She had wanted things to go back to normal. When her efforts failed, she had convinced herself she needed to be better than Chris at everything to regain her parents' affections. She had to win. But eventually Chris had decided to fight back, and the war between the two of them was born because he had to win too.

Whatever had twisted Lena as a child, Kim could feel little sympathy for the woman. She herself had once been an older sister. Only for six short years and only senior by the ten-minute head start she had on her twin, and yet her only instinct with Mikey had been to protect him, to love him.

Lena's acts against innocent people had been more brutal, more aggressive than those of her brother. There had been a part of her that had enjoyed causing harm and taking life. She didn't sense that lack of humanity from Chris.

There was no doubt that he had matched Lena crime for crime. He'd admitted every one and handed over the phone to which Lena had sent her inciting messages, but she detected no joy or achievement in his acts. He had reached out for help and had listened when she'd asked him to spare the boy.

When asked, Chris had admitted that he'd never intended to take Archie after killing his mother. In his mind, it was some kind of victory, something that Lena hadn't done; in some twisted way he hadn't wanted to leave the boy alone.

Once back at Chris's spacious home in Malvern, Archie had been taken care of. Chris had fed him, washed and dried his clothes and entertained him with toys and gadgets. He admitted that at one point he had not known what to do with the child and had considered killing him, but Kim's plea to spare the boy had reached him. When Lena killed Nicola Southall, he'd formed a plan to get her, using Archie as a distraction.

Through gentle questioning, Archie had confirmed Chris's story, and other than missing his family and being confused, he had not suffered while in the man's care.

'You had to do a bit of work to bring Ella Nock round, didn't you?' Alison asked as Kim pulled up at a red light.

'Definitely not my number one fan,' Kim admitted.

She'd had a fair bit of explaining to do to the woman: both about her front door and her suspicions. Ella had been somewhat appeased when Kim had offered to pay for the damage out of her own pocket. In fairness, the woman's main concern had been for Archie. After spending an hour with Andrew, Mia and Ella,

Kim could see how close the family was. Yes, she was bossy and forthright with a hint of dominance, but it was clear that she felt nothing but love for her niece and her younger brother.

Ella had been more gracious than Kim would have been if the roles had been reversed.

'What's happening with Sean Fellows?' Alison asked. 'Given that there's no confession from Lena yet about the sexual assault on Gemma.'

'Both Brierley Hill and the CPS are happy to move forward with the process, taking into account the lack of evidence against Sean Fellows and based on the assurance that Chris will testify against his sister.'

Stacey had been on the phone to Brierley Hill the second that Chris had admitted to the sexual assault of Lesley Skipton, in order to set the wheels in motion to get Sean Fellows released from prison.

Stacey had been right: the man currently inside Featherstone had neither attacked Lesley nor Gemma.

Unfortunately, the paperwork and process did not facilitate an immediate release for Sean, but they were talking days not weeks.

'Next left,' Alison said as Kim turned right towards Lutley Mill.

'Just pull in there,' she said, pointing to a parking area in front of a small factory that had been converted into apartments.

'So no more killers to profile, no more bollockings, no more walking around the police station and no more families to visit. Does that mean we're done?' Alison asked with a lopsided smile.

Kim genuinely hoped that the woman would give serious thought to returning to active duty, especially after what she'd witnessed today, but it was a decision she would have to make for herself.

'Yes, Alison, we're finally done,' she said as Alison got out of the car.

'Until the next time,' Kim shouted out the window before driving away.

# CHAPTER ONE HUNDRED SEVEN

Stacey collected herself before she picked up the phone in the Bowl. Her boss had offered her the privacy of her office to make a call that had been especially set up. She had been content for the news to be communicated via the normal channels, but the boss had insisted she make the call herself.

She keyed in the mobile phone number she'd been given. It was answered on the second ring.

'Hello,' said a deep voice that did not fit with the person she knew was holding the phone.

'Nathan?' she asked, checking that she was speaking with the young prison officer she'd met the other day.

'Speaking.'

'It's Detective Const—'

'I know. I've been waiting for your call. He's right here and he has no idea.'

Stacey felt a shiver of anticipation run over the bare flesh of her arms as she heard the phone being passed to Sean Fellows.

'What the fuck is?…'

'Sean, it's Stacey Wood,' she said, straight away. She was sure he was unused to being passed the mobile phone of a prison officer. 'Remember, I came to speak to you earlier in the week.'

'Yeah, I remember but this is a bit suss. You got a thing for me or something?'

She laughed. 'No, Sean, you're not my type, mate.'

'Shame,' he said, and she could imagine the shrug of the shoulders. 'So what the?…'

'Remember when you told me you were innocent?' she asked.

'Oh yeah, course I do. You gave me the same look as every other c… bugger I've told.'

Stacey appreciated his effort in minding his language.

'Well, turns out you were right.'

Ten second silence.

'You shitting me?'

'No, Sean. It's true.'

'So you ringing to tell me you believe me?' he asked suspiciously, as though she was playing some kind of joke on him.

'Oh, I believe you all right, Sean, seeing as we now have in custody the person who actually did it.'

Silence.

More silence.

'Sean, are you there?'

'Seriously, are you shitting me?' he asked with a tremble in his voice.

Stacey felt a tear prick her eye. 'No, I'm not shitting you. We know you're innocent, the victims know you're innocent and as soon as the paperwork is sorted you can get out of that place and tell anyone who will listen that you're innocent.'

'I don't… I mean… I just… is this real?' he asked, and Stacey could tell that the man was in tears.

She felt the emotion gather in her throat. 'Yes, Sean, it's real. You're getting out.'

'It's not doing the time, you know. I can cope with that. It's…'

'Being convicted of something you didn't do. Being labelled a rapist instead of the cocky bleeder you really are,' she said with a smile in her voice.

'Not so much any more,' he said hoarsely.

That arrogance had got him convicted.

As Sean pulled himself together on the other end of the phone, she took a moment of pride at her own part in this process. Even without Penn's prompting she had taken the case because of the injustice done to Lesley Skipton. She couldn't have known that following the thread of that case would lead to an even greater injustice. Most police officers she knew objected equally to the right person not doing the time as they did to the wrong person doing time. It wasn't numbers they sought but justice.

'So, Sean, take care and stay good, yeah?'

'Will do, Stacey. And… thank you.'

Stacey ended the call, wiped a tear from her eye and headed out of the boss's office.

# CHAPTER ONE HUNDRED EIGHT

Kim stood at the window of the squad room looking out of an empty office on to the car park below. Most of her team was enjoying some time at home after a physically and emotionally exhausting week. Most of her team, but not all.

Her own debrief of the case with Woody had ended only moments earlier and many subjects had been covered.

After congratulating her, Woody had informed her that West Mercia were drafting lengthy press statements that both appeared to offer support to their superintendent while putting distance between them at the same time. Kim was unsure how they were going to manage both simultaneously, but she also knew that the police force itself couldn't find Lena Wiley guilty before a jury had and so would ensure extensive legal advice had been sought before uttering one word.

The TV news was over it, but every local newspaper servicing both West Midlands and West Mercia was still spewing out the gory details and wringing every last morsel of life from the story. Frost was no exception about which Kim was not surprised. Kim knew the woman possessed some measure of morals, but she also knew she had a boss and readers to satisfy.

During the meeting with Woody, the knowledge that she had been right in her approach in reaching Christopher via the local media had hung in the air between them. Neither of them had mentioned it, but both she and Woody had come to the agreement that given recent events, most specifically her inability to follow an instruction she thought was wrong, promotion to DCI was not a viable prospect right now. Something Kim had told him at the beginning of the week.

Then they had briefly discussed career progression within her team, outlining potential opportunities for Stacey in particular.

And it was with Stacey that her thoughts had stayed. There had been easier cases to look at in the shuffles, but Stacey had chosen the toughest, most complicated case, which spoke volumes about the woman and police officer she had become. She was about to embark on a new stage of her life with her marriage to Devon, about which she couldn't now shut up since Penn had offered Jasper's services to make them a wedding cake.

She had grown in both ability and confidence far beyond Kim's expectations. There was no case they worked where Stacey didn't impress her just that little bit more, she thought as the officer herself came into view on the car park.

Stacey had asked if she could bring in Lesley Skipton to meet with Chris, if both parties were agreeable. She had felt it would offer Lesley some closure, some understanding of why she had felt certain emotions in connection with her attack, maybe even give her the chance to move on.

All parties had agreed, and the meeting had just taken place.

Stacey had no idea that Kim was watching as she hugged Lesley and then put her into a waiting taxi.

Kim knew that Stacey had no idea how far she'd come in the years they'd worked together; she had grown drastically in her ability to feel empathy, her humanity, her willingness to go a step beyond. She was a police officer to her core, a bloody good one, and she didn't even know it.

Woody knew it and she knew it, and as Kim watched the detective constable wave away the taxi, she knew it was time for things to change.

# A LETTER FROM ANGELA

First of all, I want to say a huge thank you for choosing to read *Deadly Cry*, the thirteenth instalment of the Kim Stone series and to many of you for sticking with Kim Stone and her team since the very beginning. This was a book I enjoyed writing from the moment I picked up the pencil and I hope you enjoyed it too.

If you did enjoy it, I would be forever grateful if you'd write a review. I'd love to hear what you think, and it can also help other readers discover one of my books for the first time. Or maybe you can recommend it to your friends and family… And if you'd like to keep up to date with all my latest releases, just sign up at the website link below.

*www.bookouture.com/angela-marsons*

The idea for this book was sparked while writing one of the earlier novels where sibling rivalry was touched upon in relation to child genius. The thought stayed with me and grew as questions began to form. What are the long lasting effects of such rivalry that starts at an early age? What can prompt fierce competition between people who grow up together? How far and how deep can such rivalry go?

As with all my books the more I read about the subject the more intrigued I became with the psychology behind this particular family dynamic.

In addition, I've wanted to explore the science of graphology. I have had my own handwriting analysed twice over the years and have found the results to be frighteningly accurate.

I'd love to hear from you – so please get in touch on my Facebook or Goodreads page, Twitter or through my website.

Thank you so much for your support, it is hugely appreciated.
Angela Marsons

www.angelamarsons-books.com

angelamarsonsauthor

@WriteAngie

# ACKNOWLEDGEMENTS

As ever, my first thanks are to my partner, Julie. I remember a time during this book that I spent hours upon hours grappling with a part of the plot that wasn't working for me. I didn't want to exclude it but I also couldn't make it work. With utter despair I asked Julie for a meeting (coffee on the patio) so I could share the misery I felt at what I was going to have to do. She listened, and nodded and then made one suggestion that solved everything and sent me hurtling back to the writing desk with renewed energy and enthusiasm and a solution to my problem. This one episode is symbolic of her involvement in the books and an example of why she truly is my partner in crime.

Thank you to my Mum and Dad who continue to spread the word proudly to anyone who will listen. And to my sister Lyn, her husband Clive and my nephews Matthew and Christopher for their support too.

Thank you to Amanda and Steve Nicol who support us in so many ways and to Kyle Nicol for book-spotting my books everywhere he goes.

I would like to thank the team at Bookouture for their continued enthusiasm for Kim Stone and her stories and especially to Oliver Rhodes who gave Kim Stone an opportunity to exist and to Jenny Geras who continues to champion the stories in his stead.

Special thanks to my editor, Claire Bord, whose patience and understanding is truly appreciated and always available on both a personal and professional basis. It must be said that I have almost caused her a heart attack on numerous occasions when stating the directions I plan to go with storylines and characters but I am humbled by the trust she places in me to tell the story I want to tell. And I equally place the same trust that she will always pull me back from the brink and together produce the best book we can.

To Kim Nash (Mama Bear) who works tirelessly to promote our books and protect us from the world. To Noelle Holten who has limitless enthusiasm and passion for our work and to Sarah Hardy for her contribution to the dream team.

Many thanks to Alex Crow, Hannah Deuce and Rob Chilver for their genius in marketing the books. Also to Natalie Butlin and Caolinn Douglas who work hard to secure promotions for the books. To Nina Winters who works hard on the books behind the scenes and to Alexandra Holmes who looks after the audio production of the stories. Huge thanks also to Peta Nightingale who sends me the most fantastic emails.

A special thanks must go to Janette Currie who has copy-edited the Kim Stone books from the very beginning. Her knowledge of the stories has ensured a continuity for which I'm extremely grateful. Also need a special mention for Henry Steadman (and his dog Archie) who is responsible for the fabulous book covers which I absolutely love.

Thank you to the fantastic Kim Slater who has been an incredible support and friend to me for many years now. Despite writing outstanding novels herself, she always finds time for a chat. Massive thanks to Emma Tallon who has no idea just how much I value her friendship and support. Also to the fabulous Renita D'Silva and Caroline Mitchell, without whom this journey would be impossible. Huge thanks to the growing family of Bookouture authors who continue to amuse, encourage and inspire me on a daily basis.

My eternal gratitude goes to all the wonderful bloggers and reviewers who have taken the time to get to know Kim Stone and follow her story. These wonderful people shout loudly and share generously not because it is their job but because it is their passion. I will never tire of thanking this community for their support of both myself and my books. Thank you all so much.

Massive thanks to all my fabulous readers, especially the ones that have taken time out of their busy day to visit me on my website, Facebook page, Goodreads or Twitter.

Printed in Great Britain
by Amazon

19732870R00203